Never Forgotten You

Marie Cauley

To all of my family and friends who
have supported me through all of the
moments of joy, frustration, and everything
in between – thank you for being there.

To DC, my childhood idol and the reason
this book began in the first place – I wish
you peace and light.

To JLY, for the inspiration to keep going,
so that I could finally realize my dream of
having my words and stories out in the world
for everyone to read…and the inspiration to
write new stories – I am forever grateful to you.
Never. Give. Up.

PROLOGUE

It was finally time to see HIM. After a long, busy school week filled with quizzes, homework and awkward gym classes, Karen had reached the moment of reward.

"Mom, come on, it's almost starting!" Karen pulled her mother, still wearing her ruffled yellow apron, into the living room.

"Oh, is it time for a certain show to start?" Mom teased. "Maybe…oh, I don't know…'The Amazing Anderson Boys'?"

"Of course – you know it is! Come on! I don't want to miss a minute! Dad, can I sit closer to the TV, please?"

Dad smiled. "OK, but not too close. You'll ruin your eyes."

"Don't worry, I won't. Thanks!"

"Those kids sure can sing, can't they?" said Dad. "Especially Grant."

"And he is cute," added Mom, watching Karen's softly freckled face light up.

Karen felt her cheeks get hot, then the heat spread to her arms as well. "Well, he is very cute and talented, and so much more than that! But Grant is the character's name. The actor's real name is Chris Lassiter."

The show's bubbly theme song filled the room as images of each of the boys flashed across the family television console. "I bet you know a lot about Chris, don't you honey?" Dad couldn't help himself from teasing his eleven-year-old daughter. "I'm sure you even know what he had for breakfast this morning."

"Come on, Dad!" Karen said without taking her eyes off the screen. "Although Teen Dream Magazine says Chris likes pancakes with eggs and bacon, with lots of maple syrup and butter on his pancakes."

Mom laughed. "Is there anything about that boy that he's allowed to keep a secret from the rest of the world?"

"I'm sure there is, Mom. And he's not a boy. He's twenty-one years old."

"Oh, an older man!" said Dad. "A little old for you, sweetie, don't you think?"

"It's not like she's dating him, dear," answered Mom. "She just sees him on TV and hears him on the radio and her records."

"He may be ten years older than me," stated Karen, "but you just wait till I grow up! We'll be together then!"

"You know, you're not the only girl who dreams about Grant – I mean Chris. Lots of other girls are crazy about him too," said Dad. "Don't let your imagination run away with you. You're still too young to decide that."

"There's just something special about him, Dad! I can just feel it!"

"Those other girls think he's special too, honey." Mom tried to reason with her as she untied her apron and let it fall onto the rust-colored couch. "And you've never even actually met Chris. How could you possibly know?"

Karen continued to stare at the television screen as tiny tears formed in the corners of her eyes. She knew how her heart felt. "You both just wait, you'll see!

You just wait till Chris and I are together. Then you'll understand!"

CHAPTER 1

No, no, no. This can't be happening again.

Karen pulled over onto the shoulder of the San Diego Freeway and tried to steady her breathing. It was a beautiful May day, yet she found herself fighting an overwhelming feeling of dread, accompanied by a swiftly beating heart that raced so fast she thought it would explode. She knew that something was wrong. *What is going on with me?* she thought. *This is the third day in a row. I can't get enough air. And always on my way to work. It's not like I have a dangerous job or anything. I make decent money. My boss is relatively nice and doesn't scream at people. I'm lucky to have colleagues that I enjoy working with for the most part. A lot of people would be thrilled to have a job like this. But something feels really wrong...so wrong that I'm hyperventilating on my way to the office. What's my problem?*

Karen calmed down enough to pull back into traffic. She took her usual exit ramp and made a right to get to her office building about a mile down the street. She was thrilled that her job brought her to live in California. It was always a gorgeous drive to work, warm and breezy, so she couldn't blame her strange symptoms on the weather. It seemed like it never really did rain, just like that old song.

She had always dreamed of living in the Golden State, even as a young girl. As luck would have it, the engineering firm she worked for in Indiana decided to move to the West Coast, so when her employer made her an offer, she jumped at the chance. Just hearing the word California brought to life all of the magical feelings inside of her, and sometimes she wondered if everything truly was golden there. Plus, most of her favorite shows were filmed there, and they always made everything seem so perfect.

Her family was not thrilled that she was now living so far away, but they accepted it. They were at least happy that she had such a secure job.

Karen kept trying to figure out her feelings. Was she missing her dad and stepmom? Perhaps it was because it had been so long since she'd been able to talk with her friends. It had been five months since she'd moved here and she hadn't really had a chance to catch up with them.

Maybe it was that she felt she needed to lose about thirty-five pounds for her body to be "bikini-ready". Now that she could visit the beach whenever she felt like it, it would be nice not to always go there in shorts and a T-shirt…and actually be able to jump in the water without looking like she fell overboard somewhere. The long hours she put in at the office kept her from getting much exercise, and when the weekend came she was too tired to do anything except sit on the beach, trying not to think of everything on her to do list at the office for the next week. After all of her hard work, she felt she deserved to relax. Besides, she wasn't sure about the bathing suit for, well, other reasons that she really didn't want to think about right now. That would only add to her stress level.

Karen pursued these thoughts as she pushed back a strand of her long blonde hair. *Well, these are things that bother me occasionally, but I've learned to deal with them. There must be something else making me get this way. I wish I could figure out what.*

She pulled up to the big steel and glass office building where her workday awaited. She sighed. *Oh well, time to lose myself in the paperwork as always. Maybe later I'll figure out what's bugging me.*

"Good morning, Karen." Karen cleared her thoughts as she got out of her car, finally noticing her boss standing there in the parking lot.

"Good morning, Jim! What's on the agenda for today?"

"We have two new clients that we have to put proposals together for today. They need to be ready by tomorrow morning. I guess we'll be staying late again."

Karen forced a smile. "Maybe I should just move my bed here to work."

"I'm so glad you can keep your sense of humor about all of the late hours. We really appreciate all of your hard work."

"Thank you," Karen said, determined to keep the smile on her face no matter what. "I do what's needed to get the job done."

They went into the building together, got their coffee, and reviewed the necessary information for the proposals. Karen went to work right away, taking care of as many details as she could to make the architects' jobs easier.

In what seemed like only an hour, Karen looked up and saw that it was time to go to lunch. She grabbed her purse and keys, knowing exactly where she wanted to eat.

The Hot Spot was the best diner in the area, and everyone's favorite place for lunch. Karen loved the surfing décor, and the island/beach music was just what she needed to relax on her lunch hour. Usually Karen asked a few others to go with her, but today she just really wanted to eat alone. She was still trying to figure out what was bothering her and didn't want to be lost in thought while trying to hold a conversation with her co-workers. Since they had all just eaten there a couple of days ago, she was pretty sure she wouldn't run into any of them now.

She sat at the counter and ordered, then noticed that someone had left behind the morning newspaper. As she opened the Entertainment Section, a large ad caught her eye.

COMING FRIDAY, JUNE 5th

FORMER TEEN IDOL CHRIS LASSITER

AT THE SANTA MONICA CIVIC CENTER

7:30 PM

COME REMEMBER OLD TIMES

AND HEAR SOME NEW TUNES FROM CHRIS!

Karen couldn't believe what she was reading. Chris Lassiter! It had been years since he last gave a concert. And back when he did, he and his band never got to her small town in Indiana.

Even though he hadn't been in the public eye for a while, Karen thought of Chris from time to time. She wondered what he was like now. She knew she had to go to this concert to find out. As Karen thought about it, her spirits began to lift.

Karen savored her BLT and fries, copied the concert information from the paper, and headed back to work with a smile on her face.

All afternoon, it was hard to keep her mind on work. Thoughts of her childhood watching Chris Lassiter on TV kept flashing before her. Friday nights were filled with "The Amazing Anderson Boys", a show about five young brothers honing their musical talents and taking their act on the road. As Grant Anderson, the oldest brother, Chris Lassiter became lead singer of the fictional TV band and a pop star in his own right. Karen still had every record Chris ever made, as part of the TV show or from his own solo career.

Karen wondered why Chris waited so long to make music again. She never, in all the years since, had found a more powerful, amazing voice than his. She couldn't wait to hear that voice again!

She had noticed that tickets went on sale Saturday morning, which was the day after tomorrow. *I'm going to be up extra early on Saturday, if I can sleep at all!* she thought. She shook herself out of her daydreams and resumed work on the proposals.

*****

Friday came and went quicker than she expected. Karen wondered how in the world she actually got any work done at all. Chris Lassiter was constantly on her mind.

Her feelings overwhelmed her. It was almost as if she was eleven years old again. Every thought she ever had about Chris came back to her now, plus some new ones. Now that she was twenty years older, she was thinking things she wouldn't have thought of as an innocent young girl.

Karen blushed at her own thoughts. *Wow,* she mused, *imagine if I'd been a few years older back then. Now I know where all of those high school girls' minds were. Hmm...maybe it's a good thing I was only in grade school then!*

Now it was Saturday morning, just a little after 9 AM. Tickets would be on sale in less than an hour. Even though she had worked late the night before, Karen was already on the computer, so she could be ready to get the best seat available. Buying tickets on the Internet was still new to her, so she prayed that she wouldn't mess it up. The four cups of black coffee she'd already drunk were making her jumpy and anxious for the appointed time to arrive.

Finally, it was ten o'clock. Karen typed in her request: one seat, best available. She clicked on the spot marked "continue". Suddenly the screen went blank, causing Karen to furiously pound every key in an attempt to bring the page up. She shut down and waited for the computer to reboot as she downed the rest of her fifth cup of coffee.

When she finally got the right screen to come up, she couldn't believe her eyes. Second row, center stage! The next question on the screen asked if this seat was OK. Of course it was! Karen continued on until she printed her confirmation. In three weeks she would be up close watching and listening to her childhood idol. She could not believe her good fortune. Never in her life had she been able to get such great seats for a show. Plus, purchasing tickets from the comfort of her PC sure beat standing in line for hours outside.

Now that the ticket was taken care of and a load off her mind, Karen jumped up out of her chair, too excited to even think about going back to bed. She was so wired from the caffeine that she knew relaxing was not an option. She set out to go for a walk on the beach, hoping it would help her burn off some energy and calm down.

She started out walking on the sparkling sand, but found that she couldn't stay at such a slow pace and soon broke into an awkward run. At first it felt strange to her, considering that she hadn't run since those long ago high school gym classes. But soon she began to loosen up. It was incredible to have this much energy on a Saturday, even after the long workweek. Most of her Saturdays consisted of grabbing junk food from the kitchen and sitting on the couch, too tired even to cook something for herself.

While she ran, Karen thought about her crush on Chris, along with other dreams he'd made her dream as a girl. Chris's character on the show was a songwriter, and so was Chris in real life. Ever since getting hooked on "The Amazing Anderson Boys", Karen had wanted to write songs and make music. She also secretly dreamed of getting to sing a duet with Chris.

Karen realized that Chris and the show had first awakened her to a passion for words and music. But she also realized she'd never actually put anything down on paper up to this point. Why had she not acted on this passion before? Whatever the reason, she could at least start now. She really should be working on writing some beautiful music. Maybe she was meant to create something spectacular!

This thought made her just as happy as the fact that she would be seeing Chris in concert. It was time to write down her thoughts the way she had always dreamed she would. No longer would she let life get in the way of her true dream…it was time to pursue it. But how?

The first thing she needed to do was unearth her old guitar. She hadn't played in years, so she would have to re-learn the basics. That would help with writing melodies to go along with the lyrics. She was going to find a local music shop so she could get the right notebook with places to write the notes as well as the words. Might as well do it properly and be organized about it, if she was going to get serious about it. Then even if she had a rough day at work, she would have no excuse for not being ready to work on it. Everything she needed would be ready and waiting for her when she got home.

Karen sat on the beach to rest, looking out upon the crashing waves. Suddenly she glanced down at her watch. She blinked and then looked more closely at it. She'd been running for an hour! After about twenty more minutes of soaking up the sun and watching the waves rush to the shore, she went home to shower and change so she could complete her newly discovered mission and get started again with her music.

CHAPTER 2

Chris Lassiter should have been on top of the world. He was doing what he loved, making music again after a long absence; he hadn't done so much as sing in the shower over the last few years. It had been even longer since he'd performed live in concert, and he was pacing the studio like an anxious expectant father. Time had flown by and Memorial Day approached quickly. Rehearsals were getting down to the wire, with only days left until the big event. So many nagging thoughts flooded his mind. Is it possible to really make a comeback? Would anybody still want to hear him sing? His doubts threatened to drive him crazy.

"OK everyone, let's run through this song one more time," Chris told his band. "Then we can take five."

They just stared at him, complete exhaustion evident on their faces. "Can't we just break now?" asked Jerry, Chris' bandleader and best friend for as long as he could remember. "We're dead on our feet!"

Chris looked at Jerry through his own tired, bloodshot eyes. "Humor me, please? I'll tell you what...one more run-through of this song and we'll break for an hour for dinner."

"You mean lunch, Chris," sighed Sandy. "It's five o'clock in the afternoon and we haven't eaten since those bagels were delivered first thing this morning."

"Yeah, I get what you mean." Chris managed to give her a weak smile. "Thanks, gang. I know I got carried away today."

"We're sounding great, man," exclaimed Jerry. "What are you so worried about?"

"That everyone has forgotten me and nobody will care."

"Chris, you were one of the biggest deals around – I'm sure everything will be just fine!" Sandy placed a gentle hand on Chris' shoulder, trying to appease her talented boss.

"I know. I'm trying not to be neurotic about this. But it's been a long time. I just want everything to go as perfectly as possible. And this is my comeback song!" Chris started sounding nervous again as he caught the microphone he'd nearly knocked over.

"Try to relax, please?" Jerry pleaded. "One more time, and then let's eat!"

After practicing "Never Forgotten You" one more time, Chris and the band walked down the street to a Chinese restaurant. As Chris ate his Moo Goo Gai Pan, he felt his body relax. Maybe Jerry was right…he was worrying too much about everything. Of course there were plenty of his old fans around. They'd be happy to hear the nostalgic stuff and thrilled that he was putting out new music.

But he also remembered that many other former stars tried to make comebacks and got nowhere. Then they dropped out of sight for good. He didn't want to be one of them. He loved singing and performing, and had missed it for all these years. He just wanted to make sure he did it right, even if he drove himself and everyone else crazy getting there.

"This was a great choice for dinner, Chris." Sandy laughed as she scooped up a forkful of chicken fried rice. "Although you know we'll be hungry again in a little while."

Chris smiled. "Yeah, I know about the Chinese food curse. Don't worry, just two more hours of rehearsal ahead of us. It shouldn't take as long to go over the older songs. Then we can all go grab dessert and get some rest for tomorrow."

A cheer went up among the band members. "Thank God," said Jerry, "or else we might not even have voices left for tomorrow."

After fortune cookies were read and consumed, they all walked back to the studio, with full stomachs and the evening breeze leaving them somewhat refreshed.

"Alright, now that the comeback song is ready to roll," Chris said with a wink, "let's practice some of the old stuff."

The band kicked into "Love Is the Only Way", the Amazing Anderson Boys' biggest hit. There were no problems with this song. Chris could have sung this one in his sleep. In fact, he was sure at some point in time he probably had.

"Hey," teased his bass player Rob. "For a minute I thought it was still 1977."

"Except we're all twenty years older," laughed Chris.

"Well, you were awesome then," said Sandy. "It's just that now you're twenty years better."

"Thanks. Hopefully the fans will accept the 'more mature' me!"

"Of course they will; fans like yours are very loyal. They'll be so happy to have you back," Rob said firmly. "Don't worry – just do what you're doing and it will be great."

"I know," sighed Chris, "but a lot of my fans were really young back then. Don't you think they may have outgrown me?"

"I think you should give them more credit, man." Jerry grinned right at Chris. "You never forget your first love, even if that first love was a TV star. They'll be excited to relive the past, and to have some new music that fits their lives today as adults."

"All right guys, I think you've convinced me. I'll try to relax."

*****

Chris headed home, hoping to calm himself enough to get a decent night's sleep. As he drove his convertible along the coast, the salty night air started to do the trick. He felt his nerves begin to untangle with the breeze, at least enough to make him focus on the road.

Chris pulled into the driveway of his beachfront home—a home he had only been able to afford thanks to a small inheritance from his mom. He gave thanks for getting home in one piece; he was sure that was a miracle, considering his frame of mind.

He knew that he certainly couldn't have paid for this beach house on his own. After 'Anderson Boys' went off the air, he didn't get as much work as he would have liked. He was ready to try some different, more challenging roles, but producers and directors had other thoughts. Since he was so successful as Grant, why fix something that wasn't broken?

What they didn't realize at the time was that Chris himself was broken. And he needed more fixing than anybody could have ever suspected.

So other than the occasional guest appearance and failed TV pilot, the work dried up along with the record contract that wasn't renewed once it expired in 1979. He'd already used up the money that he had made from the TV show and records. Besides, there wasn't as much money as everyone probably thought. His agent wasn't really all that savvy, and the show executives set it up so they made a lot of money off of him, with Chris only getting a small amount of what he worked so hard to have. If only he or his agent had read the fine print…

Chris didn't even want to think about how much money he could have had or how fast the money he did have went.

Now that I've finally got my head on straight, Chris thought, *I don't want to screw up my chances of restarting my career. Music and acting are my passions, and now that all of that junk is cleared out of my life, I can really concentrate on them.*

Chris turned off the ignition. He stayed seated in his car, looked out at the moonlight on the waves and let out a deep breath. *And maybe, this time around, I can enjoy it a whole lot more. Or least be aware that I'm enjoying it.*

Once he convinced himself that everything was going to be all right, Chris stepped out of the car and walked up his front steps. He let out one more sigh as he opened the door and went inside.

CHAPTER 3

Karen awakened on the morning of June 5th with her stomach in knots. She could not believe this day had finally come, and in a few short hours she would be at a Chris Lassiter show.

I don't even know what I'm going to wear tonight, Karen thought, almost speaking out loud as she sat up in bed. *I'd better have a quick breakfast and then go through my closet. I have to have something appropriate for a night out...although it's been so long since I've had one.*

After wolfing down a blueberry muffin and some coffee, Karen opened her closet doors and faced her wardrobe. She wanted to wear something fun and exciting, but as she began to pull out items from her closet, all she saw were the dark-colored suits she wore to work, along with a collection of T-shirts and sweats. And of the decent outfits she owned, the majority were black, since the ebony shades were supposed to be slimming.

Karen sighed. There was absolutely no way she could wear any of these things to the concert. She threw on her jeans and the T-shirt that read "California Dreamin'" across the front and headed for the mall.

Once she got there and walked through the open glass doors, she stood still as she became lost in her thoughts. She didn't even know where to begin. As she continued through the food court entrance, the aromas of cinnamon rolls and French fries began to make her hungry. She knew the muffin she had for breakfast wasn't much, but she shouldn't be ready for anything else to eat yet. She questioned her own sanity, as she should have known better than to use this entrance. With thoughts of slimming clothing on her mind, she kept on moving past the fast food stands into the main part of the mall. Now, which store would have what she was looking for – especially when Karen herself wasn't even sure what that was?

I can't go looking like a frump. My seat is really close to the stage. Karen's thoughts swirled around in her head. *And of course, I waited until the last minute to figure this out.*

Karen stepped into the first department store she saw, wandering around like a lost child until a salesgirl came over and offered her help. She was a redhead, petite and cute, and extremely perky. "Hi there. Looking for an outfit for a special occasion?"

Karen thought fast, not wanting to explain about the concert. "Yes, actually. It's for my date tonight."

"Well," said the salesgirl with a bright smile, "you look kind of stressed out over it. This guy must be pretty special."

"He is."

"Have you been dating him for a long time?"

"No, this is going to be the first time I've seen him again in years." *At least there was some truth in that.*

"That explains why you seem so nervous. Is he an old friend?"

Karen smiled, picturing Chris in her mind. "Yes, I guess you could say that." *It sure feels like he's an old friend.*

"Well then, you need something flirty, with some excitement, yet still appropriate and flattering."

"Exactly!" Karen exclaimed. "Exciting without looking like a streetwalker. Now what in the world do you have that fills all of those needs?"

The salesgirl laughed as her auburn curls bounced about her face. "You'd be surprised. Come right this way."

She led Karen to a dressing room and brought a variety of gorgeous things for her to try on. There were more options than Karen thought there would be, considering that every time she walked down the street it seemed like all of the women she saw left little to the imagination. She was just praying for something to fit, wishing she wore the same size as the salesgirl.

She was really sorry that she hadn't kept up with the exercise she'd started three weeks ago. She remembered how good it felt to run on the beach that day. She did run again the following day, but then came Monday and back to her daily grind. She came home late from work every day, stressed and much too tired to do anything. She hadn't had any real workouts since that weekend, and unfortunately it showed in the mirror.

Some of the clothes she tried on didn't quite fit; some did, but were definitely not flattering in any way. Karen got more frustrated every time she looked at her reflection.

Then she found it.

It was a suit. Not a suit like the boring ones she wore to work, but a cocktail suit with a sweetheart neckline and a skirt that hit her right at the knee. She was shocked at how fabulous her legs looked. The jacket complemented her curves instead of exaggerating them. And she could move around comfortably while the suit stayed put in the places that it should. There was nothing worse than worrying what might be showing that should be kept under wraps; with this outfit she could be confident that she wouldn't be exposed.

To top off the entire look, the bright emerald color brought out her sparkling green eyes.

"This is perfect! It shows off my two best features, while hiding a multitude of sins." Karen couldn't believe how wonderful this suit looked on her. It was almost as if the designer had her in mind while creating it, even though they had obviously never met. "This is the one. I'll take it!"

The salesgirl, who in her entire lifetime would probably never have to hide even one culinary sin, rang up the suit. She hung a garment bag over it and handed it to Karen with a wink and a grin.

"Enjoy your new suit – and your date tonight!"

Karen couldn't stop smiling now even if she tried. "Thank you for all of your help. And don't worry, I will!"

As Karen left the store with her purchase, she glanced at her watch. "Wow!" she said aloud. "I found my outfit faster than I thought I would. That means I have time to get shoes to match!"

Karen found that she was really enjoying herself. It had been a very long time since she had bought herself anything new to wear. It felt good to do something for herself for a change, after always putting herself last to accommodate everyone else.

She walked into the most popular shoe store in the mall. There she found the perfect pair of pumps. At least it was no problem getting shoes to fit, since her feet were average-sized. On top of that, they matched the new suit perfectly. Karen just shook her head. *It's like these shoes were made exactly for this suit. This is just unreal!*

She was really too pumped and nervous to eat now, but knew she'd better have something since she was beginning to get lightheaded. She grabbed a grilled chicken sandwich and an iced tea from the food court. After the meal, she had enough energy to get to her car and head for home.

*****

Karen slipped on her gorgeous new suit. She felt absolutely beautiful in it and still could not fathom how wonderfully it fit her curves. Sure, she would like to lose the unwanted weight. But even with those extra pounds, she had to admit that she looked stunning tonight.

Karen felt just like a teenager going on her first date. She could not get over how strong the butterflies were in her stomach.

This is unbelievable. You'd think I was still a young girl going to see Chris, not a grown woman. It is a great feeling - but it's just so bizarre! Karen tried as hard as she could to calm herself down enough to finish getting ready.

She slid her long, slender feet into her perfectly matching shoes, then put on the emerald earrings that had belonged to her grandmother. Karen's mom had given them to her for her 21st birthday. She could still remember her mother's words on that day.

"Wear these in good health, dear. Always think of Grandma when you have them on, and celebrate life as she did."

Karen couldn't help but think of her mom and grandma now. She missed them both terribly. But she knew they were smiling down on her tonight, happy that she was so excited about something in her life.

She was glad too. She had lost a lot of her zest for life lately, but now that she was reconnecting with something from her childhood, she could feel some of that old spirit coming back. She also knew that this was more than just nostalgia for her. The more she reflected on that part of her childhood, the more she suspected that it held the key to what was missing in her life. Now she just had to pinpoint exactly what that was.

Karen looked in the mirror one last time to check her makeup and hair. Then she took a deep breath and slowly exhaled. She had a funny thought – her mom was probably getting a good chuckle in heaven, watching her go all gooey over Chris Lassiter again. She reached for her purse and keys, and was finally on her way.

CHAPTER 4

Chris could hear the cheers from the audience as the band members took the stage one by one. He was itching to go on stage, yet there was a big ball of fear in the pit of his stomach that kept him firmly planted in his seat in front of the mirror, moments from his introduction.

Just then Jerry poked his head into the dressing room. "Hey Chris, we're on."

"Thanks Jer." Chris spoke to Jerry without even looking up. "I think I'm ready."

Jerry sighed. "Man, you're not still worried, are you?"

"I'm trying not to be."

"Please, Chris…relax. Everything will be fine."

"I know." Chris turned and smiled at Jerry. "I hope I'll be OK once I get on stage. I'm glad you're still by my side after all these years, man."

"Hey, if you can't count on your friends, who can you count on? Now let's rock and roll!"

Chris took a deep breath. "Ok, let's go."

They walked over to the back of the stage. Jerry joined the rest of the band, who were already playing the beginning of an old familiar song. Jerry strapped on his guitar and joined in with his first few notes. The emcee's voice rang out over the speakers:

"Ladies and gentlemen, after a long hiatus one of your favorite performers is back. You loved him on

"The Amazing Anderson Boys", and now he's ready to rock again. Please give a warm welcome to Chris Lassiter!"

Chris heard more cheers and screams coming from the audience. This was his moment of truth. He stepped through the side curtain, smiling and waving at the audience as he strolled over to his mic.

"How are you all tonight? Are you ready to have a good time?"

The crowd responded with more screams and applause. These screams actually rivaled the ones he'd last heard so many years ago. Chris was both shocked and thrilled at the same time, and for a moment he lost himself in the sound.

Chris and the band kicked in with "Girl, I Need You", a number one hit for the Anderson Boys during their heyday. Chris could feel that his voice was stronger than ever. He thought about the girls who used to swoon during his shows and wondered if that still happened with grown women.

About halfway through the song, Chris finally started to loosen up. *I'm back where I belong,* he thought to himself. *Please God, please let the rest of the night go just as well.*

As that first song ended, Chris looked over at Jerry. Jerry grinned at him with a look that said…I told you not to worry, didn't I?

Chris turned back to the crowd. He was absolutely bowled over by the response. It really did feel as if it were still 1977. If he closed his eyes, for a moment he was 21 again. He couldn't help but feel blessed to have this chance again, to entertain and sing his heart out for an audience. Even better, this audience was truly happy to see him and loving the show so far.

Chris felt he'd had his eyes shut forever, but it had only been seconds. He glanced into the crowd and saw rows of smiling faces.

"I'm so thrilled to be with you tonight. It's great to be back."

The crowd roared. Chris heard a few ladies yell to him, "We love you Chris!"

"I love you too. This night means a lot to me, more than you even know. Thank you for being here." Chris picked up his guitar and stepped back up to the mic.

"I'm getting ready to record some new music. It won't be anything like you're used to from me, but I hope you'll enjoy it. This next song is going to be the first single. Are you ready?"

"YEAH!!!" Then the audience got quiet, wondering just what kind of music Chris had in store for them.

He led the intro on the guitar, then the band joined in. Chris poured all of his emotions into the song. "Never Forgotten You" was powerful and soulful, more advanced than the music of his youth. Though the audience was quiet, he hoped they were just taking it in since they had never heard this one before.

As the tune finished, up went the screams. "We've never forgotten you, Chris!"

Just then Chris looked out and caught sight of a pretty blonde wearing a dazzling shade of green. And she had the eyes to match! Green had always been his favorite color. Strangely enough, it was the one thing the reporters from the teen magazines had never asked him. He couldn't believe they had overlooked such a simple question, but he was glad. It was at least one small thing he was able to keep private during that insane period of his life.

Chris took his focus off of the blonde and managed to get his mind back on the show. "I'd like to introduce a phenomenal group of singers and musicians; without them I would not be here today. I'm honored to have them as my band, and I'm blessed to call them my friends."

Chris turned back to the band. "On keyboard and vocals, the beautiful and talented Sandy Reynolds. On bass and vocals, the amazing Rob Madigan."

As Chris went on to introduce each band member, the audience applauded to celebrate the talent of the awesome collection of musicians that were sharing the stage with him.

Chris saved his longtime buddy for last.

"And finally, this man has been with me through it all since 1977. Not only is he a superb talent, but I'm proud to say he is my best friend in the world. On lead guitar and vocals, my band leader, Jerry Lawson!"

The appreciative audience let out the loudest cheers for Jerry, whom some of them had remembered from Chris' concerts years ago. Many others who had not had that privilege still knew of Jerry, and were reacting as much to his longtime friendship with Chris as his musicianship.

"Now," Chris continued, "I'm going to let this incredible group show off for a few minutes while I catch a glimpse of your beautiful faces." Chris stood to the side and sipped water while the band sang by themselves as they played a well-loved jazz number. It made him smile to hear the crowd's reaction, that even though he was not on stage at the moment, they recognized the talent of the other musicians playing before them.

*****

Karen still could not believe she was in the second row at a Chris Lassiter concert. Was she really this close to Chris? She wanted to pinch herself, to make sure this wasn't just a dream.

He was sounding better than she had even imagined. He was still the same Chris, yet more mature and stronger than ever.

And looking at him…well, he was still gorgeous. Even though it was almost two decades later, he still took her breath away. Watching those fascinating hazel eyes and that unbelievable smile that made her melt had her feeling like she was still a young girl in her living room watching him on TV.

Karen was sure, after Chris' new song, that he had looked right at her. It made her heart jump and sent chills right through her. She was still thinking about it as the band performed their instrumental number.

She stole a couple of glances at Chris as he waited in the wings for the band to finish the song. She had never shaken the feeling that Chris was special. It was not just his being a fantastic singer or a famous TV star. Deep down she knew it was more than that. There was just something about him. Even though she couldn't put her finger on it, she just knew.

It was good to have Chris back – and Karen could tell that he was happy to be back.

*****

At the conclusion of the jazz number, the crowd went wild. As Chris walked back on, he felt his old mischievous sense of humor coming back to him.

"OK everyone, now that you've seen how awesome the band is, I'm not needed on stage anymore. They're going to do the rest of the show on their own. Thanks for being a great audience. Good night!"

Chris walked offstage and heard the mixed reaction. A few people laughed, so he knew they must have gotten the joke. Others groaned, leading Chris to believe that they thought this was the shortest comeback concert in the history of music.

Chris waited a couple of minutes while the band started playing again. The audience members whispered and murmured among themselves.

Finally, Chris put them out of their misery. He ran back out on the stage to huge cheers from the relieved crowd.

"You didn't think I really meant it, did you?" Chris teased. "Come on, you know me better than that!"

He turned to Jerry. "Come on Jer, let's really get this party rolling!"

Chris saw the look of relief on Jerry's face as he spoke. He had been so nervous about everything lately that he knew Jerry had been worried that his smart alecky friend was gone for good. Jerry's grin told Chris that he was grateful that Chris was starting to act like himself again.

Jerry cued the band to start "Please Love Me Baby", which went number one for Chris as a solo artist back in the day. Chris felt free to be more playful and sexy, now that he no longer had to split his personality between the always sweet and perfect Grant and the real, grown-up man who was Chris.

His female audience had grown up; he could tell by the screams that they relished this side of him as much as the innocent Grant persona they had come to know.

"Wow! You know, I always appreciated those screams when we were all younger years ago. But I must admit, it sure is wonderful to hear <u>adult</u> females scream now!"

Some of the ladies screamed again, others laughed nervously.

"Just please, nobody faint," Chris continued. "It always scared the heck out of me when that happened."

Chris performed a couple more of his solo hits, all the while showing that he still had the voice, and the moves to go along with it.

Chris caught another glimpse of the blonde in the second row. She had this radiance about her, different from any other woman he had ever laid eyes on. This time their eyes met and she smiled. It was all he could do to keep singing, but as he did, he smiled right back at her.

Chris almost reluctantly scanned the rest of the audience. He wanted to please everyone there, but was also intrigued by this woman.

He moved on with the show and spoke to the entire group. "I couldn't make a comeback without picking some of my favorite songs of all time to sing for you. I didn't get to record them, but I sure wish I had."

Chris performed his favorite classics, giving them his personal spin on everything from The Beatles to The Who. He and the band did some more Anderson Boys hits, mixing them with other songs from his solo career. Then he moved on to a couple more brand new songs, which were yet to be recorded. The crowd was loving every minute of it, whether the tunes were old or new. It didn't matter, as long as it was Chris' voice singing that they heard.

"Hey everyone, it's been an absolutely wonderful night. I can't believe I'm finally back performing for all of you."

"We love you Chris!"

"Thanks for being with me on my first night back. I love you all."

For the final song, Chris had saved the biggest Anderson hit for last. He launched into "Love Is The Only Way".

The audience went completely nuts. They knew no Chris Lassiter concert could be complete without this song. If he hadn't sung it, they would have hunted him down until he had.

Once Chris finished the biggest hit he had ever known, he said good night again, blew a kiss to the crowd, and walked off stage.

The crowd clapped feverishly and chanted his name. They weren't ready for the show to end and wanted him to come back out for more.

Chris was totally spent. He had given all he had out there. But he took a deep breath, somehow gathered up some energy, and went out for an encore.

He sang another of his solo releases, plus one more Anderson Boys classic. He wiped the sweat from his face and neck.

"Thank you again. I wish I could stay here all night with you, but management is motioning to me that we've already gone over. God bless you all. Good night!"

He blew one more kiss to the audience. Some of the ladies blew one back, including the woman in green. Chris waved and left the stage.

*****

The house lights went up, and the band exited behind the curtain. The stage crew came on to pack up the instruments and equipment, joking around and making quite a bit of noise.

Karen just sat there, still going over the amazing evening in her head. Not only had the concert itself been incredible, but also Chris had looked right at her – not once but twice. And the second time, well, she couldn't help but smile right back at him. Then he smiled once more, just at her and no one else. It was the smile that had always turned her completely to jello. But this time it wasn't just a smile on a screen. It was up close and personal, for her alone.

She thought that maybe by being up front, she'd have a chance to meet Chris after the show, especially if the band had noticed her half as much as Chris did.

Unfortunately, since the show had run over the allotted time the people who were running the civic center were trying to get everything cleaned and closed up for the night. They quickly ushered everyone out of the theater.

Karen didn't know what to do with herself now that she was outside in the cool night air. She suddenly realized she was starving, having skipped dinner before the show due to all of the excitement.

She remembered passing an all-night restaurant on her way to the concert. It was just down the street, a few buildings over from the civic center. She decided she'd better stop there and have something before she got too dizzy.

CHAPTER 5

Chris was drenched in sweat, causing his shirt to cling tightly to his back as he made his way down the hall to the dressing room. Having poured his whole heart and soul into this show, he felt like he had run a marathon, exhausted yet exhilarated.

Jerry came by and gave Chris a high five. "Awesome show, man. See? You had nothing to worry about!"

"I know, I know," sighed Chris. "You don't have to say I told you so."

Jerry laughed. "Good. Now the band is famished. We really need to get something to eat."

"Sure. Just let me get a quick shower and change clothes."

Chris walked toward the showers, then turned and stopped. "Hey, are any of the fans still out there? I'd love to meet some of them, if we can keep them around a little longer while I make myself presentable. "

Jerry shook his head. "Management had the ushers clear everyone out so they could clean up."

Chris was disappointed. It had been a long time since he had gotten to talk to the fans. And his mind happened to be on one fan in particular.

"Oh, well. OK Jer, give me about twenty minutes and I'll be good to go."

As Chris let the warm water wash over him, he went over the entire show in his mind. Everything went well...in fact, better than he could even have imagined. There were no problems with instruments, no technical difficulties. Each and every band member played and sounded great. Chris felt that he hit everything right on, with strong vocals that pleased the audience.

Standing on that stage tonight, he realized just how much he had missed performing. He knew before that he missed it, but it took actually getting out there to grasp just how deep his feelings were. Performing was in his blood. No wonder he had been depressed for so long, without being able to do what he loved most. He now understood that even though he'd been trying to tell himself that he didn't miss it, it was just an attempt to make himself feel better. He also realized that it never actually worked; on the surface it helped him get through each day, but deep down he knew he'd been lying to himself.

Chris gathered his thoughts and got out of the shower, not wanting to make the gang wait too long for him. He had already gone past the twenty minutes he had promised Jerry. He quickly dried off, got dressed, and went out to join the band.

As soon as Sandy saw Chris, she called to him. "All right, boss, we're about to eat our instruments. Ready to go?"

Chris grinned. "Yeah, I hear you. Sorry it took me a little longer than I thought. Where do you want to go?"

"Rob talked to the theatre manager. He recommended this great Mexican place down the street."

"Sounds good. Let's go!"

*****

As the starving musicians attempted to pull into the parking lot of the cantina they almost ran into a long barrier. Police cars and fire trucks were all over the place, blocking every entrance into the lot or the restaurant itself.

Jerry straightened the wheel, pulled up to the curb and waved to a policeman.

"Hi, Officer. What's going on?"

"There was a big grease fire in the kitchen here. We had to evacuate the restaurant."

"Well," Jerry said, "guess we won't be eating here tonight."

"No sir." The officer laughed. "Why don't you try the place across the street? They serve great breakfasts and they're open all night. They even make a mean Huevos Rancheros if you have your heart set on Mexican food."

"Actually, breakfast does sound good," Chris said. "Thanks for your help, Officer."

"No problem. Enjoy your breakfast."

Jerry drove the van across the street to the all-night diner. Rob jumped out and went in to get someone to set up a large table for the group, to save time while Jerry found a parking spot.

When Chris and the gang met Rob inside, he told them the table would be ready in about fifteen minutes.

"They gave us some menus to look at while we wait." Rob handed Sandy a menu.

He turned to give one to Chris, but Chris wasn't paying any attention to him. He was too busy looking at the woman who had just come out of the ladies' room.

"It's her," Chris said half out loud, half to himself. "She was the one at the concert tonight."

Chris stood up from the bench as she came toward the front door. "Excuse me, miss. You were at our show tonight."

The woman looked up, and a smile immediately lit up her face.

"Yes. You were all just awesome. Chris, you're sounding better than ever!"

Chris' grin spread across his face. He felt himself almost blushing.

"Thanks. I'm so glad everything went well tonight. And it was wonderful to look out from the stage and see your beautiful smile."

Now the woman began to blush, pink hue steadily rising in her cheeks. "Wow. Thank you."

"Did you eat already?"

"Yes. I just finished and was getting ready to go home."

"Please join us anyway at our table and have coffee or something. The parking lot is a still a mess, so you probably won't be able to get out right now anyway. I'd also like to get to talk to you some more. I know the rest of the gang won't mind."

The surprise showed in her even brighter cheeks. "Sure, I'd love to join you."

The hostess showed them to their table. As the rest of the band got settled, Jerry grabbed an extra chair and placed it next to Chris' seat.

"Thanks, Jerry."

"You're welcome." Jerry grinned at her, then at Chris.

Chris blurted out his sudden thought. "I don't even know your name yet."

"Karen O'Neil."

"I'm so glad to meet you, Karen. I was hoping to meet you, and some other fans after the show – but I found out the theater kicked you all out pretty fast."

"They sure did. I was kind of surprised. We almost didn't have time to catch our breaths after the show was over."

Chris frowned over the top of his menu. "I guess I took it for granted that I'd get to meet fans. In the old days, most performers did. I never did because things got so crazy; there was fear for my safety. I was hoping to finally get that chance."

"I'm so sorry you didn't get to do it," Karen said. "Maybe you can make arrangements for the next concert so you'll have it all set up and you won't have to worry about it once you're already there."

"That's a great idea, Karen. It would be good to consider those things ahead of time. I guess things are different now, and since I can't afford someone else to handle this for me I have to make sure I take care of it."

Everyone put in their orders and then held several different conversations around the table. Karen felt privileged to share in all of the "musician-speak" and joking around. The group did everything they could to make her feel right at home.

"Do you live far from here, Karen?" Sandy asked.

"No. It was only about a twenty minute drive to the Civic Center."

"Cool," answered Sandy. "We all live close to here too. That's why Chris decided this was the perfect place for the first concert."

Karen wondered if she was hearing things right. Had she really been living this close to Chris Lassiter for months without knowing it?

She turned to Chris. "So, do you have any more shows planned?"

Chris' enthusiasm for the question showed in his voice. "Well, we're going to book some more now. We wanted to see if the first show would be a success, and it was. Plus, in a week we start recording the new album."

"You mean new CD, Chris?" Jerry teased.

Chris laughed. "Yes, Jerry. I can't get used to saying CD. I still want to call them albums. I'm showing my age."

The entire table chuckled. "Yeah, Chris," said Rob. "We have to get with the times so we don't get run over by all of the youngsters."

Chris ran his fingers through his short dark brown hair. "Well, the seventies hair is in the past, so I guess albums are too."

"The new single is fantastic," Karen encouraged. "So are the other two new songs. I'm sure the rest of the CD will be just as wonderful."

"Thanks!" Chris beamed at her. "I can't wait to get to the studio to record."

Chris wanted to go on and on about his career revival, but suddenly he felt he was focusing too much of the attention on himself and not enough on his guest.

"Please, Karen, tell us more about you."

Karen blushed again. "What do you want to know?"

"Well," Chris mused, "you said you live close to here. Have you lived here all your life?"

"No, I'm originally from Indiana."

"Really? You sure look like a California girl. What brought you here from Indiana?"

Karen thought about that for a minute. *I really wish I looked even more like a California girl...especially at the beach!*

"My company moved here from there about six months ago, so I followed my job. But I guess it was also a feeling."

Chris' eyebrows went up. "A feeling?"

Karen laughed. "I know it sounds silly, but I just had a feeling I belonged out here." She shrugged. "Maybe it was just a girlish dream of living in sunny California."

"Or maybe it's something more," Chris said. "It's always a good thing to follow your intuition."

"You're right, but the one downside so far is how much I miss my family."

Chris nodded. "That's understandable, especially if you always lived close to them before. So, what does your company do?"

"We're 'The Wesley Foundation', and our main focus is architecture. Mr. Wesley started the company when he was just an engineer for a few years. Now he's the owner, CEO, and a very wealthy man."

"Wow! Sounds like he did well for himself."

"He certainly did. I'm an executive secretary, and I work closely with his son, Jim. I plan meetings, make travel arrangements, formally prepare proposals, and a lot more. I guess I'm kind of the jack-of-all-trades person there."

"That must mean you're the 'go-to' woman. It sounds exciting."

Karen grimaced. "It used to be. It's a great job, and it pays well enough. I just don't think it's what I want to do for the rest of my life...or what I'm actually meant to do for the rest of my life."

*****

Karen suddenly sat up perfectly straight, surprised at herself. She had finally put words to some of the uneasy feelings she was having. Maybe this had something to do with her daily panic attacks. What surprised her most was that she had blurted out these words to Chris, without ever having addressed them to herself.

Chris looked like he was caught off guard. "So you moved across the country for your job, but you're not sure if it's the job you should be doing. That's got to be a scary feeling."

"That's the thing. I still feel like this is where I should be living. It's just my vocation in life that I'm trying to figure out."

"Well, I sure hope you can figure out where you're headed. I've done a lot of soul searching myself, so I know it's an exhausting process. But I also know one other thing for sure."

Karen looked puzzled as her mind took in everything she had just revealed to a group of people she barely knew. "Oh? What's that?"

Chris looked directly into her eyes. "I'm really glad you moved to California, whatever the reason. Otherwise I wouldn't have met you."

CHAPTER 6

As Karen awoke late on Sunday morning, she was pleased to see that the weather matched her sunny mood. She'd have to hurry to get dressed, but at least she'd still make it to the noon Mass at her church.

She had a "date" with Chris Lassiter later in the afternoon. Her, of all people – she was still trying to work through it in her mind. He wanted to meet her at the park at three o'clock. That gave him and the band the chance to attend what they called the entertainers' Mass at another church. It was well known among the musicians and actors who lived here that St. Cecilia's had a 2 PM service for those who "worked late on Saturday nights and really needed to sleep in". No matter what went on the night before, there was plenty of time to shake it off and get to church.

Karen almost always went to the 10 AM Mass at St. Ann's. But so far since her move to the West Coast, she had never done anything exciting on Saturday night to warrant the need to sleep in.

There was no time for coffee this morning, which was ironic since she could really have used the caffeine to fully wake her.

Karen grabbed a pair of black dress pants from her closet and pulled them on. The first white blouse she saw in there was too low cut for Sunday services, so she yanked the one next to it off of its hanger, putting it on while slipping into her black flats. She brushed her hair and applied a little bit of makeup, then headed for the kitchen.

She knew she had to eat something, so she snatched a granola bar and a bottle of water to have in the car while driving to church. Since she'd eaten so late last night, she was sure that would suffice to keep her going. The last thing in the world she wanted was to feel bloated; her dislike of being stuffed had gotten her into trouble in the past and she never wanted to go there again.

Karen didn't have much time to think on the way there, but it was impossible to get the previous night out of her head. Had she dreamed the whole thing? Well, if she had, she'd be able to pinch herself at the park if Chris didn't come. She laughed to herself at that thought as she pulled into the parking lot.

Karen finished the last bite of the granola bar, took a swig of water to release the crumbs from her teeth, and then went inside just in time for Mass to start.

She slipped quietly into a seat at the back of the church, last pew on the right at the far end. The music had already started, so Karen let out a sigh and let the harmonious sounds of the choir wash over her.

Karen always enjoyed coming to church on Sundays. She loved the rustic woodwork, the sunlight streaming through the stained glass windows, and the exquisite statues. She always felt at peace here. Her favorite part, however, was the music. It had always been that way, ever since she was a child, no matter which church she attended.

She especially loved the choir at this church. It was obvious they had been together a long time and practiced endlessly. The sound was as close to perfect as she could imagine.

She usually got to church about 15 to 20 minutes early, so she could hear the choir go over the songs and responses before Mass. It had entered her mind once or twice to find out if she could join the choir. Actually, she thought about it more often than she cared to admit. She sang along during Mass, and figured she sounded pretty good, at least not as off-key as some of the other parishioners. The problem was that she was always too nervous about not being good enough that she never got up the courage to approach anyone about it. She didn't want to be the one to mess up their perfect sound.

Besides, she thought to herself, *I'd never be able to make it to choir practice. I'm always working too late.*

During the Mass, Karen silently thanked God for her unbelievable good fortune. It was more than she could ever have dreamed up by herself, and she was going to get to have this afternoon with Chris as well.

Thank you God, Karen prayed. *Not only for getting me to such an awesome show with such a great seat, but for giving me a chance to know Chris…not just as an entertainer, but as a person.*

Karen continued to pray and sing, and before she knew it Mass was over. She suddenly got those butterflies again, knowing that in a couple of hours she would be meeting Chris at the park.

She decided to drive along the coastline on the way home. The salty air gave her a rush, even though she was already on cloud nine.

When she got home, she made herself half a turkey sandwich, got a diet soda from the fridge, and sat down to eat. She changed into casual clothes, hoping she would look presentable enough for Chris after dazzling him yesterday with the green suit. *Oh well,* she thought, *I guess he's got to see me when I'm not dressed up at some point…it might as well be now. Wonder if he'll still be impressed?*

*****

Mass had ended at Chris' church, but just as he was on his way out he heard the voice of his pastor.

"Chris, could you give me a hand for a couple of minutes?"

Chris glanced at his watch. "Sure Father, as long as it doesn't take longer than that. I have to be somewhere at three o'clock."

"You'll be all right. I just need help moving a couple of things."

Chris and the priest started moving some furniture around. Once everything was in its place, Chris started to leave so he could still make it to the park by three o'clock. As he turned to say goodbye to Father John, he witnessed the priest tripping on the leg of a chair. He fell, hitting his head with a loud thud against the floor.

"Father!" Chris yelled as he rushed to his side. "Are you OK?"

"I'm not sure," he answered slowly. "I feel a little dizzy."

"Let me call an ambulance." Chris pulled out his cell phone and dialed 911.

Meanwhile, the associate pastor walked in from outside, where he'd been saying goodbye to parishioners. He looked down at Father John, then up at Chris. "What happened?"

"Father John fell and hit his head. The ambulance is on its way. I can wait until it gets here, but I have an appointment and no way to call and let them know I'm running late. Otherwise, I'd just stay with you."

"No problem, Chris," Father Timothy said. "I'll go with him in the ambulance so you can get going."

"Thanks. Here's my cell phone number if you need anything." Chris wrote the number on a church bulletin and handed it to Father Timothy. "Once you know how he's doing, please let me know."

"I will. And thanks, Chris."

Once the ambulance pulled up and Father John was taken aboard, Chris said a quick goodbye to Father Timothy and left for Ocean View Park.

Chris hoped he wouldn't be too late to the park. *Why didn't I get Karen's cell phone number?* He banged the palm of his hand lightly against the steering wheel. *It figures that since I didn't, something happened and I needed to call her. I hope she's not upset with me!*

It seemed to Chris that he got stopped at every red light on his way to the park. He hurried as fast as he could, anxious to explain everything to Karen and praying she wouldn't leave before he got there.

*****

Karen was sitting in the park, watching a group of kids play Frisbee with their Golden Retriever. As much fun as it was to see the playful pup leap up to catch the toy in his mouth, she was getting tired of waiting. It was almost 3:30...where was Chris?

He did say to meet him by the tennis courts, didn't he? Karen thought, realizing that she had only passed this park occasionally and had never actually set foot in it before. *I hope I didn't get it wrong. There's a basketball court here too. Maybe I'd better check it out.*

Karen quickly started walking to the basketball court that she passed on her way in. Since it was closer to the entrance, she thought maybe this was where Chris said to meet. *I could have heard him wrong. Or maybe he said tennis but meant basketball, since it's the first one when you come into the park.*

She got to the basketball court, but still did not see Chris. He wasn't at either place, and it was more than half an hour since they were supposed to meet.

"I guess it's time to pinch myself," she sighed. "I should have known this was too good to be true!"

She started slowly back the other way. Why did she dare to get her hopes up? She decided to take a leisurely walk through the park, since she was already here and had never explored it before. Maybe the walk would make her feel better. Right now she felt like an idiot for believing she stood a chance with Chris Lassiter.

Karen almost walked right by the action at the tennis courts, but then she heard her name.

*****

Chris had looked up just in time to see her. "I'm so glad you're still here!"

Karen breathed out a huge sigh. "I almost wasn't. What happened?"

53

Chris, still worried about Father John, blurted out the whole story.

"Karen, I'm so sorry I was late. It wasn't very smart of me not to get your phone number so I could call in case of emergency."

"It's all right, Chris. I should have thought to give you my number…guess I wasn't thinking either. It must be from being out of practice."

Chris' sheepish grin spread across his face. "Yeah, that goes for me too."

Karen's eyes grew wide. "You're kidding!"

The stupid grin was still plastered on his face as he spoke. "I'm afraid not. I've been working so hard on the music that I haven't had much of a social life."

Karen giggled. "I know the feeling. I work so many hours at my job that I don't socialize either. I don't get to talk to my friends back home, and I haven't really made any friends since I moved here."

Chris looked sympathetically into her eyes. "That's got to be rough. I know I'd be in the same boat if I didn't have the band."

"Really?"

Chris nodded. "God bless Jerry – he's been with me through thick and thin. When we found the rest of the band members, they just clicked with us. So we've all become close."

Karen paused for a moment. "But no one outside of the band?"

"Nope," Chris said. His mind raced back in time almost two decades. "Years ago, I was surrounded by friends, but once I wasn't on top anymore, most of them decided that they weren't my friends anymore either."

Karen's shock was evident in her eyes. "Are you serious, Chris? Were all of those people really that shallow?"

"Sure were…especially in Hollywood. A lot more people were concerned with what was in it for them than worried about anyone else's feelings."

"Is it still like that?"

"I don't know." Chris shrugged. "I've stayed away from Hollywood for quite a while. Maybe I've been afraid to find out."

Karen pushed the hair back out of her eyes, as if she were trying to push thoughts of those self-centered, so-called friends out of her head.

"Well, even though you're close enough to Hollywood, I'm glad you're not living right in the middle of it. Otherwise, you wouldn't be sitting right here."

Chris gave her a smile. "I'm glad I'm here too, Karen. Looks like it was meant for us to meet."

"You know, Chris, this may sound silly, but…" She hesitated.

"What?" Chris asked, a puzzled expression on his face. "Go ahead, tell me."

"Well, I almost feel foolish even saying this." Karen's cheeks turned a bright pink.

Chris was now on the edge of the bench. "Come on Karen, now my curiosity's piqued. Please tell me."

"All right." Karen took a deep breath. "It's just that I've had this feeling, you know, ever since I was eleven years old, that you and I were going to meet one day. My parents told me it was just silly, or maybe wishful thinking. But I really, truly felt it, and no matter what they told me I couldn't shake that feeling."

Chris took her hand. "Karen, don't feel silly about that. I've gotten feelings like that before."

Karen stared at him. "You have?"

"Absolutely. And I totally believe that those feelings helped steer me away from the wrong path, toward the way that was right for my life. Some people thought I was crazy, but so far my intuition's never steered me wrong."

Karen sighed. "I'm just glad you don't think I'm crazy."

"Far from it. In fact, I had the feeling that something special was going to happen at my comeback show, something that had nothing to do with my career. The moment I spotted you in the second row, my gut was telling me that it might have something to do with you."

For a moment the two of them just looked into each other's eyes. Chris still had Karen's hand, and he gave it a squeeze. She smiled.

"Okay," Karen said. "I definitely don't feel silly anymore."

The sound of a cell phone ringing brought them right back down to earth.

"Hello," Chris answered. "Father Timothy! How's Father John – is he all right?"

56

Karen listened intently to Chris' end of the conversation.

"Oh good! Can he have visitors? I'll see you in a little while. Thanks for calling. Bye."

Chris shut his phone and looked at Karen. "Well, Father John has a huge bump on his head, but no concussion or anything. He just needs to spend a couple of days in the hospital to rest so they can make sure he doesn't get dizzy anymore."

Karen let out a relieved breath. "I'm so glad. So he's resting now?"

"He is, but he can have visitors in about an hour. Do you want to go grab a sandwich somewhere, then we can go to the hospital?"

Karen's eyes got bigger than the tennis balls whizzing back and forth behind them. "You want me to go with you?"

"Well, sure. I think Father John would enjoy meeting you. It might even help him feel better. Besides, I have a selfish reason as well."

"Oh?"

Chris took Karen's hand again. "I really want to spend more time with you. Even though this emergency happened, I don't want to cut our time short. We've hardly had a chance to talk, and I'm not ready to say goodbye yet."

CHAPTER 7

Karen tried to keep up with Chris as she followed him into the hospital, slowly catching her breath as he made his way to the information desk. "This is ridiculous," she thought. "I really need to get back to my exercise program!"

Chris quickly got the attention of a silver-haired lady working at the desk. "Excuse me, what room is Father John Granville in?"

The lady smiled and looked at her chart. "That would be room 412."

"Great," said Chris. "May we go up and see him?"

"You sure can. The elevators are just around the corner on the right."

"Thanks so much. Are you ready, Karen?"

"Ready." Karen followed Chris to the elevator, holding the vase full of red and pink carnations they had bought for Father John on the way to the hospital. She was careful not to tip the vase, which was filled to the brim with water.

When they got to Room 412, they found Father John pushing food around on his plate.

"Hi Father! Sorry we're interrupting dinner; I thought they would have fed you sooner. Do you want us to come back later?"

"Chris! No, please stay." Father John wrinkled his nose and made a face. "I don't know how much of this hospital food I can stand to eat anyway."

Chris smiled. "Well, no matter how awful it is, you have to eat something. What did they give you to eat?"

The priest looked down at his tray and shook his head. "I know I've got chewy corn, stiff mashed potatoes, and a really hard roll. But I'm not quite sure what the meat is. Or if it's actually meat to begin with."

Chris and Karen smiled at each other.

"Father, I'd like you to meet my friend Karen. She came with me to visit you."

"I wondered who this pretty young lady was." Father John winked at Chris, then turned to Karen. "It's very nice to meet you, Karen."

Karen took Father John's outstretched hand and gently shook it. "It's a pleasure to meet you, Father. I'm glad to hear you're feeling better."

"Thanks to Chris. He took good care of me until the ambulance came. He's a wonderful person – better than most people give him credit for."

Karen was a bit startled by the comment. She glanced over at Chris, who had a strange look on his face as he began to look out the window.

"Well, Father," Chris quickly answered, "I think a lot of people are better than what most people think of them."

As Karen bowed her head, hoping to stay out of what she considered a potential argument, she caught sight of the flowers that she still held in her hands.

"Father John, we brought these to brighten your room." Karen slowly placed the slim vase on the empty nightstand. The pink and red blooms provided the only color in the entire room, which was done up in the standard style and shades of hospital white.

Father smiled. "Thank you. This room's about as exciting as my dinner here. It needed some cheering up."

Chris' face registered his happiness at the chance to change the subject. "OK Father, if that's the case…maybe you'd like to eat the flowers."

Father John laughed as he set down his napkin. "I don't think so, Chris."

Chris winked at Karen as he continued. "Oh, come on, I bet you'd like it. We'll chop them up and get some salad dressing to pour over them. How about some croutons on top?"

Karen just had to join in, though she was sure she would need to go to confession for teasing a man of the cloth. "Mmm, ranch dressing would be perfect. Maybe with bacon bits too."

"Yes!" said Chris. "And don't forget the cheese. No carnation salad would be complete without shredded cheese!"

"OK, OK, I'll eat some of my dinner." Father John pushed some corn and potatoes onto his fork. "But I'll definitely pass on the carnation salad."

Karen and Chris just grinned at each other as a nurse came in to take Father John's blood pressure.

"Wow, I'm impressed." She glanced at the tray as she wrapped the cuff around his upper arm. "How did you get him to eat?"

"It was easy," answered Chris. "We just mentioned, in a roundabout way, that the food could be a whole lot worse."

"By the way," Karen asked the nurse, "where is the ladies' room on this floor?"

"Go to the end of this hallway and then take a left. The bathrooms are right there."

"Thanks. I'll be back in a couple of minutes. Hey Chris, no sneaking any of Father John's food while I'm gone!"

"Oh, all right," Chris groaned. "It'll be hard, but I'll try to resist."

*****

After Karen went down the hall, Father John finally asked questions. "So Chris, I guess your appointment today was with Karen, right?"

All of a sudden Chris shyly looked down at the floor. "Yes, you're right."

"How long have you known her?"

"Well…" Chris looked up at Father John. "The rest of the band and I met her last night after the show."

Father John gave Chris a stern look.

"I know what I'm doing, Father. All we did today was go to the park to talk. Don't get worried."

"Chris Lassiter, have you learned nothing from your years of fame? How much do you know about this woman?"

"We've talked a lot, last night and today. We're still learning about each other. I just have a good feeling."

Father John sighed. "Just don't jump into anything, Chris. You know that's gotten you into trouble before."

"But that was years ago, when I was young and didn't know any better. You know, when I let fame go to my head."

"Just don't do that to yourself again, Chris."

"Father!" Chris raised his voice, then realized where he was and lowered it back to normal. "Father, please. I've learned from the past. I'm twenty years older – and wiser. I don't want anyone to get hurt, including myself. But I'm not going to live in a cave just so I don't get hurt. I'm going to give myself a chance to get to know people. Closing myself off from other human beings for the rest of my life isn't the answer."

"Just please be careful, OK? She seems really nice, but still be careful."

"I will. Please don't worry."

They both stopped talking as Karen walked back in the room.

"Wow," she said, "it got awfully quiet in here. You guys weren't talking about me, were you?"

Chris actually blushed a tiny bit. "Well, kind of…but only good things."

"I sure hope so!" Karen laughed. "Now let's hear more about Father John."

Father John almost dropped the forkful of mashed potatoes into his lap. "About me? Really?"

"Yes. All I know about you is how you're feeling after your fall."

Chris started to form a grin on his handsome face. "Oh, I think we can tell Karen a few things about you.

After all, you're a priest. There's no wild, sordid tales to tell, right?"

"OK." Father John told stories of his life in the priesthood to Karen for a little while, but then he began to look tired.

"Maybe we'd better go and let you get some rest, Father. I'll stop by and see you tomorrow," Chris promised.

"Sounds like a good idea. I am getting sleepy," Father agreed. "It was nice to meet you, Karen."

"It was great to meet you too, Father John. You get some rest."

*****

Karen followed Chris through all of the corridors and out of the hospital. Once they were in the parking lot, they quickly located Chris' car and got inside.

"Well, Karen," Chris said, "what else would you like to do tonight?"

Karen tried to think fast. "How about a walk on the beach?"

Chris looked at the sun getting lower in the sky. "This is perfect time of day for it. I love watching the sun set over the water. Great idea!"

When Chris and Karen arrived at the beach, they kicked off their shoes and walked barefoot on the still warm sand. Karen adored the feel of the sand around her feet, but being with Chris made it even better. It seemed now that she was spending time with him, her senses were so much sharper wherever they went together.

*****

Chris tried to enjoy his walk with Karen, but a nagging feeling came over him. Was he letting the emotions of his comeback run away with him? Was it too soon to be falling for Karen? He really wanted to trust his intuition, but Father John's words kept ringing in his ears.

Chris caught Karen looking over at him with a puzzled expression. "Chris, you're so silent all of a sudden. Is everything OK?"

Chris didn't really know how to answer. "I guess so. Maybe I'm just still worried about Father John."

There was a note of truth in that, but not in the way Karen would assume he meant it. But…what else could he say? He couldn't tell her that the priest wanted him to be suspicious of her.

"I understand," she replied. "If you don't feel like talking right now, it's all right. Just walking here with you and enjoying this beautiful evening is nice."

Chris smiled at her. Maybe he should just trust his instincts, and not worry about what someone else thought. Yet this thought came from a priest, one who was only trying to protect him.

"I'll tell you what. Let's walk a little longer. Then I'll drive you back to your car at the park. We're both tired, and I'm sure you have to go to work in the morning."

Karen frowned. "Oh yeah. Don't remind me."

"And I have an early appointment with the owner of the recording studio," Chris added. "I want to be wide awake since there's a lot riding on this meeting."

"I absolutely understand. You deserve to have everything go well tomorrow."

Chris drove Karen to the park, over to the spot where she had parked her car several hours earlier. "I really enjoyed our day together, Karen."

"Me too, Chris. I hope you can get some sleep tonight."

"You too. I hope you have a good day at work. Now that I have your number, I'll give you a call tomorrow night and we can plan to get together again."

"Sounds great. Good night, Chris."

"Good night, Karen." Chris leaned over to kiss her. He started for her lips, but with Father John in the back of his mind, he turned his head slightly and kissed her on the cheek instead.

Karen smiled as she got in her car and put the key in the ignition. Chris waited to make sure it started, then they both drove away to their separate homes.

CHAPTER 8

Karen was at work on a new proposal, but she couldn't keep her mind focused on it. Instead of typing the client's name, she kept typing in Chris Lassiter. After the fifth time that she had to delete his name out of the document she stopped counting, and instead began to say the client's name over and over to herself in her head to make it stick.

Karen, you've got to get it together! She was trying hard not to say it out loud out of frustration. Thankfully she was the only one in the room. Jim was meeting with another client in his office while she was working on this proposal, so he could neither see nor hear her as she feared she was losing her mind. As much as she was beginning to hate her job, she knew she couldn't afford to get fired.

It was no use. All she could think about was the amazing way her weekend had unfolded. Not only had she finally gotten to see Chris in concert, but she also got to meet him. And on top of it all, she actually had a date with him as well! This was someone she'd been crazy about since she was young, yet this was even better. She was getting to know the real person, instead of dreaming about a celebrity. So far, the real Chris was way better than anything she could have fantasized about.

Karen hoped she would hear from him tonight. She thought everything went well, but while they were on the beach Chris seemed to have something else on his mind. It was almost like he was purposely trying to avoid her gaze.

Karen tried to shake that thought out of her head. *Chris is a busy man*, she said to herself. *It's very possible for him to have thought about something he had to do, or something like that. And of course he was nervous about his meeting at the studio, since his career comeback is on the line. It probably had nothing to do with me at all. There's no use worrying. That's not going to help me get my work done.*

She went back to the proposal, this time trying harder to focus. She made a conscious effort to type something other than Chris' name into her computer, since she really needed to make some progress before Jim was done with his meeting.

*****

"Well, Chris," Charlie said with a chuckle as he rose from behind his desk, "I have to admit my wife dragged me to your show the other night. But once I got in the right frame of mind, I really enjoyed it. You have an excellent shot with these new songs. I think it's definitely comeback time for you!"

Chris could hardly contain his happiness. He loved that he had such a huge legion of female fans, but he really wanted both sexes to appreciate his music. At this point in his life he needed to appeal to as many people as possible, and hearing positive reinforcement from another male was exactly the musical medicine that he craved.

He was in an especially good mood as he walked back to his car. Everything went better than he had expected.

"Hi Chris!" Chris turned to see an attractive lady, who looked to be about his age, walking near him in the parking lot. "I was at your show this weekend. Awesome concert!"

Chris smiled. "Thank you so much."

She continued. "Still sounding great – and still looking good too!" She gave a sly smile as she winked at him.

Chris was so surprised that he blushed. *What is it with me lately…I blush at everything!* he thought as he hoped his face would cool down. *What am I…a thirteen year old girl?*

"Well," the lady said, "I have to get back to work or I'll be late. I'm glad I got to meet you!"

"M-me too," Chris stammered. "Thanks again."

As the lady continued her way down the street, Chris attacked his thoughts. *I suppose I'll have to get used to the attention again. I wasn't quite expecting that. Not after twenty years.*

Then he thought of Karen. Would she be able to handle him getting this kind of attention from other females?

Why am I even worried about that yet? He started walking more slowly. *I just met Karen. She's wonderful, but am I getting a little ahead of myself here?*

Chris knew Father John had a valid point. Chris had his heart broken many times before, something he'd confessed to Father when he was at his lowest point. But even with that in mind, shouldn't he still follow his intuition? And his heart? He really felt that maybe God was trying to tell him something – something that was not coming in the form of a parish priest. He knew God sometimes spoke in mysterious ways; His message didn't always come from the place you would expect.

Chris found himself now standing in front of his car. He got in but couldn't bring himself to start it. He just sat there staring into space.

"I have too many different things going on in my head," he finally said aloud, now that he was shut tight in his car all by himself. "I'd better get my mind cleared before I drive anywhere."

Chris leaned back in his seat to relax. The warm sun streaming through the windows felt so good on his face. He closed his eyes, and in almost no time at all Chris was asleep.

*****

Karen buckled down, but it still took her until mid-afternoon to finish that blasted proposal. Once that was accomplished, she was able to get re-focused and everything else done on her to-do list. Now that it was five o'clock, she grabbed her purse from under the desk and quickly made her way to the door.

"Hey Karen." Jim met her right in the doorway. "Let's stay and work on that new client I met with today. We can get a jump start on tomorrow."

Karen shook her head as she slung her purse over her shoulder. "Sorry Jim, not today. I have plans for after work. Besides, my head is spinning from today's proposal. I don't think I could focus anymore."

She couldn't help but notice the wide-eyed look on Jim's face. She knew this was the first time she had ever said no to working late, and she realized he was probably in shock.

"Well...okay," he said. "I...guess I'll see you in the morning."

"See you tomorrow, Jim. Have a good evening." Karen slid the car keys out of her purse and headed out the door.

Once outside, she took a deep breath of fresh air, then let it out slowly. She got in her car and drove out of the parking lot, happy to drive away from the building while it was still light outside.

"Thank God," she said as she made her way down the freeway, "I'm not stuck at work all night again. I don't think I could have taken it today."

Karen got home, slipped her purse off her shoulder onto the couch, and went into her kitchen. She fixed herself a turkey sandwich and got a diet soda out of the fridge, determined to stick to hew new eating plan. As she kicked off her tight work shoes and sat down to eat, she felt her body begin to relax.

As she started to unwind, she also started thinking. *What am I going to do with myself all night?* As wonderful as it was to be away from the office, she couldn't help but think about how unusual this was for her. She needed to get her stressful routine out of her mind and do something else.

Maybe the beach would be a good idea…to take a nice walk and clear her mind. At least with Chris having her cell phone number now, she didn't have to sit at home to wait for his call. Thank heaven for technology!

Karen finished eating and ran upstairs. She took off her heavy work clothes and changed into a T-shirt and shorts. She slipped her feet into a pair of sandals and ran back downstairs.

On her way out, she picked up her phone and keys. Off to the beach she went, anticipating a relaxing stroll along with her important phone call. She knew full well that both of these things in combination would make her feel much better and release the work stress.

She was smart to wear shorts with pockets. Her phone went into the left pocket and her keys into the right, leaving her hands free to swing as she walked. Sunlight streamed onto the ocean, making tiny bright lights sparkle everywhere she looked. Karen stopped and slipped off her sandals. She flung them onto the sand, leaving them there to pick up on her way back.

The warmth of the sand felt amazing on her feet, loosening them up after being in cramped shoes all day. It was almost like having a free foot massage.

All right, Karen sighed. *I could definitely get used to this. I know my feet sure could!*

She walked all the way to the Pier, then back to the spot where she had left her shoes. She sat down, leaned back, and soaked up the late day rays.

A few minutes later, Karen's phone rang. Her heart jumped when she saw the number and she answered on the second ring.

"Hi Chris."

"Hi Karen. How did work go today?"

"Well…it was all right."

"Just all right?"

"Yeah. It was hard to keep my mind on work."

"Really?" teased Chris. "So just where was your mind?"

71

Karen was glad Chris couldn't see her face turning red. "Actually, it was on you, sometimes. Plus the whole weekend was just awesome. I can't remember when I've had such a great weekend."

Chris laughed knowingly on the other end. "I agree. It was an incredible weekend. And I've been thinking about you all this afternoon."

Karen almost dropped her phone, tightening her grip to keep it from falling into the sand. "Really?"

"You'd better believe it. Once I got home from the meeting, I kept thinking about you. And the meeting, of course."

"So, how did it go this morning?"

"Better than I could have ever dreamed. He's even going to give me some extra studio time to experiment with some soul, some R & B."

"That's great, Chris! You could sing just about any style of music you want anyway."

Chris hesitated. "Well...I know I like to sing different styles. I'm just not sure what the public will think."

"Chris," Karen said gently, "you have to please yourself first. If you enjoy singing it, people will notice and they'll love it too."

"Hmm...that makes a lot of sense. I just know it will surprise a lot of people."

"Well, it's good to keep them guessing. Besides, I've always said that you could record 'Chris Lassiter Sings The Phone Book' and it would be a hit."

Now Chris laughed out loud. "Now <u>that</u> would be an interesting album." There was a second of silence. "Oh, excuse me, I mean <u>CD</u>."

Karen's laugh was loud enough for other people walking by on the beach to hear. "I guess you'll just have to get used to this new-fangled technology."

"Yeah, I want everyone to think I'm still hip – or whatever word means 'hip' now."

"Chris, you're not <u>that</u> old!"

"I know. But I'm not twenty anymore either."

"You're getting better with age."

"Kind of like wine?"

"Absolutely," Karen stated. "And just as intoxicating."

Chris was stunned. "Oh wow, Karen. I'm flattered."

"And I mean every word." She was blushing from head to toe, but since she was giving the compliment over the phone it didn't matter one bit.

"So…what time do you get off work, Karen?"

"Today I left at five o'clock. Most days I've wound up working late. In fact," Karen said proudly, "this is the first day I've ever told my boss I couldn't stay late."

"Karen…honestly?"

"Oh yes, it's true. I really shocked Jim. He didn't know what to say."

"I'll bet he didn't!"

"It just felt so good to not be stuck at work and actually have the evening to myself," Karen gushed. "I should have done this sooner!"

"Well, why didn't you?"

It was quiet on the phone for a moment while Karen mulled that over. "I guess I never really thought I had a choice. I thought it would make me look bad, like I'm not a team player."

"So…what made today different?"

Karen immediately knew the answer to that. "I finally realized that my job is not my life. There are other things that are important other than work. This weekend made me understand that. I've been so burned out at my job, it made me too numb to do anything else. It's an awesome feeling to know that there's more to life!"

"I'm so glad, Karen. It sounds like you really need to get away from work."

"I really do, otherwise I may just go insane."

"Well, in case you do go insane," Chris said slyly, "you'll look awfully cute in that straitjacket."

"Chris! That's just terrible!"

"Maybe so, but it is the truth."

"Thanks. That's really sweet. But," laughed Karen, "I'd rather keep my sanity and wear something a little more stylish."

"So does this mean the end of late nights at work?"

"Kind of. I might stay a little bit, here and there. Just not so late, maybe just an hour sometimes. I don't want them to totally go into shock!"

"That's true," said Chris. "I guess you have to let them get used to it a little at a time."

"Exactly," Karen agreed. "I really can't afford to have them think I'm looking for another job."

"I didn't mean it that way, Karen. Besides, they should realize that you're not a slave."

"I know. I just meant that I can't go losing this job without having another one lined up."

"Do you have any jobs in mind at all?"

"No, not really. I think I'd like to do something different. I know I'm restless." Karen stared out over the ocean. "The problem is figuring out what that something different is that will make me happy."

"I get it," Chris said. "But in the meantime, if you're planning on staying at work tomorrow, how about afterward we meet for a late dinner?"

"That would be wonderful, Chris. Are you sure you don't mind having dinner late?"

Chris just laughed. "Now, remember, I'm a musician. I have no problem being up late, and we eat at all hours of the day most of the time anyway. Besides," he said, "I don't have to get up till the crack of noon."

"True," said Karen. "I forgot about that. Silly me."

"Yeah, it's great! You ought to try it sometime!"

"Sure, Chris," Karen snickered. "First let me get used to not working into the night."

"Gotcha. Let's meet at seven. How about Mexican?"

"Sounds delicious. There's a great place called Carlita's. It's about two blocks from my office."

"It's a date," said Chris. "See you tomorrow night."

CHAPTER 9

Karen got more work done than she could have hoped, considering the lack of concentration that had plagued her the day before. Maybe all she needed was some motivation…in the form of Chris Lassiter. She wanted to make sure there was no reason that she couldn't leave the office at a decent hour for her dinner date.

This was really happening, to her of all people. Even Chris called it a date. Karen still had trouble believing it was real; this kind of thing never happened to ordinary people like her.

Then again, now that she was getting to know Chris, she found herself starting to believe it. She just had to replace the fantasy from long ago in her mind with the real thing. As amazing as the scenarios formed in her girlhood imagination were, the reality that was upon her now left her in awe.

I guess someone up above is watching out for me. Obviously He knows how things should go better than I do. And He knows what He's doing!

Her thoughts were interrupted by Jim, who was standing in her office doorway, leaning against one side with his arms crossed. "Hey Karen. Will you be able to stay later tonight?"

Karen let out a light sigh. "Well Jim, I do have some plans for later, but I can stay until 6:30."

Jim stood straight up, his head almost reaching the top of the doorway. He put on his usual polite, tight-lipped smile, which Karen had seen him give to difficult clients. She wondered if he was now putting her in the same category.

"OK, that will at least help a little bit," he said quietly. "Thanks, Karen."

"Sure, Jim." Karen knew she was throwing her boss for a loop, but she wasn't ready to share any more information with him just yet. This was all still new to her as well.

As Jim turned to walk away, Karen could see the bewildered look frozen on his face. She put her hand up to her mouth as if to cough, attempting to keep Jim from seeing the little smile that was forming on her lips.

Once Karen got her original tasks done for the day, she met with Jim in his office. After going over his notes, she set to work on the new proposal.

Maybe, Karen thought while she worked, *what we really need is to hire another person. Then the rest of us wouldn't be overworked and burnt out. I bet we would all do a better job if we weren't overwhelmed.*

The clock hands seemed to move at a snail's pace for Karen. As she typed she kept glancing over, but every time she did it was only a couple of minutes later. It only made the day feel longer than it already was, but she couldn't keep herself from looking at the moving hands over and over again.

Finally! It was 6:30, and the extra time she'd grudgingly given to her boss was over. Karen took the part of the proposal she had finished over to Jim's office, promised to finish the rest of it in the morning, and said good night.

Karen let herself exhale at last once she was inside of her car. It was good to be free! Making the moment even sweeter was thinking about Chris waiting for her at the restaurant. She could hardly wait to see his sparkling hazel eyes looking into hers.

In a few minutes time, she was in the parking lot of Carlita's. Standing near the front door was Chris, looking casual and cool in jeans and a dark green shirt.

Karen wondered if she would be overdressed. She was still in her stuffy suit from work, and she hadn't thought about bringing a change of clothes with her for a casual restaurant setting. She made a mental note to remember that for the future.

As Chris spotted Karen getting out of her car, his entire face lit up with a big smile. He waved to her.

"I was worried that your boss wouldn't let you out on time," he said.

"I was kind of worried about that myself. I know he wanted me to stay even later, but he didn't stop me from leaving. I think I have him stumped. He's too confused to really say anything about it." As she remembered the look on Jim's face, Karen broke into a fit of laughter. "Even though I feel a little guilty about it, I'm enjoying his confusion. I just can't stop myself from getting a kick out of it."

Her laughter was contagious, and Chris found himself joining in right away. "Well Karen, you just might be entitled to enjoy it a little. After all, look at how much of your time you've given to the company…time that should have gone into your life instead of your job."

"Very true," said Karen, "but it's still a bit weird to be feeling this way."

"You are human. I think anyone in your position would be at least slightly amused. Come on, Karen, you know that you've been taken for granted."

Karen looked right into Chris' kind, sympathetic eyes. "You know, you hit the nail right on the head. It just took me a long time to realize it myself. Too long."

"Or...just too long to do something about it."

"Exactly. Since I'm on salary, they've basically been getting all of the extra time out of me for free."

"And it's time for that to stop. Now, there's something else we have to do something about," Chris said. "I'm starving!"

"Me too. Let's go in!"

Chris and Karen found a table in the corner by the window, giving them some privacy to talk. Karen ordered an orange-mango margarita.

"I'll have one too, but make it virgin," Chris told the waiter.

Karen's eyebrows went up, even as she was trying to act nonchalant. "Are you not feeling well, Chris?"

As he hesitated, Chris let out a sigh. "I'm all right. It's just that...well..."

"You don't care for tequila. That's OK, they have beer and wine here too."

"No, that's not really it." Chris took a deep breath and went on. "Back in my younger days, I used to drink too much. All of that 'big star' stuff, I guess, going to parties and overdoing it. I was never actually an alcoholic, but still didn't keep control of myself like

I should have. So, I try to limit any alcohol to very rare occasions."

"Oh." Karen thought of her own choice of beverage. "Will it bother you if I have one? You know, will it be too tempting?"

"No, don't change your order for me," Chris said. "Back when I first cut down, it would have been a problem. Now I have better willpower and self-control. It doesn't bother me."

"OK…if you're sure. I think I can count the number of times I have a drink on one hand, so it really wouldn't be a problem for me to skip it."

"Positive. Besides, the non-alcoholic one still tastes great."

Karen was surprised by this revelation, but she tried not to let it bother her. She knew that Chris was not the first person ever to go through something like this. Besides, he seemed to have the issue under control, which is what really mattered.

The waiter came back to the table with a basket of tortilla chips and Carlita's special recipe salsa. "I'm so hungry I could eat the whole basket of chips," Chris said.

"So could I." Karen looked down wistfully at her hips. "But I have to make sure that I don't eat too many."

"Karen, don't worry about that. You're beautiful just as you are."

Karen smiled at Chris shyly. "Thank you, but I could still eat healthier."

"Well, I'm sure I could too. I try, but sometimes you just have to relax. You can't make yourself nuts over it."

Karen's nervous laugh threatened to give her away. "I guess you're right." She held the menu to her face as she bit her lip. *If only he knew.*

"So," Chris said, snapping Karen back into the present. "What's good here? There are too many appealing choices for me to narrow it down."

"Well, I've never had anything here that wasn't good. I do have two favorites though. The shrimp and crab enchiladas are to die for, and the chicken burrito with green sauce is awesome."

Hmm, I've never done the seafood thing at a Mexican restaurant. I think I should branch out a little and try that."

"I'm willing to bet that you're going to love it."

"You know," Chris said, "after the concert, the band and I were going to have Mexican at the cantina over by the Civic Center. We wound up at the diner because there was a kitchen fire and the cantina was closed."

"So that explains all of the police cars and fire trucks that night! I'm sorry they had a fire, but I'm glad it brought you to the diner…otherwise we wouldn't have met."

"I have the feeling that God was setting up our meeting." Chris smiled, never taking his eyes off of Karen. "And right now, I have another feeling."

Karen's stomach felt like it dropped to her knees. "Oh? What do you mean?"

"I mean...I have this feeling we're going to suddenly be surrounded by music."

The mariachi band started up behind her, and Karen jumped out of her seat as if she'd sat upon a pincushion.

Chris chuckled. "Are you OK? I meant it as a surprise, not to send you into shock!"

"I'm fine." Karen took a deep breath. "Maybe it's just the surprise attack from behind."

It took a minute, but the color finally came back to her face. Chris breathed a huge sigh of relief. "You're sure you're OK now?"

"Yeah, I'm fine. It's a great surprise, it's just..."

"The sneak attack. I'm sorry, I didn't think about them coming up from behind."

"That's all right. I'm over it now. I notice the band has never stopped playing, even through my meltdown."

"You're right." Chris glanced up at the mariachi players, all with smiles plastered on their faces as they performed. "They must be used to the different reactions from customers by now."

Then one of them spoke. "Now, a special song for the beautiful senorita."

The band began to play "Spanish Eyes". Karen immediately felt her heart rate slow.

"This is one of my favorite songs. I've loved it since I was a girl. How did you know?"

Chris shrugged. "This one was just a lucky guess. They asked me if I wanted a special song, and I couldn't think of too many, since I don't really know you that well yet. This is the one that popped into my head first. I'm glad I chose the right one."

"You certainly did! You should make lucky guesses more often."

Karen closed her eyes and breathed in the music. It took her back to when she was young, a true romantic even then. She supposed this song was coming back to haunt her, but in a good way.

Chris stared intently at Karen, trying to look through her closed eyelids and into her brain. "OK Karen, a penny for your thoughts."

Karen smiled, eyes still closed. "I was remembering how I used to listen to this song when I was younger. My parents had a couple of different records with this song on it, and I used to listen with them. I started to love the records so much that I used to put them on myself, even if my parents were busy doing something else. While the music was on, I used to dream."

"About what?"

Karen almost wished she hadn't let out that last sentence, but she decided to go on. "I dreamed of my own little romances. Sometimes they were about whoever was singing the song I was listening to, sometimes someone else."

"Oh? Like maybe a boy in your class?"

"No, not really." Karen drew in a deep breath, then let it out slowly. "It…was you. I had it so bad for you. No matter who else I started thinking about, it always came back to you."

At that moment the server brought out their meals. Chris looked happy to see the food; Karen was sure that he needed the extra minute or two to contemplate what he just heard from her. Once the server walked away, he spoke.

"I guess I knew that girls dreamed about me since they saw me on TV, and of course I remember the completely insane concerts. But I never realized that someone so young, who was not even a teenager yet, could feel that way."

Karen was relieved that Chris finally said something. She also felt that she needed to explain herself further.

"I was about ten when I started having those feelings. I was still pretty naïve at that age, but other than that I knew what I felt. I guess it sounds weird, doesn't it?"

"It's not really weird, just hard to fathom. I knew kids liked TV stars, this is just…wow."

"I know," Karen said, her stomach in knots at this point. "Sometimes I can't even believe how intense my emotions were at that time. I just know that they were."

"How long did you have these feelings?"

"For years. It went way beyond your show going off the air. No one else after you ever compared."

"What about boys your age – like at school?"

"Well, there were a couple of guys I liked; there was one especially in junior high. But neither one was interested. Greg, the guy from junior high, really rejected me big time. It came out that a big part of that was because of my being chubby then. That was one thing a lot of the guys just couldn't handle."

Chris' face fell. "That's awful, Karen. As beautiful as you are now, I'm sure you were really cute then. It's a shame that young, immature minds can't get past that."

"Some adults can't get past it either. Anyway, real life romances never got off the ground. I knew I hadn't actually met you, but I felt something special about you. I just couldn't help myself."

"Wow," Chris said once again. "I'm just taking this all in. Most of those screaming girls moved on to the next big thing once the show was done. What made it different for you?"

"I'm still not really sure, other than having this feeling that there was more to you than being a big star. So I guess it wasn't about me being attached to someone famous. It was about you as a person, so it felt wrong to go crazy about just any other celebrity."

"Karen, I'm just so overwhelmed by this. I have to say, I am impressed with your loyalty. I've dated fans in the past, but this is different. I feel a real connection with you."

Karen smiled at him through her tears. "I feel the same way, Chris."

"It just might take me a little while to absorb all of this, that's all. When I dated other fans, it was during my time in the spotlight. I didn't ever have to deal with something like this before."

Karen nodded. "Believe me, I understand. I suddenly dropped a lot of strange information on you."

"Well, I did too…you know, about the alcohol thing. We just keep learning new things about each other."

"We're full of surprises, aren't we?" Karen blinked back another tear.

"Don't cry, honey. It's all stuff we need to know about each other so it's going to come out at some point. It's better we share it with each other than to keep it a secret."

"I know you're right," gulped Karen, "but it still makes me a nervous wreck."

Chris sighed as he took Karen's hand. "I know, but let's just both try to relax. We can finish our dinner, then how about a moonlight walk on the beach to help us clear our heads?"

Karen nodded again and held tightly to Chris' hand. She just hoped they could work through all of this. It was still so early in their relationship; would their feelings for each other be strong enough to overcome unexpected revelations?

Karen prayed with her entire heart that they would.

CHAPTER 10

Friday came with disbelief from Karen that she had made it to the end of the workweek. For the last few days, she could have sworn she'd been on the world's longest roller coaster ride.

She and Chris had agreed on Tuesday night to each take a couple of days for themselves. Chris had a lot to take care of before going into the recording studio next week, and they would have some time to take in all that had happened between them in a few short days.

Karen's head was spinning and her stomach was turning, in combination with her regular panic attacks every morning. Chris had told her that he was blown away as well, though she had no idea if he was having the same physical symptoms. She was also sure that this was just the beginning…and there were more startling revelations about each other yet to come.

Karen's heart felt like a cement block sinking down to her stomach, nestling itself among the series of knots that had formed there. She knew for a fact there were more surprises in store for Chris. Since she and Chris were going to meet for dinner after she got off of work tonight, her mind put her through a series of both excited and anxious thoughts. She wasn't sure what to expect.

The roller coaster ride would continue on. Karen knew that even though she was frightened to death, she did not want to get off.

At least there's one thing I know for sure, Karen thought. *I'm not going to be staying late at work anymore, no matter what happens with Chris. I've had enough of that.*

Even though she hadn't spent time with Chris the last couple of nights, she still left work on time, except for the measly half hour she had stayed on Wednesday. That was just to complete a project that was almost done, so she wouldn't have to deal with it the next morning. It would be one less thing to panic over.

It's time I have a life outside of my job. Whether I'm with Chris or someone else, or I even want to spend time by myself, I have a right to that. No more being taken advantage of!

Once she'd grabbed a quick sandwich and taken a walk on the beach that Wednesday evening after her "overtime", Karen went home and accomplished something else.

Karen put pen to paper and poured out her heart. Everything she was feeling about Chris came together as the lyrics of a new song, the first set of lyrics Karen had ever completed.

She had written down ideas before, a few words or titles here and there, but had never actually done anything else with them. Despite the promise she made to herself only a month ago, the only thing she had done was buy that music notebook.

Now that her mind was free from work in the evenings, Karen had time to devote to writing. Why not start with the man who inspired her love for music in the first place?

Karen stared at the paper in front of her. The lyrics were in place. Now…what about the music?

Karen discovered that she hadn't packed her old guitar for her move to California. She called her dad back in Indiana, who informed her that since she had left it behind, he had given Karen's guitar to a young relative who wanted to take lessons.

At least it's being put to good use, Karen thought, *but now I have to find a new one.*

On Thursday after work, she went to the nearest music store, the same one where she bought the notebook. She picked out a brand new acoustic guitar. It was even more beautiful than the one she had as a girl. The honey-colored instrument had gorgeous Southwestern detailing, and the minute Karen touched it she fell in love.

It certainly didn't take much convincing from the salesman, who sold her the works – case, strap, and everything she needed for the complete package. Karen smiled all the way home, then immediately went to work on the music for her new song. She didn't get the melody entirely worked out, but she was well on her way.

Karen went over all of this in her mind as her workday neared its end. Soon she would be with Chris at the restaurant. She knew they had a lot to talk about, but she wasn't ready to mention the song just yet. Besides, it wasn't complete.

The clock on her desk hit five on the dot. Karen said goodbye to Jim, who was still curious but didn't even dream of asking her to stay now. She left for the restaurant with confusion in her mind and unrest in her soul.

*****

Chris had Karen on his mind. Actually, she had never been off of his mind since Tuesday night. No matter where he was or what he was doing, he could not stop thinking about her.

He hoped he hadn't frightened her. She looked like a deer caught in the headlights at the cantina, and he knew she had to be wondering what he was really thinking about her revelations.

Chris himself wondered exactly what he was thinking. He knew a lot of girls had crushes on him, but Karen's crush seemed so…well, intense. He thought that was a little unusual, especially considering she had never even met him until a few days ago.

Father John's words still haunted him. *Am I jumping into something too soon with a fan…a fan who had been fixated on me when she was younger?* Chris sighed at his own thoughts.

Even with knowing all of that, he still had strong feelings for Karen. Maybe there was a reason all along for her feeling that way so long ago. Besides, he'd dropped some surprising news about himself on her too.

Chris' head was starting to throb. He really cared about Karen. She was special – very special. Still, perplexing thoughts were swirling around in his head.

As he sat waiting for Karen at the bistro, Chris sipped mineral water, anticipating the evening ahead. Yet he wondered just what he would be able to eat as his stomach nervously competed with his mind for attention.

*****

Karen headed into the bistro, feeling the shaking of her knees as she walked slowly to the front counter. As she made her way over to the maître-d, he looked up and smiled.

"Miss O'Neil?" he inquired.

"Yes," she answered, surprised. "That's me."

"Let me show you to your table. Mr. Lassiter is already seated."

"Thank you," Karen said, following him.

As they walked through the restaurant, Karen caught sight of Chris. Their eyes met, and Chris grinned at her. That smile, ever since she was ten years old, had always made her feel that everything was going to be all right.

Karen swallowed hard, trying to push the feeling of her throat tightening out and away. She prayed that was still the case. She nervously smiled back.

The maître-d pulled out Karen's chair and she sat down. "Thank you so much, sir," she said.

"You're quite welcome, Miss O'Neil. Have a good evening."

As Karen looked at Chris again, she sure hoped it would be.

Chris closed his eyes, quickly opened them, and took Karen's hand. The touch of his hand caused a warm feeling that ran all the way through her, and Karen felt her body start to calm down.

"I was worried you wouldn't be here," she said.

Chris' smile faded a little. "Actually, I was nervous that you wouldn't show up."

"I would never do that to you, Chris. Never."

Chris let out a long, deep breath. "I'd never do that to you either, but that thought crossed my mind, awful as it was."

"Believe me, I get it. Guess that's just part of our learning process," Karen said. "So, we both made it here. I propose we just take it from there."

Chris' face brightened again. "Sounds like a plan. So what's new in the last couple of days?"

"Well," Karen started, "let's just say I didn't throw myself into my work."

"OK Karen, what does that mean?"

"I'm done with staying late. I mean, the one day I stayed a little just to finish something up, but that was only twenty minutes or a half hour at the most. I decided I need to start doing other things, like get some exercise or work on some things around the house."

Karen didn't elaborate on exactly what "things" she was doing around the house, and to her relief Chris didn't ask.

"That's great, Karen. There's more to a person's life than a job. Is this new way of thinking still baffling your boss?"

Karen nodded as she reached for her water goblet. "He doesn't ask, but I know he's still wondering what's going on with me."

"It is your right to have your own life after hours. There's no need to explain to Jim; it's really none of his business anyway."

"My thoughts exactly." Karen grinned. "Now, how's it been going at the studio? Are you ready for next week?"

The knot in Chris' stomach loosened into a feeling of excitement. "So far, awesome. All of the details are worked out. Of course, there are always some things you work out as you go, but that's normal. I can't wait for Monday. I wonder why I waited so long to start recording again."

"It's obvious you've really missed it all this time."

"I guess so. I just never realized how much until I started getting involved with it again."

"Why did you wait so long?"

Chris hesitated. He didn't know if he wanted to drop anymore bombshells on her right now. "It's kind of…a complicated combination of things. One reason is that I kept wondering if my time in the spotlight had come and gone. I didn't know if anyone would really want to hear me sing again."

"Really?" Karen said. "You're such a phenomenal singer. How could you be so concerned about that?"

"Now remember, most of my fans were teenagers and younger, like you. I thought they had grown up and most likely outgrown me."

"OK. I guess I can see what you mean. But rest assured, we may all have grown up, but we still know a great voice when we hear it. Believe me, you haven't been forgotten, not by me or anyone else who adored you back then."

Chris felt tears coming to his eyes, but he managed to blink them back quickly. "Thanks, Karen. That's my hope, but it's really good to hear it spoken out loud."

The waitress came by to take their order. They quickly settled on a couple of Cobb salads, though Chris asked her to leave the bleu cheese off of his. Chris requested another mineral water, while Karen ordered an iced tea.

"Now," Chris ventured, "I think I'm ready to hear more about those records…you know, your parents' records that you listened to."

Karen felt like she had to swallow to get her heart back down to its proper place. "Are you sure? You really want to go there?"

"Yes. I know I wasn't quite ready a couple of days ago, but I've had time to think. It's part of what makes you tick, Karen, and I'm intrigued by anything that's a part of who you are."

It was Karen's turn to blink away tears. "Wow Chris, that makes me feel so much better. I'm glad I didn't scare you away."

"That's all right, honey. I was worried I'd scared you when I freaked out the other night."

"Well, you did just a little bit, but certainly not enough to keep me away."

"Good," Chris sighed. "So let's pick up where we left off with that."

"OK. My parents had a decent record collection, and there were a few that we played on the stereo all the time. You know, one of those big console stereos, the kind that took up as much room as a couch or other piece of furniture."

"Ah, yes. I remember those. They opened from the top and the speakers were built into the wooden front."

"Exactly," Karen said. "And there was a wide section inside next to the turntable to hold your albums. We had more albums than that could hold, but my mom's and dad's favorites went in there so we could just pull one out and pop it right on."

"Sounds just like my mom's stereo," remembered Chris. "She kept her favorites in there too."

"My parents had a variety of favorites. There was Irish music for my dad, polkas for my mom, and some other stuff they both liked. A couple of the albums we listened to all the time were male singers. I guess you could say they were my mom's idols, closer to her age. But a lot of it was very romantic music."

Chris nodded his head. "That definitely sounds like my mom's collection. There were a lot of romantic singers, the kind that could make a girl swoon back in the day."

"My mind tuned in to that very early on. Even though I was really young and didn't know the facts of life, per se, I knew people went on dates, fell in love, got married, that kind of stuff. The words and music were so powerful…it got my imagination going. I've always felt things deeply, so I really got into the songs."

"That does make sense. Music is such a powerful force."

"And then," Karen went on, "along came 'The Amazing Anderson Boys'. Even though a lot of people called it bubblegum, it was great music and well written. When you released your solo records, it confirmed your talent for me. Hearing you sing made me want to sing. Your voice was so amazing; you nailed every song on all of those albums. And the fact that you were so gorgeous definitely didn't hurt."

Chris began to blush. "That still gets me. I mean, I never thought I was bad-looking, but the response I got from girls – it was just overwhelming. I certainly thought there were better looking guys out there than me."

"I could only imagine how crazy it seemed for you," said Karen. "There was no doubt that you had 'it'. You were the total package…great looks, great voice, great sense of humor, and more. It was so easy to fall for you, and I fell hard. I don't think even my parents knew just how hard. So when I'd listen to <u>their</u> romantic songs, I naturally thought about you then as well. When I'd think about us together, I always imagined myself as being a few years older, because obviously a young adult male and a not yet teenage female together was not right. So I imagined us being about the same age and falling in love. I'd dream of us dancing together to those songs."

"Sounds like you had things well thought out, definitely beyond the realm of a hysterical, screaming teenager."

"I was always more mature for my age than most," Karen answered. "And I have to say, I've never in my life been accused of being shallow. I always knew there was more to you than just being a star."

"Funny," Chris said, "that's something I wanted so badly when I was on the show. I always wanted people to realize that I was a real person with real feelings, not just this idol placed on a pedestal. Although there were a few ways I was like my character, there were many ways I was not like Grant. I think some people actually thought my name was Grant."

"I must admit, sometimes I did dream of you in character, because it was so easy to just insert myself into the storylines. But I also knew the difference…dreaming of you quite often as Chris, you know, yourself, like maybe we had met after you were done with work on the set, and I got to be a part of your real life."

"This is all still sinking in," Chris replied, "but I'm not so freaked out anymore. I do still have to absorb all of this information, you know."

"Of course, Chris. I don't pretend to snap my fingers and expect us to understand everything perfectly. There's a lot to each of us. We've only known each other really about a week; it will take some time. I'm sure I have a lot more to learn about you too."

Chris tried his best not to look uneasy. *You don't know the half of it,* he thought, while all he actually said was, "That's true."

They both fell silent as the waitress arrived with their salads, but Karen picked up where she left off once they were alone again.

"For the record, a couple of years after the show was done…when you got engaged, I was kind of bummed, but I was also really happy for you. I knew I was still really young; I didn't have a chance anyway because you were an adult. I was glad you found someone."

"Thanks," Chris said ruefully. "But as it turned out, we never did get married."

"I did eventually find that out. I never heard anything about the wedding. It was probably two or three years later that I heard the engagement had been broken."

"Yes. That was a very painful time."

"Oh Chris, I'm sorry," Karen said sorrowfully. "I should have thought better of it. I'm so sorry I brought it up."

"It's all right Karen, really. It's a part of my past, so you have a right to know what affected me as a person."

Karen hesitated. "Do you…want to talk about it? Or if it's too painful, I understand."

"Well, I won't go into great detail right now, but …" Chris sighed deeply, feeling it all the way through his body. "I really thought she loved me, that we were two of a kind with our singing careers and all. It turned out she was using me just to make a bigger name for herself. I found out she never really loved me at all. She sure put on a good act though. She had me fooled."

"Chris, that's absolutely awful. It makes me sick to my stomach that someone could treat another person like that."

"That's just it. She didn't care about me as a person, or consider that I had real feelings. She only cared about herself – what was in it for her."

"That is just plain disgusting. You didn't deserve that. No one does."

"Thank you. You're absolutely right." Chris took a bite of his salad, then went on. "That's a big part of the reason I dropped out of sight for a while as well. Between my ex-fiancée and those so-called friends I had, I found it hard to trust anybody."

Karen took Chris' hand in both of hers and held onto it tightly. "I can certainly see why you felt like that."

"The only people I trusted were my mom and Jerry." Chris thought back and smiled. "Jerry's been with me through my best and my worst. I thank God every day for giving me a friend like Jerry. I would never have made it through that time without him."

"Oh Chris, I'm so glad you have Jerry too. Everyone needs a friend like that."

Karen broke eye contact with Chris, looking wistfully into the distance. "I sure could use a friend like that. I have a couple of good friends back in Indiana, and we try to keep in touch by e-mail, but it's hard sometimes." She looked again at Chris. "And nothing beats having a friend that lives close by, so you can actually see each other face to face and do stuff together. Plus you can really, physically, be there to help each other out."

"Well maybe," Chris said, "now that you're not always stuck at work, you'll be able to make more friends out here."

"I am glad I'll be able to do things other than just work. To be able to see friends? That would be wonderful."

As they ate, Karen had a great idea. "So Chris, how would you like to see my place after dinner? Believe it or not, you'll be the first person ever to be over there with me, except for the movers when I came here."

"Seriously?"

"Honest, Chris. My company paid for everything, so I didn't have to make my family drive out here to help me with any of the moving. They've never seen my house, unless you count the pictures I sent to them. Since I've practically lived at work, I hardly know my neighbors. No one's been over, and you're my first real friend here. Will you do the honors?"

Chris' face lit up with a giant grin. "I sure will. I would be proud to be your first guest. And I can't wait to see where you spend your time when you're not at that office."

CHAPTER 11

As they walked toward the etched glass double front doors of her house, Karen fumbled in her purse for her key, almost spilling its contents.

"Wait here, Chris. I have to straighten some things up. It should only be a couple of minutes."

"Come on, Karen," teased Chris. "It can't be that bad. I'm sure I've seen messier houses in my day."

"Humor me, please? Just for a minute."

Karen ran in quickly and hid the sheet music with her new song on it under a chair cushion, straightened her sofa pillows, and ran back to the door. "All right, it's safe to come in now."

"Are you sure?" Chris chuckled. "Nothing's going to jump out and bite me?"

"No, smarty pants, you'll be fine. Come on in."

Chris came through the door and looked around at the spotless house, dumbfounded. "Karen, you were only in here for a couple of minutes. What could you possibly have had to clean up?"

"Oh, not much really. I just cleaned some paperwork up. Come have a seat."

Chris sat down on the rust-colored sofa, close to the shade of canyons in Utah, or perhaps New Mexico. As he looked around the living room, he noticed detailed Southwestern pottery, along with breathtaking artwork displayed on the deep beige walls. Turquoise and rust patterned curtains completed the scene.

"Karen, this room is amazing!" Chris exclaimed. "I love the look. I feel like I'm in Santa Fe!"

"I'm so glad you like it. I've been to New Mexico and I fell in love with everything about it. I visited a few years ago and really want to go back. I guess if I couldn't live in sunny California that would be my next choice."

"You know, a couple of years ago I took a trip to Santa Fe. I went alone. I needed to get away to think, to decide what I wanted to do next. I had been thinking about getting back into music, but I wasn't sure if it was the right thing to do. So I spent a couple of weeks there, praying and thinking. I knew God had given me my answer when I was sitting out there on the hotel balcony, and a new song came to mind as I took in the scenery. I hadn't written anything in years; it was a long, tough period in my life and my mind couldn't even focus on music. But then this song came to me in Santa Fe. I wrote the whole thing, words and music, in half an hour. It was the fastest I'd ever written a song in my life. For it to come that quickly...I knew it came as a gift from God, as His answer as to what direction to take with my life."

"Chris...you're giving me chills. Wow. That's really amazing."

"It was amazing, and still is when I think about it today. The long dry spell was over, all because I had given control over to God instead of trying to do it myself, beating my head against the wall. My depression began to lift; I felt like there was meaning to my existence once again."

Karen sat there with her eyes closed, tears streaming down her cheeks. When she opened her eyes, she saw the tears in Chris' eyes as well.

"You know, Karen, for years I've been trying my best to let God lead me where I need to go. I don't always succeed. Sometimes I still get caught up in my own thoughts and my mind gets carried away with worry, but I do know that when I just let Him take control, things always turn out for the best...not just for me, but for other people too."

"I try so hard to do that too," Karen admitted, "but I always let my thoughts run away with me until it all snowballs and I feel like I'm going crazy. I really need to take your advice, slow down my mind, and let Him handle things."

Chris smiled as he wiped away the stray tears. "It happens to all of us, honey. We're all human, so it can't be helped sometimes. Believe me, I know from many, many years of experience. What counts is that we keep trying...always."

"I know He's always at work in us, even when we don't realize it," Karen added.

They were both silent for a minute, then Karen stood up from the sofa. "Chris, I never even offered you anything to drink. I'm sure we could both use something now. Why don't you come see my kitchen, and you can choose what you like?"

"Sounds good." Chris followed her into the kitchen, decorated in bright, Southwestern tiles to compliment the living room. He felt right at home in this oasis of creativity and spirituality.

Karen opened the refrigerator. "I've got iced tea, diet pop, and bottled water. Not much else. Oh, I mean diet soda...sometimes I still forget that I'm not in the Midwest anymore."

"Diet soda sounds great," Chris decided. Karen brought two cans over to the counter where Chris was standing. She used her fingernails to pop the tab on hers and took a sip.

*****

Chris watched Karen's every move, not even realizing that she'd set his soda on the counter. The conversation they had just had, along with the other feelings he was having, made him sure about more than just his music career.

He reached over and took Karen's hand. As she looked up into his eyes, Chris pulled her into a gentle embrace. He could feel her let herself be drawn in closer and her heart beating faster with every movement. His lips closed in on hers for a long, tender kiss.

*****

Karen felt as if she'd been waiting for this moment all her life. God had been leading her all right, out to California and to the right man. He really was at work in her, all the way back to when she was a girl. She just didn't know how it would all come together until now. God's perfect timing.

Karen lived this moment in time for all it was worth. She held tightly on to Chris and did not let go, enjoying the warmth of his lips on hers. She didn't want the kiss to end. Nothing had ever felt so perfect.

After what seemed like the longest kiss she had ever experienced, Karen still held on to Chris, noticing that he didn't want to let go either. The look Karen saw in his beautiful hazel eyes made her heart leap.

*****

Chris couldn't help but look at Karen with wonder. He'd always tried to figure out why he couldn't find the woman he was supposed to share his life with, but now he knew that God had found her for him. He had just waited until they were both ready for each other and the time was right. It was hard to believe all of the incredible things that were now happening in his life. Everything was starting to come together musically, and now here Karen was in his arms.

"I almost can't believe this is happening," sighed Chris, "but I'm so glad that it is."

Karen smiled at him, her eyes lighting up like the lights of Albuquerque. "So am I, Chris. I've never felt like this in my life." She seemed to tilt off balance and tried to steady herself. "Can we please go sit together in the living room? I think my knees are about to give out on me."

"Just what I was thinking. You go sit down. I've got the sodas."

Chris carried the drinks into the living room and set them down on the coasters Karen had placed on her coffee table. He joined Karen on the couch and pulled her back into his arms. They sat snuggling together comfortably, relaxing into each other. Karen laid her head on Chris' shoulder, and he kissed her softly on the forehead.

Chris closed his eyes and breathed in the scent of Karen's perfume, letting it linger through his nose and into his head. He held her even tighter as he listened to her heartbeat.

When he opened his eyes again, a gleam of light caught him by surprise. Leaning in the corner of the room was a beautiful, shining acoustic guitar. "Karen," he asked, "do you play?"

"Kind of…well, I used to play a long time ago. I'm teaching myself to play again."

"Oh. How long have you been at it now?"

"I've wanted to for quite a while, but actually just did something about it recently. I decided I had to make the time for it."

Chris walked across the room and picked up the guitar. He noticed how it matched the décor in Karen's living room, marveling at how flawlessly Karen had coordinated every single item here.

"Do you mind if I play?" Chris asked cautiously. He knew how some musicians could be about letting other people touch their instruments.

"Please do," Karen told him. "That guitar's probably just waiting for an expert to play it!"

"Expert? Well, maybe yes, maybe no…but definitely someone who loves to play."

As Chris fine-tuned the instrument, he looked over at Karen, whose eyes were still shining. "So, how long has it been since you really played?"

He saw Karen's smile turn into a slight frown. "Since I was nineteen. I can't believe I let it be so long before playing again."

Chris brought the guitar back over to the sofa and began softly playing a melody. "If you don't mind my asking…why did you wait such a long time?"

"Well, one reason was that I starting working. My parents couldn't afford to send me to college, so I got a job right out of high school."

"OK," Chris said. "Was there another reason?"

A single tear rolled down Karen's flushed cheek.

"Yes, there was. After I'd been working for a few months, my mom got sick. It turned out that she had cancer. I helped my dad take care of her."

"Karen, I'm so sorry." Chris stopped playing and took Karen's hand.

"She actually did well for a couple of years; the treatments were working and everything. She was in remission." Karen swallowed hard. "Then the cancer came back with a vengeance. Nothing the doctors tried worked anymore. I made sure I spent every single moment with her that I could, not knowing how long she was going to be here. She fought hard and lasted almost another year, but the cancer just kept spreading until finally we lost her."

Karen now had more tears streaming down her face than she could count. Chris gently kissed her cheek.

"That was a lot to deal with, honey. I lost my mom about five years ago, but she had a heart attack and was gone just like that."

"I'm sorry, Chris. I'm at least glad she didn't suffer for a long time."

"That's true," Chris said, "but at least with your mom, knowing it was coming, you got to show her how much you loved her."

"You're right. Wow Chris, I guess I hadn't thought much about that before."

"Well, not too many people get the ideal chance to say goodbye. I guess we just have to live with whatever happens." Chris sighed. "Not that it's easy."

"Definitely not easy." Karen wiped her cheeks with her fingertips. "I was still pretty young and I didn't take it well at all. Plus, I was trying to help my dad get through it. I was so wrapped up in my grief and his that I couldn't even think about picking up my guitar."

Chris nodded at her. "I understand that more than you know."

"I had my two best friends for support, and my company…well, they were really good about everything while my mom was sick. So, I've been very loyal to them. In fact, I'm so loyal that I moved to California."

Chris stared with wide eyes. "You mean you've been with the same company all of this time?"

"That's right. Mr. Wesley was very good about the move, and I actually always wanted to live in California anyway. But now…"

"But now what?"

"Even though they've been so good to me in the past, I'm burnt out on the job…even if I feel a little guilty about it. Deep down, I know that it's not what I'm supposed to do with the rest of my life. I'm not quitting yet, but I'm trying to figure out what's next for me."

"Sounds familiar. Which way to turn?"

Karen smiled. "At least I know I need to get on my knees and pray now. I've been pushing this stuff around in my head for a while, and I'm driving myself crazy with it. I won't find the right answers unless I ask for God's help. "

"I'll second that." Chris squeezed her hand. "And there's something else."

"What's that?"

"I'm really glad you started playing the guitar again."

"Me too. I know my mom would be glad as well. She's looking down on me, smiling, and happy that once again I'm doing something that I love."

Chris started playing again, this time picking out "Spanish Eyes". He began to sing, and Karen couldn't resist joining in.

"Karen," Chris said when they had finished the song. "You have such a beautiful voice!"

Karen's shock was evident all over her face. "You really think so?"

"Honey, you should be singing all the time. Didn't you realize how good you are?"

"Well," she said with a shrug, "I guess I knew I could carry a tune, you know, that I wouldn't break anybody's eardrums or anything. But no one's ever really complimented me on my voice before, so I've always been afraid to try to sing in front of any kind of an audience. I figured maybe I was OK, but not good enough for that."

"Oh Karen, don't ever be afraid to try. You should share your talent with the rest of us."

Karen felt her heart jump again, this time for a completely different reason. To think that she could do something she's loved since she was young…and that people might actually want to hear her?

"I always sing in the car," Karen admitted, "and around the house. It's been a long time since I sang for another person, unless you count singing along at your concert."

"If you love to sing, you just have to do it." Chris looked at her sadly. "I should know. I've been holding back for years. Now it's time to share again with everyone."

Karen pondered that for a minute. "Of course, I really should have thought of that before. God wants us to share our talents, not bury them because we're afraid."

"We're just stubborn humans." Chris laughed. "You're right, but I guess sometimes He has to hit us over the head with it before we really understand."

Chris started strumming Karen's guitar again as thoughts floated around in his mind. "Now, what would you like to sing this time?"

"How about 'Can't Take My Eyes Off You'? I've always loved that song."

"So have I. I've heard several versions, but it's such a great song that it's wonderful no matter who sings it."

They sang the classic while Chris played. He watched Karen's shoulders relax as the song went on, and he hoped she was becoming comfortable singing for him.

"All right," Karen offered once the song was complete. "Now you pick something."

Chris thought quickly and began to play the first notes. Karen's beautiful green eyes lit up, just like he thought they would.

*****

As they made a duet of "Love Is the Only Way", Karen realized that one of her young girl dreams was coming true. It took singing the Anderson Boys hit for her to fully absorb that she was singing with the one person she'd always wanted to sing with. Now that it was happening for real, it was even better because now she had a real connection with Chris.

Their voices blended together perfectly, like two souls in an embrace. Even Karen, who had envisioned this since she was eleven, was astonished by the sound of both of their voices together.

"Karen, you take my breath away," Chris said. "Well, actually from the moment I met you that was the case. But now…"

"Oh Chris…"

Chris leaned over the guitar and kissed her sweetly. "Now I'm speechless," he said. "Right now the way I feel is beyond words."

Karen opened her mouth to speak, but found she didn't know what to say either.

She finally responded the only way she could. She reached over, gently touching Chris' face. As she held his face in her hands, she kissed him as if her life depended on it.

When she drew away from him, she saw a look in his eyes that was more than she could ever have dreamed up…from Chris, or any other man.

Karen felt her voice coming back to her. "Way before I actually knew you, you've always made me want to sing. You bring out the best in me, in more ways than one."

Chris looked into her eyes with a twinkle in his. "Thank you, honey. I know we haven't been together that long, but it feels like I've known you forever. You bring out my best too."

Karen came up with another song for them to sing, then Chris thought of one. This kept going on and on, and they almost sang the entire night away. Chris finally said good night as they realized daylight would soon be coming over the horizon.

CHAPTER 12

Karen had never been so relieved that it was Saturday. Chris had left her house so late that the sun was ready to come up. They were having so much fun singing together that it was hard to stop for the night, or the morning, as it turned out. She'd made Chris call her so she would know he got back to his own house all right. Somehow she still managed to get eight hours' worth of sleep, but of course that meant it was past noon when she woke up.

Karen dragged herself to the kitchen and made coffee. As her bagel was toasting, she searched through her cupboards looking for something to go with it. *I'll have to go to the grocery store today,* she thought. *There's not much left in the house to eat, not even butter or jelly for my bagel. I hate eating them dry!*

Usually she didn't allow her food supply to get this low…but then again, she usually didn't have love on the brain either. She thought she might have to pinch herself to see if this was all really happening.

Karen had a jolt of warmth run through her entire body which had nothing to do with her morning java. She had truly never had feelings like this before in her entire thirty-one years. She'd dated, she had friendships with other men, but this was like nothing she had ever experienced.

As she tried to wash down the plain bagel with her coffee, she looked out of her kitchen window. It was a bright, completely cloudless day. She couldn't wait to go out and enjoy it. She finished her meager breakfast and ran up the stairs to change into a T-shirt and shorts. The groceries would have to wait while she took a stroll on the beach.

Karen walked down to the shoreline and slipped off her shoes. She made her way to the cooler sand, where the waves had lapped up and lowered the ground temperature. The sandy moistness felt like a balm on the soles of her feet.

She glanced at her toes as she walked on the sand. Since she was going barefoot more often now, she really could use a pedicure. *Maybe I can stop by the nail salon and make an appointment.* The thought made her feel like she was taking better care of herself already.

Karen kept on walking, and soon her thoughts turned from her toes to Chris. *Has it really only been a week that I've known him? It sure feels like I've known him my whole life.* Even if she counted what she knew about Chris when he was on TV, she still hadn't really known him.

In this short time, they had come to find out a lot about each other. The week felt like a year, maybe longer. It was like she didn't even remember a time that she didn't know Chris.

Karen did know what she felt in her heart, and nothing before even came close to how she felt about Chris. To think that Chris had the same kind of feelings for her…well, that just about knocked her over. The two of them clicked from that first moment at the diner, and Karen was enjoying every single minute, just taking it a day at a time.

She had something else to think about now as well…her music. Did she dare actually consider pursuing a music career? Chris certainly left no doubt that he loved her voice; of course, maybe he was biased. But what if she really did have a shot as a singer?

It was time to become more proficient on the guitar and write more songs. She knew she had a lot of songs in her just waiting to come out. She could always still write, even if someone else got to sing the songs.

But what would her family think? She knew they would probably think she was crazy. Better to have a "real job" and have security than to go chasing dreams…she could just hear it now.

In what seemed like no time at all, Karen had traveled a long distance from where she had started. She stopped to sit for a while and think. There were so many creative ideas spinning around in her head that she had to try to sort them out.

Karen sighed as she looked around. She couldn't get enough of the beach. It was so beautiful and peaceful…yet so powerful. Not only had God created an incredible world, but amazingly He brought her to live in a place like this, where nature was at its best and ready for her enjoyment.

Between her feelings for Chris and her wonder at God's creation, Karen had a new song coming to mind. She was afraid she would forget the words before she got home. What could she do?

She suddenly realized that she had her grocery list and a pen in the pocket of her shorts. She pulled them out and started to jot down the words on the back of the list.

She wrote down everything she could think of, her pen sailing across the paper. All of a sudden she found the melody was forming in her head. Darn it! She didn't have her guitar, or anywhere to write the notes even if she'd actually had the guitar. The words had already taken up most of the limited space on the page.

She folded the paper and stuck it back in her pocket along with the pen. She started walking back the way she came, humming her new melody over and over as she headed back toward the street where her car was parked. The music just felt right in her head. Karen didn't feel like her feet were even touching the sand!

Abandoning her original plan to go right to the market after the beach, Karen decided instead to go home first. If she didn't write the melody down right away, she might lose it forever.

She drove home and practically leaped from her car right through her front door. She took the lyrics out of her pocket and set them right next to the notebook. Grabbing her guitar and still humming the music, she worked it out until it was written down exactly the way she wanted it. She played and sang the new tune a couple of times through, making sure it was perfect. Her heart was pounding so hard that she could feel it in her ears; she had no idea how she was going to calm it down.

She began to breathe slowly and deeply, her heart rate slowing with each breath. After about ten minutes, Karen felt collected enough to go to the store.

*****

As Karen pulled into the shopping center and saw the sign for the nail salon, she remembered about her toenails. Sand-n-Surf Nails was only two doors down from the market, so she stopped there first. The platinum blonde receptionist, with perfect coral nails herself, was happy to schedule Karen's appointment for Monday after work.

Once that was all set, Karen walked over to the market and got a cart, pushing it into the produce section to fill it with plenty of fruits and vegetables. She had to start making healthier food choices. She still wanted to lose some weight and wanted to make sure she went about it the right way. She sure didn't want to resort to the more dangerous methods. She had already been down that road…and it hadn't been pretty. She had to make sure she didn't go there again.

Once her cart was loaded up with fresh produce, Karen went to pick out some lean meats. She was comparing packages of chicken breasts when a sound came up from behind her. It was a foreign, yet somehow familiar voice.

"Karen? Karen O'Neil?"

Karen slowly turned around to discover a man about her age. It didn't take her long to realize who it was. It had been fifteen years since she last saw him, but there was no doubt that standing before her was her junior high crush.

"Greg Richards?"

"That's me," Greg said. "What are you doing out here in California?"

"My company moved here, so they asked me to move with them. What about you?"

"I live here now too. I followed my girlfriend out here two months ago, but it turns out that wasn't such a good idea."

"Oh?"

Greg frowned as he looked down at the floor. "She's already found a new man. And since he's a 'real California guy', I just can't compete. So...now I'm on my own."

"Wow," Karen said. "Sorry to hear that."

"Thanks, but I don't know what possessed me to follow her out here in the first place," Greg admitted. "Things weren't going that well for us already, before we moved here, so it was kind of stupid for me to move across the country for her."

"Do you have a job here?"

"Not yet, but I've got a couple of interviews this week."

"Well, good luck. I hope everything works out for you."

"I sure hope so." Greg looked into Karen's eyes and smiled. "You look great, Karen. It was good to see you."

"It was good to see you too, Greg. Take care."

"You too." Greg walked away, still smiling.

This is unbelievable, Karen thought. *Greg Richards wound up here in California, in the same city I live in. And he actually said I look great. That's the first time I've ever heard anything like that from him. He certainly didn't feel that way fifteen years ago.*

Karen quickly made her way through the store, finished her shopping, and headed for home. Chris was going to pick her up for dinner in about two hours, and she wanted to relax a little before he got there.

Just the thought of Chris made her feel better. Karen couldn't wait to take a nice hot shower and figure out what to wear for her date tonight.

*****

Karen had just finished getting ready, adding a final swipe of lipstick as she heard Chris' car pull into her driveway. After a last minute look in the mirror, she met him at the door.

"Hi gorgeous," Chris said with a big smile. "You certainly take my breath away."

Even though Karen was getting used to compliments from Chris, she still found herself blushing. "Chris, you're going to make my head so big that I won't be able to fit through the door."

"If your head got that big, it would still be pretty. Besides, I can't imagine you ever getting conceited."

"I certainly hope not." Karen grinned. "But if I ever do, I give you permission to smack me silly."

"It's a deal," Chris said, laughing. "Now let's go. I'm starving."

"Actually, I am too. So, where do you want to go?"

"I have someplace in mind." Chris looked at her slyly. "But it's a surprise."

"Oh, really? How about just a little hint?"

"Sorry, no can do. All I can say is that we have a reservation, so we'd better get going."

Chris held the passenger side door of his yellow convertible open for Karen to get in. The top was down, as it was most of the time. Karen was convinced that California weather had to be the best climate on earth.

After Karen was settled into her seat, Chris got in and started the car. He turned up the radio, which was tuned to a station playing sweet smooth jazz.

"Can't you give me just a tiny clue?" Karen begged.

Chris smiled at her, reaching over to push the hair out of her eyes. "Sorry, sweetie. I really want it to be a surprise."

Chris took Karen on a long drive along the shore. Breathing in the salty air was making Karen even hungrier, but she was enjoying the gorgeous view of the ocean, and of Chris. If it meant she had to starve to hold on to the moment a little longer, that was all right by her.

Karen felt the wind on her face and her hair blowing around freely. She closed her eyes and absorbed the sounds of the saxophone coming from the radio. She could have sworn she was actually floating above the car, instead of riding in it.

As she soaked in the experience so deeply, she didn't even notice Chris had pulled off the road and into a parking lot. She finally opened her eyes when Chris turned off the engine and she could no longer hear the radio.

She couldn't believe what she saw in front of her. A castle?

"Chris, it's beautiful! Where are we?"

"Welcome, my dear…to 'The Sandcastle'. They serve the best seafood I've ever tasted, and wait until you see what else they have going on in there."

"A castle right along the beach," Karen sighed. "It's perfect."

"And I'm the luckiest guy in the world," stated Chris, "because I have the perfect woman to share it with."

"Oh, I think I'm the lucky one," Karen said as Chris took her by the hand and led her into the castle.

Karen thought this place was beautiful from the outside, but the interior was simply magical; the sparkling crystal chandeliers, the intricately carved furniture… all of it was just something out of this world. Karen tried to take it all in, looking around to see ivory carvings on the walls, while below her feet were natural stone floors fit for a king and queen.

As the two of them were seated, Karen couldn't help but feel that she was living in a fairy tale. It certainly felt like her prince was sitting beside her.

"So, what do you think so far?" Chris inquired with a smile.

"I think I should pinch myself," Karen answered. "I must be in a dream."

"Hey, there'll be no pinching allowed," Chris teased. "No bruising that delicate skin."

"That's OK. If this is a dream, then I really don't want to wake up."

A waiter in a regal purple and black tuxedo brought over a couple of menus and a wine list. Karen glanced over at Chris with an uneasy look on her face. "Were you planning on having a drink tonight?"

Chris kept the smile going, refusing to show any of his mind's dilemma on his face. "Well, actually tonight I figured I could allow myself one glass of wine. But remember honey, even if I don't have any, that shouldn't stop you from doing it. It really doesn't bother me."

"All right." Karen turned toward the waiter. "I'll have a glass of the house Chardonnay, please."

"And I'll have the same," Chris responded. "Thank you, sir."

"You're quite welcome," the waiter replied with a smile of his own. "I'll be back with the wine in a few minutes."

Karen began to look over her menu. There were so many choices, and they all sounded good. Picking only one of these entrees was going to be a challenge.

"This place is really incredible, Chris. I'm so glad you kept it a surprise."

Chris' eyes twinkled with mischief. "Just you wait. There's more to come."

Karen could feel her eyebrows going up. She knew so far that Chris' surprises had been wonderful. She'd just have to wait and see what was coming next, trusting it would be just as good as the others.

The waiter came back with the two glasses of white wine. Karen finally decided on grilled scallops while Chris chose the crab stuffed prawns.

As Karen sipped her Chardonnay, Chris laughed. "You know, I always used to crave the taste of alcohol. But now that I hardly ever have it, I don't really miss it.

I mean, I'm enjoying this glass, but the taste of it doesn't make me want to have it all the time anymore."

"That must be a great feeling." Karen stared at the loaf of bread on the table and sighed. "I'm trying to get to that point with food."

"Karen, you don't look like you have a problem."

"Not as much as I used to. I still haven't completely gotten a handle on it, but at least I don't have as many issues to deal with as I used to."

"Really, honey? I had no idea."

"That's OK," Karen said. "There's more to the story, but I'll save it for another day."

"I'm curious, but I understand."

"Thanks. I guess it's just not a subject I want to discuss while we're at dinner, of all places." Karen laughed to herself at the irony. "So, how anxious are you to start recording on Monday?"

"I want to camp out at the studio," Chris said. "Does that answer your question?"

They were both laughing as their salads arrived. "Mmm," Karen said. "These salads look almost too good to eat." Then she picked up her fork. "Almost."

"Everything is delicious here. I've never had a bad meal at 'The Sandcastle'." Chris took one more sip of his wine, then pushed it toward Karen. "Do you think you could finish this?"

"Why?" Karen looked at Chris with great concern. "Is something wrong?"

"I just think I'd better stop now. I guess sometimes having a few sips does make me want more after all. I don't want to push my luck."

"Sure Chris, I'll finish it. You have to do what you have to do."

"Thank you. I'll call the waiter over in a minute to request something less dangerous for me. So much for having a handle on things."

"Chris, don't get down on yourself about it. Nobody is perfect. I know I'm sure not. Sometimes making a decision like this before making the situation worse is having a handle on it."

"Thanks," said Chris as he let the forced grin drop. "I guess you're right."

"So what do you still have to do before going into the studio on Monday?" Karen asked, getting back to the subject at hand.

"I just have to go over a few more things with the band. I'm so happy that I get to record this album with them. The studio musicians are awesome performers, but there's nothing like recording with your own band."

"I would think so. You all know each other so well, since you work together more often than with the studio musicians. And it must be extra special having Jerry there."

"It is. He's been in the studio a couple of times before, you know, years ago. Back then he just got to observe the process. Now he actually gets to be a part of it."

"I'm glad…for all of you." Karen smiled wistfully. "It has to be so exciting."

Chris was pretty sure that he knew what she was thinking. He wanted to let her in on another surprise, but for now he bit his tongue. *I have to wait until a little later in the evening for this one,* he thought.

A server came by to clear the salad plates and bring the entrees. Karen had never seen scallops that looked so good. As she looked over at Chris' plate, she was equally impressed.

"I think I'm in seafood heaven," she joked. "Don't worry, I'll refrain from pinching myself again."

Strolling violinists suddenly appeared at their table. They started playing a familiar song, and Chris began to sing softly. As he reached for Karen's hand, she smiled, then joined in singing "Can't Take My Eyes Off You". They gazed lovingly at each other, with the words becoming truer than they had ever been before. It dawned on Karen that she was actually living the words of a song she had loved since she was little, and she truly felt like she was living in a dream.

When they finished, Chris squeezed Karen's hand. "See, I told you I had more up my sleeve for tonight."

"You sure did. Do you have any more sleeves I should know about?"

His eyes shone with that familiar mischief. "Maybe. You'll have to wait and find out."

They thanked the musicians and got back to their dinners. "Did you and your band rehearse this afternoon?" Karen asked.

Chris nodded as he chewed, then swallowed. "We did. We still have to tweak things a bit." He took a sip of water. "I forgot to order something else to drink. Oh well, water's better for me anyway. So how did you spend this afternoon?"

Karen was suddenly in another world, thinking about her strange encounter earlier.

"Karen," Chris called as he lightly tapped her hand. "Earth to Karen."

Karen blinked, as if to snap herself back to the present. "Sorry. It's just that I had something really weird happen today."

"Weird? How do you mean?"

"I ran into someone. Someone that I haven't seen in a long time."

"A friend?"

"No, I wouldn't say that."

"Oh. An enemy?"

Karen laughed nervously. "I wouldn't say that either."

"All right, honey. Now I'm confused."

Karen wasn't sure how to describe this. "It's a guy who went to school with me."

"High school?"

"No, junior high. Remember how I told you about someone named Greg that I had a crush on?"

Chris recalled that conversation very clearly. "You mean the guy who rejected you for not being a small enough size for him?"

"Yes, that's the one." Karen frowned, thinking back to a decade and a half ago. "He's living out here now."

"What brought him out here? Work?"

"No, he's still looking for a job, I guess. He moved here because his girlfriend did, but now they're on the outs."

"Well…that's a pretty interesting development."

"Yeah." Karen shook her head, trying to shake away thoughts of Greg. "Anyway, I don't even really want to think about him anymore."

"It still hurts to think about the past, doesn't it?" Chris said sympathetically.

Karen nodded, unable to speak for the moment.

"Believe me, I know that feeling." Chris took her hand again, looking directly into her eyes. "We have to move forward. Now we have each other, so none of that matters."

Karen put her other hand on top of his, rubbing it gently. "You're absolutely right. Let's just enjoy this magical evening with each other."

"My thought exactly," Chris said. "Plus I have at least one more surprise for you tonight."

Karen couldn't help but laugh a little. "Today has sure been a day of surprises for me."

"Well, you may have had an unpleasant one this afternoon, but I promise that all of mine will be pleasant."

"So far they have been. I can't believe there's still another one."

"That one will come shortly," Chris told her. "Let's relax and enjoy dinner first. The next surprise won't happen until after dessert."

CHAPTER 13

After a slice of creamy key lime pie to die for, Karen and Chris were back in his car driving toward downtown Santa Monica. Karen couldn't imagine what on earth could top their evening at The Sandcastle. Everything had already been pretty close to perfect.

She looked over at Chris. His dark hair blew in the wind as he was driving and whistling along with the radio. She knew without a doubt that she was on her way to Surprise Number Three. Chris seemed even more excited than he had been before.

"You're enjoying the suspense, aren't you?" she asked.

Chris tried his best to look innocent. "Oh, whatever gave you that idea?"

"Hmm…I'd call it intuition, but the look on your face gives it away."

Chris laughed. "Then it's a good thing I don't play poker."

Karen reached over and playfully smacked Chris on the arm.

"Hey! I might want to use that arm later."

"Then maybe you'll finally give me a little hint."

"OK." Chris thought it over for a moment. "We were kind of talking about it earlier this evening."

Karen she tried to think back over their dinner conversation. "We were?"

"In a way…we're almost there anyway, so just relax and enjoy the ride."

They were driving through a part of town Karen had never seen before. It was a beautiful neighborhood that led right into a very eclectic business district. Of course, there were quite a few sections of the city Karen hadn't had a chance to visit yet. She resolved to go see new places and try new things more often. She knew she'd spent too long holed up in her house or stuck in her office. It was time to get out and explore what the city had to offer.

Chris pulled up in front of a cool, artistic-looking building topped with a neon bluebird. With its own funky style, it had definitely been built in the right part of town.

"We're here," Chris announced. "California Songbird Studio!"

"Studio?" Karen said, her heart pounding. "You mean the studio where you're recording your new album?"

"You are correct, my dear." Chris put his arm around Karen's shoulders to steady her. "I thought you might like to check out the place, and maybe learn a little about the recording process."

"Would I? You bet I would." Karen just about jumped over the car door without needing to open it.

"Now Karen, don't hurt yourself. Allow me." Chris came around and opened her door. Karen was too excited to remember to thank him.

"Chris, I've never even been near a recording studio before! Just don't let me break anything!"

"Don't worry, that's why I'll be your guide for the evening. I asked Charlie, the owner, to come out here tonight so he could let us in and help me show you around."

Chris hit the buzzer at the front door. "Hello," came a deep male voice from the speaker.

"Hey Charlie, we're here."

"All right, buddy," answered Charlie. "I'll be right there to let you in."

In a less than a minute, Charlie was there holding the door open. Once they were all inside, he locked it behind him.

"Karen, this is Charlie, the owner of California Songbird Studio. Charlie, this is my girlfriend, Karen."

Karen felt electric chills running through her body. *Chris introduced me as his girlfriend. It sure has a nice ring to it!*

"It's a pleasure to meet you, Karen." Charlie put out his hand. "Chris has told me a lot about you."

"Oh?" Karen felt that familiar warmth coming to her cheeks. "I sure hope it's all good."

"Definitely," said Charlie as Karen shook his hand. "I couldn't imagine there would be anything bad to tell."

"It's a pleasure to meet you too, Charlie. I'm so glad you and Chris are working together. I know how excited he is about this project."

Nothing could have wiped the grin from Chris' face at this point. The two best things in his life were coming together. He was so thrilled that he could hardly stand still.

"All right, young lady, let's show you around this joint," Charlie said. "There's quite a bit to see."

As Charlie went through the studio, Karen followed him around like a kid in a candy store. She was fascinated by everything she saw.

Charlie and Chris explained the process of recording an album. When they got to the soundboard, Karen was in awe. "Goodness, Charlie! How do you keep all of this straight?" Karen looked up and down the board at all of the various knobs, buttons, and controls.

Charlie laughed heartily. "Years and years of experience, my dear."

"I would love to learn how this all works," Karen said. "I've been curious about it for as long as I can remember."

"Maybe sometime soon I can show you a few more things about it," offered Charlie. "I could go into more detail then if you would like."

"Oh Charlie, that would be fantastic!"

"In the meantime," Chris said, "we have another surprise for you."

"Another surprise? I don't know if my heart can stand another one!"

"Then we might have to call the paramedics for you, sweetheart," answered Chris. "I'm sure you'll think the trip to the ER is worth it."

"OK, now you're scaring me. Tell me before I really do need an ambulance."

The two men exchanged grins like partners in crime, then they turned back to Karen. "I hear you're quite a singer, Karen," Charlie said. "Chris has been raving about your voice."

"I do love to sing. I guess the first professional opinion I've ever received is from Chris."

"Chris and I thought we'd take that a step further. How would you like to make a recording?"

Karen stared at Charlie, then at Chris. "Are – are you serious?"

Chris looked deeply into Karen's eyes. "We couldn't be more serious. Your voice is a gift. You should share it with the world."

Karen stood there in shock, unable to move and barely able to breathe. Something she had thought about since she was young, something she'd never thought could actually happen for her...could it really be coming true?

"Karen?" Charlie snapped his fingers. "Karen, are you with us?"

Karen blinked and focused on Charlie again. "Sorry. For a minute I thought this was a dream."

"Oh this is real, if you want it to be," said Charlie. "So what do you think?"

"I would love to. When shall we do it?"

"Since I was hoping you would say yes, I already reserved Thursday and Friday evenings for you, after Chris has his recording sessions during the day. That way his band will still be here to work with you."

"Is the band all right with that, Chris?" Karen asked.

"They sure are. Jerry checked with everyone and they're willing to help out. Besides, I carried on so much about your voice at practice today, they can't wait to hear you sing."

Suddenly Karen's nerves began to flare up. "Oh, great. No pressure, right?"

"Don't worry honey," Chris assured her. "You're going to knock 'em dead."

"What am I going to sing?"

"We'll try a few standards," Charlie said. "If all goes well, we'll figure the rest out from there."

"Sounds like a good starting place, Karen." Chris put his hand on her back and rubbed it gently. "What do you say? Does it sound like a plan to you?"

This is all happening so fast, she thought. Then she took a deep breath. "It does. I'm still a little anxious, but I could never pass up this opportunity."

"Of course," Charlie added, "I'm dying to hear you sing now, after all of the good things I've heard about you."

"So…you want me to sing for you now?"

"That would be cool. Let me get my guitar from the office for you to use."

As Charlie ran to get his guitar, Karen began to pace the floor, taking deep breaths and letting them out slowly. Chris walked over and stopped her in mid-pace.

"Honey, just relax. You're a natural. Just pretend that I'm the only one in the room with you."

"I'll try," sighed Karen.

Charlie came back with the instrument and handed it to Karen. She gave it a strum to make sure it was in tune. "OK," she said. "What shall I sing?"

Charlie thought for a moment. "How about a song everyone knows? Let's try 'America the Beautiful'."

"Perfect...I actually know the chords to that one." Karen silently sent up a quick prayer and started the song. She glanced up as she sang, in time to see Charlie look over at Chris with his jaw dropped, and Chris' I-told-you-so look in return.

Karen finished her song as exhilaration took over for nervousness. She had never realized what a rush it could be to sing for someone else. She thought she felt that way the other night just because it was Chris...but now after performing in front of Charlie, she knew she could really come to enjoy singing for people.

"Karen," was all Charlie could say, almost in a trance-like state.

Karen wasn't sure what to think of Charlie's reaction. "What? What did you think?"

Charlie cleared his throat and found his voice. "I think you should quit your day job."

Karen laughed. "So I take it that you liked it?"

"Liked it is an understatement. You need to lay down some vocal tracks, girl. That voice is just begging to be heard."

Karen began to cry tears of joy. She felt Chris slip his arms around her as he spoke softly into her ear.

"See sweetie, I told you. Your voice is amazing. Now you have a second professional opinion to confirm it."

Karen wiped her eyes and caught her breath. "Thank you so much, Charlie. This means more to me than you could really know. And thank you, honey, for setting this up. I don't know how I can ever thank you enough."

Chris hugged her again. "Just share the gift of your voice with the world. That would be all of the thanks I need."

Karen started to play the guitar again. She and Chris launched into a song together, smiling at each other all the way through.

Charlie steadied himself against the soundboard. This was just too good to be true.

"You two are the perfect vocal blend for a duet. You should sing together more often!"

Chris grinned at him. "Thank you. We plan to."

"And Karen," Charlie said, "I'd like to hear 'America the Beautiful' again…but this time acapella."

"Oh, OK." She sang the patriotic melody sans guitar.

As she finished, Charlie clapped furiously. "My dear, I'd be willing to bet you're going to book a lot of 'Seventh Inning Stretch' gigs."

Karen smiled. "I think I could handle that."

"Just wait till they want you to do 'The Star Spangled Banner'," Chris offered.

"That would be a little more nerve-wracking, but I'd be willing to try it."

"Well," Charlie said, "let's take one step at a time. What time can you be here on Thursday, Karen?"

"I get through with work at five…so let's say six to be safe."

"Six it is. Now why don't you two go out and enjoy the rest of your evening. I'll close up shop."

"Thanks, Charlie," Chris said. "I'll see you at ten o'clock on Monday."

"I'll be here. I can't wait to get started."

"Feeling's mutual, man. Good night."

"Good night, Chris. Good night, Karen."

"Good night, Charlie. Thanks for everything," said Karen as she and Chris headed out into the cool night air.

*****

Chris and Karen were settled back into the convertible and down the road when Karen finally lost her composure. She was laughing, yet tears were streaming down her face. Chris noticed that she was also shaking all over.

"Honey?" he asked. "Honey, are you all right?"

Karen tried to calm herself down, but it was no use. "I guess," she said, then began another fit of laughter.

"Do I need to pull this car over? I think you've lost it!"

Karen took a full breath to stop her laughter, but the tears were still rolling down her cheeks. "I'm sorry. This is so overwhelming. When you said you had more surprises for me, you really weren't kidding."

"I told you it would be a pleasant surprise, right?"

"Oh, it certainly was." Karen breathed in and out again slowly, trying to relax her trembling body. "Just really unexpected. This has been a lot of excitement for one day."

"That's true." Chris softly caressed her arm in an attempt to sooth her frazzled nerves. "I promise that was the last surprise planned for today, so please try to relax."

"OK." Karen felt the shaking begin to subside. "It's just that…you don't know how long I've dreamed of doing this. Seems I've always wanted to sing and make records, but I never really thought it would ever happen for me. You and Charlie are helping to make my dream come true."

"Sweetheart, don't ever sell yourself short. God gave you your voice for a reason. Believe in your gift. He wants you to share it, otherwise He wouldn't have given it to you."

"I know you're right. Maybe I've just always been too afraid of failing, that maybe I don't have what it takes."

"Karen, just trust God. He gave you the voice. He'll be your strength; He believes in you. Believe in Him…and yourself."

Karen reached over and put her arm around Chris. "How did you get to be so wise?"

"Many, many years of trial and error. I had to go through my own insecurities to find the truth. I still go through it, but I get past my fear faster when I remember that God is on my side."

"He does work in mysterious ways," Karen said. "I guess He's full of surprises too."

CHAPTER 14

Karen lay blissfully in bed, looking through her small bedroom window to a Sunday that lived up to its name. She knew even if it had been raining, the sun would still be shining in her mind.

She was still recovering from the many surprises of yesterday. Only now, she discovered there was less anxiety churning in her stomach. It was being replaced by excitement and hope.

Last night had been topped off by an incredible evening on the beach with Chris. He had a blanket stashed in his car just for such an event; they spread it out on the cool sand, enjoyed the sound of the waves and talked for a long time. There had been quite a breeze blowing in, but that was fine with Karen. It just brought them closer together, snuggling to keep warm and holding each other tight. Karen even thought that an angel of love may have created the windy night just for that purpose.

They confided in each other, sharing their wildest dreams and envisioning their thoughts for the future. They discussed music they both enjoyed, other than the obvious Chris Lassiter and Anderson Boys records. They spoke about their favorite books both in childhood and as adults, and the lessons they had learned from them.

It was amazing just how much they really had in common, and the differences they discovered only deepened their interest in each other. It felt as if they'd known each other for a lifetime, yet they still learned new things. This created the perfect combination of comfort and excitement for both, keeping them away from the boredom or fear that could have set in.

Karen felt her heart pounding when she thought about how the incredible feelings that she had for Chris when she was young, yet mature beyond her years, had been an indication of what was happening now. She had realized her feelings went way past the typical girl's feelings for her favorite teen idol then. Now she was sure there had been a reason for that all along.

Karen pulled her pillow close to her as she remembered what happened after Chris had brought her home from the beach. Knowing neither of them had really gotten enough sleep the night before, he decided he'd better not stay too late. Of course, this was easier said than done. Karen lost count of how many times they kissed good night. When Chris was really finally leaving for home…well, that kiss seemed to go on forever. Karen secretly wished it had.

Karen rose from her bed with that thought and dressed in her Sunday best, going downstairs to sneak in a late breakfast. Soon she would be on her way to noon Mass once again.

She thought about how she usually went to 9:30 AM Mass. *The people who usually see me at 9:30 are probably wondering what happened to me. I hope they don't think I'm just skipping church.*

Karen took another bite of her blueberry muffin. *Oh well, I shouldn't really worry what they think. What counts is that I still get to Church, and that God knows I'm there.*

*****

Karen gave thanks when she arrived at church a little earlier than she had the Sunday before. She was able to enjoy most of the choir practice, which put her in an even better mood. The choir sounded extra sweet to her, as she was experiencing greater love and happiness in her life, along with eliminating a little bit of the stress.

She laughed to herself, thinking about the night before at the studio. Here she had been apprehensive about joining the choir, while in the meantime God had a plan in the works for her voice to be heard.

Mass was about ready to start. Some last minute people were coming in as the opening hymn began. *That was me last week,* Karen thought as she watched them scramble to find seats.

A man came to sit in Karen's pew. She took a couple of steps to the right to let him in, all the while concentrating on her hymn book and the sound of her voice.

As the song ended, she heard the man's voice whisper. "Karen?"

She looked to her left to see the one and only Greg Richards standing next to her. Karen felt a huge lump forming in her throat. "Long time, no see," she whispered anxiously.

"Yeah, I guess so," Greg whispered back. They turned back to face forward toward the altar as the priest spoke.

Karen tried her best to pay attention to what Father was saying, but the uneasy feeling moved from her throat to her stomach. Did she really have to run into Greg two days in a row?

Her mind drifted back to her junior high days and going to Mass with her parents. Greg was an altar boy at their church. The weekly bulletin always gave the servers' schedule; Karen usually tried to arrange which Mass her family attended according to that schedule. That way she was able to see Greg on the altar as much as she possibly could. Even after he rejected her, she still stuck to that schedule. She was hung up on him for a long time, and she knew at least at Mass she could see him without him telling her to go away or saying nasty things to her. He had to behave himself up there on the altar with the priest. Even if he didn't like seeing her there, he couldn't do a darn thing about it.

All these years later, here she was sitting next to Greg at Mass…and all <u>she</u> wanted to do was get away from <u>him</u>. Being that Mass had already started, she couldn't. She was trapped there with him, just like he had been stuck with her at church so long ago.

Dear God, she silently prayed, *please help me make it through this Mass. I'm uncomfortable being next to Greg, so please help me make the best of it. And I need your help getting my focus back on Mass, so I can pay proper attention and learn from your Word.*

She still felt some discomfort as Mass went on, but her prayer helped to ease some of the tension. She was finally able to absorb some of what the priest was saying. She did her best to ignore her old crush and think about Jesus.

She was fine until it was time for the sign of peace. Karen extended her hand to the woman on her right and said, "Peace be with you." Then she turned to Greg. Instead of putting out his hand, he embraced her and whispered in her ear, "Peace."

Karen didn't need to look in a mirror; she knew she had turned bright red. It felt as if she had stepped into a giant oven. The heat spread from her face to her arms, and then to the rest of her. She found it hard to breathe.

She remembered this feeling well also. Many times back in school she felt embarrassed; giving speeches or presentations especially freaked her out.   Sometimes she hid it well, but when things didn't go according to plan and something came at her from completely out of the blue, her whole body felt like it was on fire and someone had sucked the air out of the room.

Once again she asked God to help her as she prepared for communion and tried to calm herself. As she walked up to receive the Host, she noticed that her body temperature was returning to normal. Knowing that she was cooling down, she was able to relax enough to breathe properly.

Karen returned to her pew to find that Greg had left immediately after communion. She felt the release of the rest of the tension that had still been in her body.

Then she began to wonder. *What was the reason he left early? Did he have to be somewhere else, or did he sense my uneasiness and decided that he'd better leave?*

She was sure that Greg would have noticed her red face, since it was a familiar sight to him as well. It seemed most of the time when Karen got embarrassed in class, Greg was present to see her blush. It looked like some things would never change.

As the closing hymn ended, Karen headed out to her car. She really had no idea what to make of the way Greg was acting. The only thing she was going to let herself think about was going home and changing into jeans to meet up with Chris and the band later. If she didn't focus on something pleasant, she knew she would give into the sudden craving for a double cheeseburger and large chocolate shake.

And if she gave into that craving…well, she didn't want to start a chain reaction that would lead her down that old, self-destructive path. She had come too far to wind up there again.

*****

Chris was in his car, on his way to his favorite Mass. He would almost bet that a lot more people would make it to church every week if their churches had a mid-afternoon service.

Chris was also eager to check on Father John. He tried to give him a call a couple of times, but Father John had either been sleeping or out of his room for tests. Chris knew that he needed his rest, and Father Timothy assured him that Father John was slowly getting better. Since he had finally been released from the hospital, Chris hoped he would see Father today.

Chris assumed that Father Timothy would still be saying Mass; Father John wouldn't be up to that much activity yet. Maybe he could stop by the rectory afterward to see him for a few minutes. He didn't want the priest to overdo it and get weaker again.

Chris always enjoyed this Mass, not only for the fact that it was at two o'clock, but also for the musical selections. They still sang the beautiful hymns, but instead of traditional organ accompaniment, the songs were performed on guitar and piano, with additional instruments if the choir director felt the arrangement called for it. There was no doubt that the musicians at this church had found a creative way to make a joyful noise unto the Lord.

Chris had an idea for a Christian song that had been rolling around in his head for some time now. He'd never written anything like that before and he wasn't sure how to go about it. Would he be able to do it justice? And with the wild life he used to lead, would anyone out there even accept such a song coming from him?

For now, he thought, *I'll just enjoy the music.* He closed his eyes and took it all in, thinking about how good God was being to him. He offered up his own quiet prayer of gratitude for his second chance with his musical career, and for meeting Karen. Life was exciting again, in so many ways, thanks to now having Karen in his life.

Chris couldn't wait for the next day to arrive so he could be in the studio and start recording again. It had been almost twenty years since he had a record out. Also, Karen was going to get her chance to record this week. First he'd fallen in love with the woman; now he cherished her voice as well.

He felt a smile stretching across his face from the irony of it. Now he was on the other side of the coin… he discovered what it was like to utterly and completely fall in love with another person's voice, like so many fans had done with his.

The hymn came to a stop, and Father Timothy began to say Mass. Chris tried hard to keep his mind on Father's words, but it wasn't really working. He heard bits and pieces, but not everything.

He knew why his mind was elsewhere, but he still felt awful. *Please God, forgive me for my wandering mind. I know I need to focus on You. I'm just so excited about everything, and I want You to know I'm thankful for all You're doing in my life.*

Between trying to concentrate on the Mass and his roaming thoughts, the service was over before Chris even realized it. As he left the church, he spotted Father John sitting on a bench shaking hands with the parishioners. It was so good to see him talking to everyone!

"Father John! I'm so glad to see you feeling better." Chris reached out to shake Father John's hand.

"How are you doing, Chris?" Father John gave Chris a quick but firm handshake.

"I'm doing very well, Father. We start recording tomorrow."

"That's wonderful. I'm happy for you." Father John thought for a moment, then added, "Are you still seeing that woman…Karen, right?"

Chris beamed. "Oh, definitely yes. Things are really going well between us."

Father John mustered up what energy he had to shake his finger at Chris. "Chris, I told you to be careful, remember? You look like you've already fallen in love."

Chris was taken aback. He noticed that other parishioners were watching them closely. He could feel several sets of eyes burning into the back of his head.

"Father, I am falling in love, but I also haven't lost my mind. Don't you think I know what's best for me?"

"Chris, I think you've been wanting love to come so badly that you're jumping into this too quickly. You have to watch your back. You know what happened to you before. You can't fall for her just like that!"

"Father…" Chris started, then he felt his stomach do a flip. He knew what he felt, but what if Father John had a point? "Father, that was all in the past. I'm looking forward to the future."

"And you couldn't possibly already know that your future includes Karen."

"Now, just because I know I'm falling in love doesn't mean I'm not watching my back. I refuse to live in a cave just because someone hurt me in the past. I appreciate your concern, but I pray about this all the time, and I feel God is leading me. Please just be happy for me and trust that I will do what is right."

"OK, Chris," sighed Father John, shaking his head. "Just don't say I never warned you."

Chris forced a stiff smile. "Well anyway, Father, I'm glad you're feeling better."

With that, Chris walked to his car and took off for home. He turned up the radio, hoping the music would push Father John's words out of his mind for the rest of the day.

CHAPTER 15

The band members skillfully tuned their instruments at the rehearsal studio as they waited for Chris and Karen to arrive. Jerry glanced nervously through the glass front door. "I'm sure they'll be here any minute," he said, hoping his statement would make it true as quickly as possible.

Jerry turned his gaze toward the other musicians and started the group up for an instrumental run-through of the first song planned for the next day's session, all the while keeping one eye on the entrance to the studio. What could be keeping them?

None of them could ever remember Chris being late for anything; normally they didn't have to worry about him. Now they couldn't help but be anxious as they hoped nothing bad had happened. It was almost thirty minutes past the appointed time.

As they finished the third run-through, Karen and Chris walked through the door. Jerry could see right through their frozen smiles. "Hey guys! We were getting worried about you. Are you two OK?"

The couple looked right at him, without even a sideways glance at each other. "Sure Jer, we're fine," Chris answered. "Mass just ran a little late, that's all."

Karen stared at Jerry and swallowed down the lump in her throat. He didn't buy the explanation Chris came up with, and one look at Karen confirmed that he was right. Now he began to wonder what the real story was.

Chris went over to his microphone and checked to make sure it was working properly. He adjusted the mic stand to a comfortable position as he cleared his throat.

"All right, everyone," he said. "You were sounding good when we came in. Let's take it from there."

The band took it from the top, this time with Chris finally at the mic.

Karen found a stool to sit on, and Jerry could tell that she was trying to lose herself in the music. Little did he know that she kept rehashing the conversation she just had with Chris over and over in her mind.

Chris and the band did a flawless rendition of the new song. He at least looked pleased about that.

"Well," he said, "I think this song's ready for tomorrow. Let's work on 'Never Forgotten You'. I think we may want to tweak a few things on it."

*****

As the band began working on what would be Chris' first new single in years, Sandy caught a glimpse of Karen sitting over in the corner on her stool. Karen was watching everyone <u>except</u> Chris, fighting back tears the entire time. Her original smile had turned weak; her hands were clenched into tight fists in her lap.

Sandy couldn't help but wonder what was going on. All she ever heard from Chris was how wonderful Karen was and how well things were going with her. All of a sudden, something wasn't right. What in the world was happening?

Chris and Jerry played around with some of the arrangements, working it out between them before presenting the new version to the rest of the group.

"No major changes," Jerry announced, "but this should improve upon what was already an awesome song."

All together, they practiced the new improved version of "Never Forgotten You". Jerry and Chris exchanged grins, nodding their approval in time to the music.

*****

As they all practiced the updated song a few more times to make sure they all knew it, Karen's thoughts drifted back to the concert, where she'd heard this song for the first time. That was the beginning of something wonderful; now she was wondering why Chris had jumped down her throat on the way to rehearsal.

Karen had never seen him like that before. Even when they worked through the other issues that came up, Chris might have been afraid or confused, but never really angry…certainly not as angry as he got today.

Karen lifted her head to find Sandy looking over at her. She tried her best to brighten her expression. It certainly wasn't Sandy's fault that she and Chris had a fight.

Sandy smiled back. Her expression seemed to invite Karen to come to her, as if she knew that Karen really needed a friend.

*****

After "Never Forgotten You" was perfected, Chris told everyone to take a twenty minute break. As the musicians scattered, Jerry followed Chris outside.

"What are you doing out here?" Jerry inquired.

Chris sighed. "Oh, I just needed some fresh air."

Jerry placed his hand on Chris' shoulder. "So, do you want to talk about it?"

Chris tried to give Jerry an innocent look. "Talk about what?"

"Whatever's bothering you. Whatever the reason is that you and Karen can't even look at each other."

"Oh." Chris hung his head down. "You noticed that?"

"Of course I did, man. Everybody did. You two were really giving off some bad vibes."

Chris kicked a stone across the sidewalk, sending it into the middle of the busy street. "Here I thought I was hiding it well."

Jerry laughed. "You've never been able to hide it well. Now what's going on?"

"You know...I'm not really sure. I mean, a part of me feels like I'm being too hard on Karen, but then there's another part of me that's just really confused and angry."

"All right, Chris. You know that doesn't really tell me a whole heck of a lot. This is Jerry you're talking to. Spill it."

Chris started to speak, then just shook his head. "I'm not sure if I can explain it when I don't really understand it myself."

"Give it a try. Maybe if you talk through it you can make more sense of it."

"OK...here goes." Chris took a deep breath. "We both had gone to Mass. She went to her church and I went to mine. Then we met up to come over here."

Jerry reached up to scratch his chin. "So far everything sounds normal."

"Oh, that's the easy part. That's only the beginning." Chris stuck his hands into the pockets of his jeans. "She was kind of jittery on the ride over, so I asked if something was bothering her. She said this guy she knew from school showed up at her church."

"Is that a problem?" asked Jerry, hand still on his chin.

"Well…that's where I'm not really sure. It could be. She actually first bumped into him yesterday. He moved here from Indiana a month ago, but Karen never knew he was in town until she ran into him yesterday at the market. When she mentioned it last night, she told me how he hurt her and broke her heart back when they were in junior high together. She seemed to be upset that he lived here now, like she wanted nothing to do with him."

"That would make sense," Jerry said.

"I thought so too," Chris agreed. "But then she mentions the guy again today."

"I guess it would be weird to run into someone you haven't seen in a long time," Jerry said, "especially two days in a row."

"Yeah, but…" Chris found a larger rock and kicked even harder; this time it made it all the way across the street. "Why did Karen bring his name up again? Am I supposed to be jealous?"

"Maybe it's that she's really spooked by seeing him again, especially if this dude was such a jerk back then."

"Or maybe," Chris mused, "she still has feelings for him."

"Now don't go jumping to conclusions, man," said Jerry. "If Karen was hurt so badly by this guy a long time ago, maybe she was glad to be rid of him. And at that age it <u>really</u> hurts to have your heart broken."

"She said she didn't want to be around him anymore," Chris said. "But of course, I kept pushing her and questioning her. She wound up crying and wanting to know what I was so mad about. I guess after the conversation I had with Father John, I've been in a strange frame of mind."

Jerry gave Chris a curious look. "What conversation with Father John?"

"The one I had with him after Mass today, which sounded just like the last couple of conversations I've had with him. He's adamant that I have to watch it with Karen so I don't wind up hurt again. He thinks I'm too trusting."

"Well Chris, I'm sure Father John means well and he thinks he's helping you, but you have to go with your own instinct. He's not living your life, he's not always with you every minute of the day to know everything…and he's not inside of your head. If you want my opinion, I think you should take his advice with a grain of salt."

"I'm trying to, Jer," Chris said. "But, he is a priest. Maybe he really does know what he's talking about."

"Even priests aren't perfect, you know. I'm not saying you shouldn't ever listen to him. Just listen, pray, and let God lead you. God's the only One who's always right."

"So, I should go over Father John's head and take it to his boss?" Chris finally managed a slight grin.

Jerry laughed. "Exactly. Now let's not keep everyone waiting too long. Back to work!"

*****

As Chris and Jerry took their break outside, Sandy found Karen in the ladies room. She was crying softly, drying her eyes with the coarse brown paper towels stacked next to the sink.

"Karen?" Sandy inquired. "Are you all right?"

Karen looked up into Sandy's eyes. "No, not really, but I guess you already figured that out before you came in here."

"I did," Sandy admitted. "That's why I came looking for you. I thought you might need someone to talk to."

"You did?"

"Call it woman's intuition. And since I'm the only woman present other than you, no one else but me has it."

"Thanks." Karen smiled a little through her tears. "It's really hard to sit through rehearsal, listening to Chris sing and act as if everything is perfectly fine."

"Something didn't look right with you guys when you came in today. I could tell. Is it something you feel like talking about?"

Karen inhaled deeply, then slowly exhaled. "If you don't mind listening, I'd like to get another female opinion. And you know Chris better than I do."

"I'm all ears, Karen. What happened?"

"Chris came to my house to pick me up after Mass. He was a little late getting to my place, but he told me that Mass at his church ran a little bit longer than usual. I had him come inside to have a quick sandwich, since he hadn't had a chance to eat yet. Then we got in his car and headed over here."

"So at least he told the truth about Mass running late," Sandy said.

"Yes, that part was true. Chris just didn't let everyone in on the rest of the story."

Sandy nodded her head. "I knew there had to be more to it than that."

"A lot more." Karen started to tear up again. "And it definitely wasn't pretty."

Sandy grabbed more paper towels from the bathroom counter and handed them to Karen. "It's OK, hon, I understand. Please go on."

"So we started driving and Chris asked how Mass was at my church today. As it turned out, something strange happened to me at church."

"Strange? What could be strange at church?"

At the thought of Greg, Karen's mouth formed an automatic frown. "It was the person who wound up sitting next to me. I went to junior high with him back in Indiana. His name's Greg. Anyway, I bumped into him yesterday first at the grocery store. He said he moved here about a month ago because of his girlfriend, but that now he wasn't getting along with her that well."

"Oh, that's interesting. He moved across the country for a girl that he didn't have a stable relationship with?"

"Yeah, well, that actually sounds like something Greg would do. He wasn't exactly stable when I knew him. Of course, I didn't find that out until after I fell for him."

"You had a thing for this guy?"

"Oh, yeah. It was a pretty big crush. That's a whole story in itself, so I'll save that for another time."

"For a guy you had a crush on...you sure didn't look happy when you mentioned his name."

"That would be correct. The condensed version of the story is that he wound up being really mean and nasty to me. Basically he broke my heart. I would have been perfectly happy if I never saw him again."

"Ooh ...sorry to hear that. I do know where you're coming from. I remember dealing with my share of jerks during my school years."

"Thanks, Sandy. I was definitely over Greg a long time ago. It's just that seeing him again brought back all of the bad experiences, plus the negative feelings I wound up having about myself. I still hope not to ever see him again, but now that I've discovered that he goes to my church, I'm afraid I'm going to have to deal with it differently."

As Karen explained the whole Mass incident to Sandy, she started shaking uncontrollably. Sandy's jaw dropped. "Wow! He actually had the nerve to hug you in church instead of shaking your hand?"

"Yes he did. Now, I've seen people hug during the sign of peace, but it's couples and families…you know, people who are close and love each other. I did not expect to be embraced by someone I haven't seen in ages that I did not get along with, that's for sure."

"Now I understand all of this stuff about Greg," Sandy said. "Just where does Chris come into this?"

"Well, I told him yesterday about bumping into Greg at the market. Then I see him again today. I'm so unsettled by all of this that I went on blabbering about it to Chris. He started yelling at me, coming down on me that I was talking on and on about old boyfriends. Greg was <u>never</u> my boyfriend. I had made that very clear to Chris. I also let Chris know how much Greg hurt me, but the more I explained it, the angrier Chris got."

Sandy twisted a strand of her long brown hair around her finger. "Hmm…that sure doesn't sound like Chris."

"I didn't think so either. I figure you've known him a lot longer than I have, so I'm glad I got to run this by you because I'm not sure what to make of it."

"Actually, Karen, I really don't know what to make of it either. He's still mad even after you told him everything?"

"Extremely mad," Karen said. "He kept saying – actually shouting – that I must still have feelings for Greg and that it sounds like I still want to be with him. No matter how much I assured him that wasn't the case, he just kept freaking out about it."

"I wonder what it was that really set him off," Sandy said. "There has to be more to his ranting than just what you told him."

"Yeah, I'm interested in finding out about that myself. It really scared me the way Chris was acting. Thanks for letting me vent with you."

"No problem, Karen." Sandy smiled and grabbed Karen's hand, giving it a sympathetic squeeze. "Hey, us girls have to stick together, you know. We're way outnumbered here."

That managed to make Karen laugh a little. "I guess we really are. We can be a pair of Amazons, taking on the men."

"Sounds like a plan to me," answered Sandy. "Take a deep breath, then let's go back out there and prepare for battle. I'm sure somehow we'll figure out what's going on inside that man's head."

*****

As Chris went over the next song with the band back in the rehearsal room, he caught sight of Karen getting settled in the corner. He got an awful feeling as he noticed her red nose and puffy eyes. He was already starting to feel guilty for screaming at her, but he was still confused about the events of the day.

Something dawned on him as he rechecked his microphone. After they were done with the songs for Monday's session, Karen was supposed to practice a couple of tunes with the band. Would she still feel up to it? Would all of the crying she'd been doing affect her voice?

"OK…are we ready?" Jerry asked, causing Chris to snap back into the moment. He nodded. Jerry counted out, "One, two, one two three…"

They kicked into the third number, the one that if all went well with the first two, would be included in Monday's recording session.

Chris' vocals started out strong, but by the second verse his voice was beginning to crack. This was the tune he had written in Santa Fe, the one God led him to write as he prayed about the decision to get back into music. He was getting into the emotions of that moment; soon he even forgot he was at rehearsal. Eventually he choked his way through the song.

"Sorry, gang," Chris said as he dabbed at the corners of his eyes with the tips of his fingers. "This one just means an awful lot to me."

"It's all right, man," Jerry said. He was the only person who knew about Santa Fe other than Karen, only Karen didn't know which song was the one. Jerry did.

Chris and the band started again, this time with Chris' mind on the song, not the story behind the song. This run-through went much smoother than the first.

"One more time and I think I'll be ready to call it a day," Chris announced. "Then you guys can have some practice time with Karen."

"Sounds like a deal to me," Jerry said, giving Karen a wink.

*****

Karen took a deep breath and turned her eyes toward the ceiling. Once the song was over, she swiftly rose from her seat. Now that the moment was upon her, she was eager to get started. Chris met her halfway to the stage, mic in hand. He managed a quick smile as he handed it to Karen.

"The band's all yours. Just let loose and go for it."

"Thanks, Chris." Karen took the mic, attached it to its stand and made her adjustments. She turned to Jerry. "OK Jerry, what's up first?"

"We thought we'd go with 'Can't Take My Eyes Off of You'."

"OK," Karen said. "Let's do it!"

Jerry kicked off the band while Karen prepared to start. Chris grabbed the stool that Karen had been using and took his seat.

Karen took Chris' advice and just let go. Her voice came through clear and powerful. With each note she became more relaxed, giving a more than convincing performance.

"That was solid, Karen. I'm impressed." Jerry reached up to give her a high-five.

"Thanks. I wasn't as nervous as I thought I would be."

"You're a natural, Karen," Chris offered from his seat. Karen smiled anxiously, but not because of her performance. Her stomach did a flip in spite of her efforts to remain calm.

"Let's try something else," Jerry said. "I guess Charlie suggested 'Can't Help Falling in Love'."

Karen just stared at him. "The Elvis song?"

"That's the one. You know it, right?"

"Sure do." She closed her eyes and took a deep breath. "All right Jerry, I'm ready."

Karen came through beautifully on the tender ballad, causing Chris to be the one who blinked back a few tears.

Jerry sighed. "The King would be pleased."

"You think so?" Karen was finding it difficult to get used to all of this praise, considering she'd never really had much of it before.

"Absolutely," Chris chimed in. "That was breathtaking, honey."

Karen wasn't sure she heard that right. *Did he say honey? Like maybe…it's possible he isn't so mad anymore?*

"Thank you, Chris. That means a lot to me."

"Karen, feel free to sing with us anytime," Sandy added, giving Karen a big thumbs-up.

"I know we're out of time for today," Chris said. "See everyone tomorrow at eleven AM."

Chris came up to Karen with a sheepish look spread across his face. "I guess I'm still kind of confused about what happened today, Karen. Can we take a couple of days away from each other to sort things out?"

Karen frowned. "Well, that may have worked last time, but that's going to be a problem now. Charlie wants me at the studio for the next three days after work so he can observe me before my session on Thursday, remember?"

Chris closed his eyes. "That's right, I forgot. Well, I'll figure something out. But for now I have to get out of here." He gave Karen a small peck on the cheek and went outside. She could hear his car radio clearly as he drove away down the street.

Sandy came back in for her equipment. "Karen, how are you getting home?"

"Oh, no! I forgot Chris drove me here!"

Sandy shook her head. "I really don't know what's gotten into that man. Why don't I give you a ride home?"

"Oh, thank you Sandy. I'm just happy that you hadn't left yet."

"Me too," Sandy said. "The thought of you being stuck here with no way home just makes me sick."

Karen helped Sandy carry her equipment out to the car and load it in the trunk. They got in and took off for Karen's place, with Sandy still shaking her head over Chris' behavior.

CHAPTER 16

Karen pulled up to the curb at California Songbird Studio with mixed emotions. Luckily the excitement of recording outweighed the dread of wondering how Chris was going to behave, but she still had that anxious feeling in the pit of her stomach.

The night before when Sandy drove her home, Karen invited her in to hang out for a while. Both women were curious to see if Chris would realize that he'd left Karen stranded at the rehearsal studio. Sandy was sure Karen would get a visit from Chris, or least a call to apologize.

The two women threw together a couple of chef salads in Karen's kitchen, eating and talking about all sorts of things to get Karen's mind off of Chris. Yet in the backs of their minds, they kept anticipating the ringing of either the doorbell or the telephone.

Karen was so thankful that Sandy was there for her. After her move to California she sorely lacked girlfriends; her two best friends back home were hard to keep up with other than the occasional letters. And right now she needed a friend who didn't live a couple of thousand miles away.

Sandy kept Karen company until about eleven o'clock, then she headed home…but not without first giving Karen her cell phone number so she could let Sandy know in the morning whether Chris contacted her or not.

Unfortunately when Karen called Sandy in the morning, the answer was no. Sandy was very disappointed in her boss, wondering how she was going to deal with him for the rest of the day. She was on her way to meet the rest of the band at the recording studio.

Now it was early evening, and it was Karen's turn to wonder how she was going to handle the situation. She had already dealt with it badly during the day, buying a bag of chips and three candy bars from her office vending machine and scarfing them down in less than 15 minutes. Afterward, it was all she could do to keep herself from running to the bathroom and immediately getting rid of the junk she'd just put into her system. Very little work got done as she wrestled with the part of her brain that was trying to make her get back into old, damaging habits.

Karen parked her car and sauntered into the studio, silently making her way over to Charlie and the soundboard. She didn't want to startle him while he was working the board, since Chris and company were in the middle of performing "Never Forgotten You".

Karen stood back as she watched Charlie make adjustments at the board, his hands flying everywhere at a second's notice. She still couldn't imagine how he knew exactly where to go on the board to adjust what needed adjusting. She had never seen anything with so many buttons, bells, and whistles in her life. She always knew there was a lot to the recording process, more than just what was shown on TV. Still, she never realized just how much was involved until she got a look at all of the equipment. There sure was a lot to keep in order. Besides all of that, you had to have an ear for what sounded right, and what didn't sound right so you could fix the problem. Karen was completely absorbed in watching Charlie at work.

*****

With Karen's eyes riveted on the board and Chris being totally in the moment with the song, all was well for the moment. At least that's what Sandy thought as her eyes darted back and forth between the two of them. She wondered what would happen once the song was done.

None of this affected Sandy's keyboard work or background vocals; she had been a professional musician long enough to know that no matter what is going on around you, you learn to make sure it doesn't interfere with the music. She'd been through stranger situations than this during her career and had always maintained her composure. She wasn't about to let that change now.

The song finished as Charlie went to fade out. "All right everyone, that sounds like the one."

A collective sigh came across the sound system. "Those are the most beautiful words I've ever heard," Rob said. "I'm not sure I could have handled another go."

Charlie's hearty laugh was just what the band needed to hear. "Congratulations gang, after nine takes the tenth was the charm. We have a new single ready to roll."

"Then I guess," Chris said as Sandy watched him glance over at Karen, "a break is in order."

"I'd say so," agreed Charlie. "Be back in twenty minutes."

*****

Karen quietly stood behind Charlie until he turned around to see her there. "Hey," he said. "I didn't notice you come in."

Karen smiled. "I didn't want to scare you."

"Good thing too. If this take wouldn't have stuck, I think they would have been ready to kill me."

"How many takes do you usually need?"

"Four or five would be about the average. Sometimes you get lucky in one or two. Every once in a while, there's a session like this one."

The door opened very slowly. Chris' face appeared in the doorway of the control booth with a solemn expression. "Karen, can I talk to you for a minute?"

Karen closed her eyes as she spoke, trying to hide the emotion behind them. "Sure, Chris. I'll be right out."

As Chris pulled the door shut, Charlie shot Karen a worrisome look. "Karen, are you guys having a problem? I don't mean to pry, but Chris just hasn't been himself today."

Karen's eyes opened, revealing the fear she didn't want Chris to see. "It's a long story. I do, but yet I don't want to know what he has to say."

Charlie smiled, in a way that Karen interpreted as encouraging. "Good luck, my dear."

"Thanks." Karen quickly slipped out the door, into the hallway to speak with Chris.

"Hey Karen," he said softly. "I'm so sorry about last night."

"Sorry, huh?" The fear was being pushed out of her eyes by anger. "I'm not sure you are. I know for some reason unknown to me you're still angry with me, but ditching me and leaving me stranded…well, how do you justify that?"

"I know nothing I can say would be a good excuse," Chris pleaded, "but let me try to explain. When I took off, I fully intended to come back for you. I meant to just drive around for a few minutes and cool down. When I came back you were gone. I figured that you were so upset that you didn't want me to drive you home and you got a ride with someone else."

"You were so mad when you left, Chris. How was I supposed to know you were coming back? You never said anything except that you had to get out of here!" Karen was now so exasperated that her hands were flying all over the place as she spoke. "Nothing in the way you were acting led me to believe you were still coming back for me. Sandy saw you drive off and thought the same as I did. She offered to drive me home. We both thought I'd hear from you last night, but that sure didn't happen."

"I know that now," Chris answered, head down. "Sandy really laid into me this morning. Once she explained all that, I realized I wasn't very clear about what was going on. I should have told you I'd only be gone a few minutes. Honestly, Karen, no matter how angry I was, I would never just leave you stranded without a way home. You've got to believe me. I'm still not sure about everything that happened between us yesterday, but I would never do that to you. Please believe me. I'm so, so sorry." Chris' shoulders began to shake as he turned pale.

"Chris, I still don't quite understand why you're still upset with me. I'd really like to believe you wouldn't just ditch me like that."

"Oh, honey…never!" Chris was still shaking and his voice quivered. "I love you! It breaks my heart that you think that of me!"

Karen opened her mouth to speak, but her original thought had left her. "Chris…what did you just say?"

*****

Chris looked straight into her emerald eyes. "I love you. Karen, honey, I love you so much. I've never had feelings this strong before, and everything's happening so fast with us. I guess that frightened me and I got spooked by some things." He swallowed hard. *I can't just come out and tell her that a priest told me to be wary of her.* He let out an aggravated sigh. "And when I got spooked, all kinds of thoughts started going around in my mind. I'm still trying to understand my own thoughts, let alone the things we talked about yesterday. The only thing I know for sure is that I love you."

Chris saw tears being to form in Karen's eyes. "Oh Chris…I love you too. I agree that things are moving really quickly, but whatever you're feeling, whatever thoughts you're dealing with…I wish you would talk to me about it instead of lashing out at me. I was so hurt. Of course I was angry as well, but just more hurt than anything, because I love you so much."

They came together in an embrace, crying and holding each other. Chris wished they didn't have to let go and head back into the studio.

"Honey," Chris asked as he brushed tears from Karen's face and blinked back his own, "can we go somewhere to talk after the session's done?"

Karen nodded as she blinked and brushed her fingers over the tears that had already begun to leave makeup streaks on her face.

"Good. Let me tell Charlie we need a few more minutes to compose ourselves. Then maybe we can lay down another set of tracks for the day and go talk this all out."

"I'd really like that. Let me go to the restroom and try to make myself presentable again. "

Chris gently kissed her cheek, then headed back into the control room to speak to Charlie.

*****

Chris knew that the next song they were scheduled to record required emotion to make it work. He channeled his current emotions into his vocals, nailing the track in just two takes.

Charlie stood behind the glass with his mouth hanging open.

"I think," he finally said, "this was a gift from above to make up for all of the problems with the single."

Chris managed a weary smile. "I'm sure you're right about that, Charlie."

"Well," said Jerry, "then I'm thankful for Divine Intervention."

"I'll second that." Rob was already packing his bass. "I think we could all use a good night's sleep before tomorrow. Good night all."

"Good night Rob." Chris turned to Karen. "I'm sorry we ran so late that you didn't get to practice tonight."

"That's OK. I think all of us are emotionally drained."

"Are you ready to go?"

"I sure am." Karen reached for her purse. "I just need to speak to Sandy for a minute."

"No problem." Chris smiled as he gently touched her arm. "I'll meet you outside."

*****

Everyone had already headed out, leaving Karen and Sandy alone to talk. "Hey girl," Sandy said. "How did your conversation go with Chris?"

Karen tried to hold back the waterworks that were still just below the surface, ready to spring from her eyes at any moment. "I was a mess to start with, but after a few choice words, I think it went pretty well."

"I had a few of those words for him myself this morning. I guess guys don't always think things through."

"I guess not," Karen said, pulling a tissue from her purse. "We're going somewhere to talk now, so maybe we can finally get to the bottom of this."

"I'm glad, hon." Sandy gave Karen a quick little hug. "I sure hope you can work it all out."

"Thanks, Sandy. For everything."

"Anytime, Karen. If you ever need me for anything, just let me know."

The two women went outside into the warm evening air. Sandy bid Karen good night and waved to Chris as she got into her car.

Chris motioned for Karen to get in his convertible. "Let's drive over to the little coffee shop down the street. I'll bring you back to your car afterward."

"OK…sounds good." Karen got in, and before she had time to think, they were inside the Daily Grind.

"Karen, honey, why don't you find a table for us while I get our drinks?"

"All right. Could you get me a decaf hazelnut with cream and sugar?"

"You've got it. I'll be over there in a few minutes."

Chris strode to the counter to order the coffees. Karen walked through the café, spotting a small table in the corner that looked like it might give them some privacy. Chris soon joined her with two steaming hot mugs.

"I know I've been a bad boy," he said. "Is that why you're putting me in the corner?"

Karen chuckled. "Well, that's not why, but it does make some sense. I thought nobody would bother us back here. That way we can talk without an audience."

"Great idea. But if you want, I'll see if the manager has a dunce cap that I could wear."

"Now, now." Karen smiled. "That won't be necessary. Just come sit with me."

Chris carefully set down the full mugs, then pulled a chair over from the nearest table and sat next to Karen.

She gently slid her coffee closer and cupped it with both hands, deeply inhaling the sweet, nutty aroma.

"This smells like heaven right now." Karen peered over into Chris' mug. "What did you get?"

"Just the house blend, fully loaded. It's been a long day and I need the caffeine to stay awake on the way home. I didn't sleep well last night."

Karen set her mug down on the table, still holding it with both hands. "I can relate," she said. "I didn't get much sleep myself."

Chris sighed. "My mind was so messed up. I didn't know a man could ever wind up crying so much. Suddenly I didn't know what to think about anything anymore."

"You're definitely going to have to explain. Honestly, when you started going off on me the other day, I didn't know where it was coming from, or why."

"I know, Karen. You deserve a full explanation. Please bear with me, because I have to straighten it all out in my mind as I tell it. I almost have to explain it to myself as much as I do to you."

Karen placed her hand on his tense shoulder. "I'm not quite sure if that makes me feel better or not."

"Yeah, I know. Believe me, it's hard to realize that your own brain is trying to unscramble what's going on inside itself."

Karen inhaled slowly, then exhaled even more so. "OK, I'm ready. Explain away."

"I guess the first thing that bothered me was that we wound up talking about this Greg guy two days in a row."

"But Chris, that was only because I ran into him two days in a row, otherwise I wouldn't have brought him up again."

"I know that now," Chris said, "but at the time I couldn't process that. All I kept thinking was that you were going on and on about this other guy, a guy you once wanted to be with."

Karen's hand froze with the coffee mug halfway to her lips. "That was such a long time ago! And don't forget he treated me like dirt!"

"Sweetie, I realize that. But I know from experience that a person does not automatically stop wanting someone just because that person treated them badly."

"Oh." Karen set her coffee down and looked directly into those kind hazel eyes. "This has something to do with that ex-fiancée of yours, doesn't it?"

"I'm afraid that's a big part of it. I still had moments, even after Andrea hurt me, that I wanted her back in my life. I really thought I loved her…and after spending that much time with her, well, it's really difficult to shut that part of your heart and mind off."

"That's true. But you and I, I believe, are both long over the people who did us wrong."

"Yes we are. I also know that those incidents will somehow always be a part of us. They're part of what shaped our lives."

"I can agree with that…but also know that the events that shaped our lives have now brought us together."

Chris looked at her sadly. "Karen, I'm so sorry. I should never have compared our relationship to the ones from my past. It's just that…this time I had a little help from someone else."

Karen suddenly felt a strange sensation in her stomach, as if she was bracing for a kick to land there. "Oh? Like who?"

Chris took a deep breath and let Karen in on his unusual conversations with Father John.

"No wonder you were confused, Chris," Karen said. "This advice came from your priest."

"Tell me about it. His voice kind of echoed the negative little voice in my head, the one I was trying to push as far back as possible."

Karen shook her head. "Wow, I thought he liked me."

"Oh, I'm sure he does, but…" Chris swallowed hard. "I think he thought he was looking out for me. He's known me for a long time and doesn't want to see me get hurt. I tried arguing with him about it, but he kept insisting that I couldn't be too careful."

Karen's lips started to form a tiny smile. "You defended me to Father John?"

"Of course I did. And if it makes you feel any better, I truly believe he would have said these things to me whether it was you or some other woman I might have met and started dating."

Her smile grew with each word. "Thanks. That does help a little."

"The rational part of me was wrestling with my irrational inner voice, plus Father John's voice." Chris covered Karen's hand with his own. "I'm sorry that it was the irrational voice that came out of me the other day."

"Well," Karen said, "at least now I know where it came from."

"I feel like a heel, Karen. All of these thoughts seemed to make a lot more sense yesterday. Now after explaining myself, it doesn't make as much sense as I thought it did."

Karen laughed. "This may scare you a little…but I actually understand you better now."

"Let's see if I can get this straight." Chris' left eyebrow arched upward. "I understand myself less, but you understand me more?"

Karen shrugged her shoulders. "Looks like that's the case." She took another sip of the smooth, sweet hazelnut coffee. "Just relax. Maybe soon it will fall into place for you."

Chris took both of her hands in his, gently rubbing her fingers. "Hopefully it will. I feel better knowing you understand."

"I do." Karen let her mind drift for a second. "I have an idea, if it's all right with you."

Now his right eyebrow went up. "My curiosity is piqued," he said. "Just what do you have in mind?"

Karen could not conceal her sly grin, nor did she want to.

"I think I should accompany you to Mass at your church this Sunday. That way I don't have to see you-know-who…and Father can see us together in a much better setting. He can't very well find fault with us going to church together, can he?"

Chris' smirk matched Karen's, with his eyes following. "I think it's a brilliant idea, honey. This will be the perfect way to cap off an amazing week. And hopefully it will improve these other situations."

CHAPTER 17

With everything going on both with her and around her, Karen could have sworn that she blinked and it was Thursday. Not only did she get plenty of rehearsal time at the studio earlier in the week, but she also eked out some practice at home with her guitar so she could be more prepared for her upcoming sessions.

This singing opportunity came about so fast that Karen really hoped she was ready. While there were moments when she wrestled with wondering if she actually had the talent, she tried to remind herself that God wouldn't have presented her with this big chance if He didn't feel she could handle it.

Even with all of her positive thoughts, a problem threatened to burst her joyful bubble. Karen was so excited that she called home to share her good news. Her father was less than enthusiastic.

"You're going to do what?" he asked in an astonished tone. "What brought this on?"

"It's an awesome opportunity, Dad. It's something I've always wanted to do, and there's no way I could pass up the chance."

"Do you really think you're any good? Seriously, honey, don't you think you're too old to be chasing little girl dreams?"

Karen was taken aback, nearly dropping the receiver as his words hit her. She knew her father would have some questions. She just never imagined it would feel like she'd been smacked in the face.

"Now Dad, come on," she said in as calm of a voice as she could muster. "Chris and Charlie really love my voice. I've been practicing and I have confidence in myself. It's better to at least try and do your best than to never do it and wonder for the rest of your life."

"Wait a minute," Dad said abruptly. "Just who are Chris and Charlie?"

Karen slapped her forehead as she realized that he had no idea that she was dating Chris. She was going to be springing this on him as well. Her dad was probably going to think something strange was wafting through the California air, possibly from L.A. smog or people "smoking funny stuff", as he called it.

"Well, Charlie owns the recording studio," Karen started, then looked up to heaven and took a deep breath. "Chris is Chris Lassiter. We met out here and now we're dating."

"Chris Lassiter." Karen's dad was silent for a minute. "You mean that TV star you had a crush on way back when?"

"One and the same," came her reply.

"Isn't he a lot older than you, dear?"

"Just ten years, Dad. Once you get to my age that's not really a big difference anymore."

"Hmm…well, maybe then he's just praising your voice to make you feel good."

Karen let out an exasperated sigh. "Chris is not like that, Dad. He brought me to Charlie to get his opinion, and Charlie agreed with Chris. I'm going to start recording tomorrow night."

"Oh." Her dad seemed to hesitate for another moment, which to Karen felt like forever. "Anything else you need to tell me?"

Karen choked back tears, but somehow still managed to speak. "I bought a new guitar and started playing again. I'm writing songs again too."

"Yeah, I remember you playing around with that stuff when you were younger. Now what I really want to hear about is how your job is going."

Karen was now leaning her head on her free arm, eyes closed. "My heart's just not in that job anymore."

"Don't even tell me you quit your job!"

"No, I haven't quit…but I certainly need to think about pursuing other avenues."

"Like what? Singing?"

Karen was starting to wonder why she even bothered to call home.

"Well, possibly. It all depends on how things go." Karen swallowed down the gigantic lump in her throat. "Please be happy for me, Dad. At least I'm getting the chance to try something I've always dreamed of doing."

"OK, honey. I'll try to be happy. You know your ole Dad's got to be skeptical. I worry about you."

"I know, but please just trust me."

"I'll work on it," he allowed. "I hope you know what you're doing. I do wish you luck, honey."

"Thanks Dad. I love you."

"I love you too, Karen. I'll talk to you soon."

"OK. Bye Dad."

Karen knew she would never forget a single word of that conversation. The problem was that it depressed her enough that she would rather not think about it.

She was also trying not to imagine what her other family members would say about her once they found out the news from her dad. The more she tried not to dwell on it, the more it popped into her head and threatened to drive her out of her mind.

She was thankful for Chris and Sandy, both of whom she called later that night for moral support after crying thousands of tears. They got her to calm down and think positively again.

Now on her way to the studio, Karen attempted to push the phone call with her dad out of her thoughts. She preferred to think of her mother and grandmother up in heaven. She just knew they were smiling down on her, cheering her on.

Dear God, she prayed. *I know You're the One who brought this opportunity into my life. Please help me clear all of the negative thoughts out of my head so I can make the most out of what You've given me.*

*****

When Karen walked into the studio, she found three gifts waiting there for her. What surprised her the most was that they were from three different people.

First was a fragrant bouquet consisting of two dozen velvet-soft red roses and sweet, abundant baby's breath. She pulled the card attached and read: *A voice like yours deserves a room filled with roses, but then there would be no room left for you to record. Knock everyone's socks off, honey. Love, Chris.*

Karen inhaled the lovely scent and gently touched the soft petals. Then she noticed the next gift. It was an 8 x 10 pencil drawing of Karen at the mic. The detail was remarkable, as if Karen were watching herself come to life. Beside the picture was a note: *When I'm not living out my musical dream, this is my hobby. Now it's time for your musical dreams. Go for it girl! Love-n-friendship, Sandy.*

Wow! Karen had no idea Sandy was such a talented artist. She liked her even more now than before.

The third present made Karen laugh. It was a bottle of sparkling grape juice, with yet another note: *I'm thrilled to have you aboard! This is to celebrate because I know you're going to be awesome…Charlie. P.S. Sorry – you can't drink it until after the session, unless you wish to burp through your song!*

Well, Karen thought, *that would be an original form of musical expression!*

Karen walked over to the control room and rapped rhythmically on the door. When Charlie opened it, Karen found Chris there with him.

"You guys…thank you so much for my surprise welcome!"

Chris flashed his trademark smile, and Karen was sure it lit up at least the entire state of California. Forget solar power…all of the warmth and light needed for energy conservation could come from that grin. "Hi honey!" he said. "I'm so excited for you…I can't wait to see how it goes."

"Hey Karen," Charlie chuckled, "you didn't drink from that bottle yet, did you?"

"No way, Charlie," Karen answered. "That is <u>not</u> how I want to make my debut."

They all laughed together as they watched the band tune up. Karen hit the speaker button. "Hello everyone!"

"Hey Karen!" came the group reply.

"Sandy, thank you so much for the drawing. I didn't know you were such a brilliant artist!"

"You're welcome, hon," said Sandy. "I'm a woman of many talents."

"Now Sandy," Rob called out, "I don't think you should discuss those here."

"Hey, that's not what I meant!" Sandy turned a deep shade of crimson as her hands froze above the keyboard.

"I know," Rob said. "But that was just too good of an opportunity to pass up."

Sandy sighed. "Men!"

Jerry looked up into the control booth and winked. "So Karen, are you ready for your debut recording session?"

"No one's ever probably really ready, but I'm as ready as I'll ever be."

"Cool. We're just about set out here. I know Charlie's got some things to fill you in on before we get started, so we'll see you in here after that."

Charlie laid out the ground rules for the session. Karen listened intently, absorbing as much information as she could and hoping she could remember it all.

"Now Karen, final advice…keep your mind on what you're doing, but not so much that you stress yourself out. It will show up in your voice. Just relax and enjoy."

"Thanks, Charlie," Karen said, taking a deep breath as she tried to get the butterflies in her stomach to stop fluttering around.

With a high five from Charlie and a kiss from Chris for luck, Karen made her way to the other side of the glass. She adjusted her mic, silently sending up another prayer to the One who got her here. She gave a thumbs-up to Charlie and a nod to Jerry.

Jerry counted off, and Sandy's fingers began playing the beautiful strains of the true classic "Without You." Karen closed her eyes, concentrating on the music for her cue.

"No I can't forget this evening, or your face as you were leaving," began Karen, becoming more confident with each note. Before she even realized it, she was belting out the chorus, with more emotion than she even thought she had in her.

*****

Chris and Charlie grinned ridiculously at each other. It wasn't often that a voice like Karen's came along, and here they had this incredible talent right under their noses. It was like finding a wooden chest full of buried treasure.

As Karen finished strong, Charlie stopped the tape and held up his hand. He could see the fear in Karen's eyes; he knew she had to be wondering if she had messed something up.

"Great first take, gang," Charlie called out over the speaker. "How about a little lighter on the percussion this time?"

"Gotcha," said Marcus, the veteran drummer who kept beat for the band.

"And Karen…it was perfect except for the very beginning, which I attribute to first time nerves."

"Don't worry, Charlie. I have no illusions about being flawless on the first take."

Charlie laughed. "Good thing you've been hanging around musicians. Now that you've got your studio legs under you, I know the start will be just as amazing as the finish."

Karen smiled and blew Charlie a lighthearted kiss. He was pleased to see her loosen up and relax a little bit.

"Let's do it again." Charlie pointed to the band and rolled tape, and Karen was right on from the start this time. But a sudden popping sound broke the flow, causing Karen to jump and stop singing.

"Sorry everybody," Jerry said ruefully. "I broke a string."

"Hey Jerry, it happens," Charlie consoled. "How about we all take ten while Jerry gets tuned up again?"

*****

Once they came back at the end of the break, Jerry tested his strings for durability. "All right guys and gals," he announced. "We should be good to go. Sorry about all of this, Karen."

Karen smiled at him. "It's fine, Jerry. Anything can happen during a session, which I'm learning as I go."

After one more adequate take, the fourth one was the charm. When Karen glanced over at Charlie and Chris, she saw the grins on their faces that told her everything she needed to know.

Karen felt it too. Such a feeling of complete peace came over her; her soul was soaring within her in a way she'd never known before.

There was a calm, quiet moment after they finished, then Charlie called out, "That's our winner!" Karen and the band started a round of high fives.

"OK," Charlie interrupted. "Let me play it back for you." They all listened intently, ecstatic over the sound of their performance. Karen looked through the glass at Chris, who was beaming at her. Now her heart skipped a beat for two very different reasons, although Chris was definitely involved in both of them. It was nice to have things come together for a change; it had been a long time since she felt anything was really going the right way in her life.

At the end of the playback, applause broke out in the studio. Karen's smile spread from ear to ear, all the way through her entire body. Could this kind of bliss really be possible?

"Now," said Charlie with eyes twinkling, "I think it's time to break open that bottle!"

"Great minds really do think alike." Chris was in the doorway, bottle already in one hand with a tall stack of paper cups in the other.

After the bubbly juice was poured, Charlie raised his cup. "I would like to propose a toast – to Karen and the band for a super session." He winked at Karen and continued. "And especially to Karen, who took her first recording session by storm and showed us all how it should be done. I've never in my life seen anyone's first session go so well. Congratulations, Karen!"

Karen absorbed the compliment as the group raised their cups to Charlie's. She took the statement as a sign from above that she was on the right path.

"Thank you, Charlie, and thank you everyone. This is a dream come true for me. I'm glad you're the people here with me to make it happen."

"Believe me, it's our pleasure," Jerry said.

"You've got the voice, girl," Sandy added. "That's for darn sure."

"You are amazing, Karen," Charlie said. "But I must interrupt this love fest to go over some things."

Karen grinned. "Fire away."

"I know that you know your two other songs for tomorrow night. If we finish the first one and have time, we'll work on the second."

"Sounds great."

"However, we have a brand new song for you to learn for next week."

"Really?" Karen asked, wide-eyed. She thought they were only going to work with classic songs. "What is it?"

Chris came over to her and handed her some sheet music. Karen didn't even notice a title at first. The part that caught her eye was "Lyrics and music by Chris Lassiter".

"Karen," Chris said as he put his arm around her, "would you do me the great honor of recording my song?"

Karen brushed a teardrop from the sheet of music before her. "Wild horses couldn't stop me from recording this song," she replied.

Chris hugged her tightly. "Don't worry, this weekend I'll be going over the song with you, so by next week it will be second nature."

"Good. Oh Chris, I can't wait to get started!"

"Well, Karen," Charlie said, "you'd probably better go home and get a good night's rest. It's been a long, exciting day for you, and tomorrow will be more of the same."

"Good idea," Karen answered. "I think the exhaustion is starting to set in."

Everyone bid each other good night. Chris walked Karen out to her car and opened the driver's side door for her.

"Honey, I'm so proud of you. You were completely amazing!" Chris pulled her in close to him and kissed her, with a mixture of sweetness and passion that took her breath away.

"Chris," Karen said when she could finally talk, "I loved every minute of it. I'm thrilled you want me to sing one of your songs."

"I wrote it with you in mind. In fact, while I was thinking about you, it practically wrote itself."

Karen smiled at Chris' words, but suddenly found herself attempting to stifle a yawn without much success. Chris stroked her long blonde hair. "You'd better go get some sleep, baby. I'll see you tomorrow."

After one more quick kiss good night, they got in their vehicles and drove to their separate homes. Karen barely made it to her house with her eyes open, praying all the way there and thanking God for keeping her awake. As much as she wanted to read through the new song, she knew it would keep her from getting enough rest. It would have to wait until morning.

She walked into her kitchen and saw the bright red light blinking by her telephone on the counter. She had two new messages.

Karen pressed the button to listen. Message one turned out to be from Greg, wanting her to call him. *OK,* she thought, *how in the world did Greg get my number? I never gave it to him.*

She put that out of her mind as she retrieved the second message, which was from her dad. "Hi honey. I hope your recording session went well. Just don't get your hopes up about making a living at this, OK? But I still hope it all went well. Love you."

Karen sighed. Why was there always somebody or something trying to rain on her parade?

She refused to think any more about it right now, and she was too sleepy to deal with it. It was too late at night to call either of them back anyway, especially her dad, who was a couple of time zones away. She went to her bedroom, laid down, and was asleep as soon as her head hit the pillow.

CHAPTER 18

On Friday morning, Karen made sure she started her day by thanking God and asking for His help to get through this last day of her work week. With all of the thoughts she had swimming around in her head, she was grateful that she wouldn't have to do it again tomorrow. *I'm not used to having so many things going on in my life,* she thought, *and all of it happened within a matter of days. Crazy!*

Now on her morning coffee break, she was about to add another event to the mix. She had been putting this one off for much too long already. She took a deep breath as she picked up the phone and dialed the number written on the business card in front of her.

"Hello? Yes, I need to make an appointment for a mammogram and ultrasound. This is Karen O'Neil. My physician in Indiana sent you my most recent films a couple of months ago. Sorry it's taken me so long to make an appointment. I know it's late notice, but is Tuesday good? At lunchtime? Great – I'll see you at 12:15 on Tuesday. Thank you for fitting me in. Bye."

All right, Karen, she told herself. *Exhale and relax. At least it's all set up now. You have to have regular checkups to stay on top of this. It does run in your family.*

Karen put the card back into her wallet and placed it in her purse. Like it or not, she knew this was always going to be a part of her life. She had to deal with it no matter what. Trying not to think about it at all would not make the issue go away, as much as she wished it would.

Karen got back to the project at hand. While she sorted papers into their proper piles, her thoughts shifted to another subject that had nothing to do with either her job or her upcoming appointment. How in the world did Greg Richards get her phone number?

Karen hardly ever gave out her number; when she did it was her cell phone number. Besides her family and boss, only Chris and Sandy had the home number. Plus, Karen didn't have her address or phone number listed in the phone book. Since she lived alone, she didn't want the information out there for the entire public to see.

With her head bent over her desk, Karen pressed on with her work. She made a few minutes' worth of progress when she was struck by an alarming thought. *Since Greg now has my phone number, does that mean he knows where I live too? My phone is unlisted, how did he find it?*

She tried to focus on her computer screen, but the paragraph she had just finished typing became a blur to her. Suddenly she was very sick to her stomach. She tried to control her breathing to calm that feeling in her gut, but it seemed that all of the oxygen had left the room. The feeling was similar to the daily panic attacks on her morning commute, and she was sure that she was going to throw up right there on her desk.

Jim came to her doorway and knocked. He was surprised to find Karen with her head in her hands, unable to even look up at him.

"Karen, are you all right?"

Karen finally leaned on one hand and made an effort to turn toward Jim. She knew if she raised her head all the way up it would trigger the reflex in her stomach that made her feel like gagging. She also knew that reflex was extra sensitive in her, ever since those days in the past when she made herself throw up when she shouldn't have.

"Karen, you don't look so good. You're as white as the sheet of paper I have in my hand."

"I'm not feeling very well right now. My stomach's all over the place and my head is starting to hurt."

"Well, you were probably due for the flu bug. I can't remember the last time you were sick."

"I'm sorry, Jim. I can't even focus on what I'm doing. It's all I can do to keep from throwing up right now."

"Why don't you go home? You probably need some rest. I'll see you on Monday."

"What about this proposal?"

Jim smiled. "We really don't have to have this one ready until Tuesday afternoon. You're good…you'll have it done in plenty of time."

"Thanks Jim," Karen said, sighing. "If I would have felt this way when I got up this morning, I wouldn't have come in. It just came on all of a sudden."

"It's no problem, Karen," Jim reassured her. "It happens sometimes, you have no control over it."

*****

Karen went to the restroom, closed her eyes, and tried to calm herself down. Once she felt able to, she left work and drove to the nearest convenience store.

She bought a two-liter bottle of ginger ale, hoping it would soothe her troubled tummy.

She started toward home, but her paranoia took over. *What if Greg is waiting for me at my house when I get there? He could be, if he's impatient because I haven't called him back.*

Karen got on her cell phone and called Sandy, hoping she was still at home. She knew Chris' session for the day didn't start until one o'clock.

"Hello?" Sandy answered.

"Sandy, it's Karen. Can I come over and talk to you before you go to the studio? It's really important."

"Karen, aren't you at work? What's going on?"

"I left work sick. My boss thinks it's the flu, but it has nothing to do with that. I'll explain more when I get there, if it's OK."

"Sure, hon. Let me give you directions."

Sandy stayed on the phone, guiding Karen through each turn and stoplight all the way to her house. When Karen's car pulled up, Sandy was at the front door already waiting for her.

Karen stepped inside the house, ginger ale in hand. "Thanks, Sandy. I just couldn't go home right now."

"You're quite welcome, hon, but please tell me what's wrong. You don't look good at all."

Karen explained the message from Greg, telling Sandy about her growing fears. "Sandy, I'm so worried that I actually made myself sick. My boss, Jim, assumed it had to be the flu from my pale complexion and stomach problems. I guess I just let him keep on thinking that, since I didn't feel I could tell him what was really going on. I'm still surprised that he was so understanding and let me leave for the day."

"Well, I can see why you're upset. It _is_ really creepy."

"So now I'm at a loss as to what I should do. I certainly thought I hadn't given Greg the impression that I ever wanted to see him again."

Sandy thought about that for a few seconds. "I'll tell you what. Why don't you hang out here until you need to come to the studio later? You can rest and try to calm down before your session."

"That would be wonderful," Karen said. "Are you sure it's all right?"

"Definitely. If your stomach settles down and you feel like eating, help yourself to whatever you want in the kitchen. I think I still have some saltine crackers in the cupboard, if you don't think you can eat anything else. When you leave, just lock up. I want to do whatever I can to help."

"I'm so grateful, Sandy," Karen said. "But I have another question for you. Do you think I should tell Chris about this? I really, really don't want to bring up Greg's name again, especially after the last incident."

"Oh yeah...that's right," Sandy replied. She paused for a minute as she contemplated Karen's question. "I do think he needs to know. He's going to notice that you're worried about something, and you could possibly be in danger."

Karen folded her hands in her lap to keep herself from wringing them anymore. "So, how do you propose I tell him?"

"That's where I'm stumped. But very carefully, for sure. Between us, hopefully we can figure that out before you get to the studio."

"OK. Oh, by the way, guess what the other message I had last night was? My dad, hoping everything went well at the studio, but basically giving me a 'don't quit your day job' talk."

"Lovely," Sandy said. "Well, only you can decide what's best for you. I know it would be great to please your dad, but he's not living your life. You are, so try not to think about it."

"I know you're right, Sandy. I'm trying."

"I know you are, hon. And I also know how difficult it is when your family doesn't support your dreams. Now, I'd better get to the studio. Get some rest and I'll see you later."

"Thanks."

While Sandy took off for Chris' session, Karen settled in on the couch. She pulled the blue and white striped afghan down over herself and settled in for an afternoon rest.

*****

Chris and the band were finishing up his session just as Karen arrived at the studio. She still wasn't sure how to tell Chris about the situation with Greg, but there was one thing that made her a little less tense. She talked to Sandy before leaving the house, and Sandy said she told Chris about Karen leaving work

197

sick and coming to Sandy's house. She also told Chris that Karen was very worried about something, but that Karen wanted to tell him herself.

Karen couldn't wait to give Sandy a big hug. At least Chris was prepared for a strange conversation; Karen wouldn't just be going into it cold to tell him.

After Karen heard them wrap up the song they were working on, she went over to Sandy and gave her a squeeze.

"Were you able to eat anything?" Sandy asked.

"I had a turkey sandwich at about four o'clock," Karen replied. "I skipped the mustard and mayo so I wouldn't make my stomach upset again. Thanks for the use of your place today."

"Hey, you're welcome anytime. Just glad I could help out."

"After I ate and became coherent, I noticed the drawings around your living room. Are they all your work?"

"Sure are." Sandy smiled. "Pretty soon I'll have no wall or table space left."

"Anytime you run out of room, you can fill my house. They're all so beautiful."

Chris walked over to Karen and put his arm around her. "Sweetheart, how are you feeling? Sandy gave me some info but said you have more to tell me."

Karen gave Chris a kiss on the cheek. "Since you finished early, I can tell you now."

"Good. Let's go into Charlie's conference room so we have some privacy."

The conference room was bare except for a long table and a few chairs. Karen felt like she was in a crime show episode, being led in to be interrogated by the police.

Chris quietly pushed closed the door until it clicked shut. "OK honey, Sandy's got me all worried about you. What's bothering you?"

Karen felt a hot tear roll down her cheek as she spoke. "I'm not sure where to start. You know my boss thinks it's the flu, right?"

"That's what Sandy said."

"Well, it's not. Something happened that made me so nervous that I'm worrying myself sick. I probably should have told Jim that I know it's not the flu, but I thought he would assume that I was just being ridiculous."

"About what?"

Karen swallowed hard, only partly looking up at Chris. "I had a very strange message on my answering machine when I got home last night, from someone I did not want to hear from in any way, shape, or form."

Chris took Karen's hand in his, lifting her chin up with his other hand so he could look her in the eyes. "I'm guessing that you mean Greg?"

"Yes." She sighed.

Chris gently touched her cheek. "Were you afraid to tell me because it was Greg?"

Karen nodded solemnly, trying to keep any more tears from falling.

"Oh, honey." Chris pulled Karen in close, holding her gently and lightly rubbing her back. "I'm very sorry. I don't want you to be scared to talk to me about anything. I know I went off the deep end about Greg last time, but I promise I won't do that to you again."

Karen held on to him, hugging him tighter. "Are you sure?"

"I must admit it bothers me to hear his name, but I know it's not your fault. You haven't done anything wrong."

"Thanks Chris, only now you really won't like hearing his name."

Chris could feel the tightening in his chest as he braced himself for what Karen would say next. "Why?"

"Number one, I never gave Greg my phone number, and I'm not listed in the telephone book."

"All right...so how did he get it?"

"I wish I knew. It's been bugging me all day, and I'm getting creeped out."

"Hey, I understand. It's kind of giving me the chills too."

"I kept thinking about it at work, then I started wondering if he knows where I live now. I don't want a visit from him. After I left work, I was afraid I would find him waiting for me. That's why I called Sandy."

"It does seem like Greg might be stalking you, since you didn't invite him to call or visit you."

"That's exactly what I'm afraid of."

"Your first stalker," Chris laughed nervously, "and your record isn't even out yet."

"Chris!" Karen scolded him, but caught a giggle coming from herself as well. The whole thing did seem oddly humorous.

"Sorry, honey," Chris said. "It just came out. Remember, I've had experience with that sort of thing in the past."

"It's all right. It's not funny, but yet it is. And of course Greg doesn't even know I'm making a record."

Chris and Karen both thought it at the same time, only Karen couldn't vocalize it. Chris, with panic in his eyes, did.

"Unless he's been watching you, and he does know."

Karen's tears began anew. "Why is he so adamant about staying in contact with me now, when for all those years he couldn't have cared less about me?"

"Good question. I don't know what he wants, but I don't want you to stay at your place by yourself."

"I don't either, but what am I going to do?" Schedule you guys to take turns babysitting me at my house?"

Chris thought that over. "I have a better idea. Why don't you come and stay at my place for a while, until we see what's really going on with this guy?"

Karen's heart felt like it was going to stop. "Wh- what did you say?"

"Relax, honey. I have a guest bedroom you can sleep in, or you can sleep in my room and I'll go to the guest room. Whichever you prefer."

"Oh, good," Karen sighed, a wave of relief washing over her. "It's just that we've only been dating a short time and …"

"I know what you're getting at. I've learned my lesson from the old days, and I don't do that anymore. It wouldn't be right…and I don't want to mess up a beautiful thing."

"I'm glad you understand, sweetie," Karen said, blushing. "At least we're on the same page about this."

"So, what do you think about staying with me?"

"Sounds like a great idea. I'll just have to get some clothes and stuff from my house."

"I'll follow you over there after the session, just in case you-know-who is waiting for you."

"Thank you, Chris. I appreciate this so much. I would be a total wreck if I went home by myself right now."

"Honey, I'd do anything for you. I want you to be safe."

Chris and Karen heard a faint knock. The door opened slightly and Charlie peeked in. Are you two all set?" he asked. "Ready to start session two, Karen?"

"You'd better believe it. I can't wait to focus on my music instead of my problems."

*****

Karen took her position at the mic while Charlie and Chris got everything ready at the soundboard. All of the band member re-tuned their instruments, giving Charlie the signal once each of them was ready.

After recording such a beautiful ballad yesterday, it was decided that Karen would go a little bluesier on this next song. The unanimous choice, across the board, was the Linda Ronstadt classic "You're No Good".

As Karen made her adjustments, she began laughing out loud uncontrollably. Everyone in the band stared at her in wonder.

Finally, Rob couldn't take it anymore. "All right Karen, you've got to let us in on the joke."

Karen managed to get herself under control. "Sorry, guys. I couldn't help thinking what an appropriate song choice this is for today."

"What do you mean?" Rob said.

Karen looked over at Sandy. "I'll have to fill you in at the end of the session. Right now I'm just going to use it for motivation."

As Jerry counted off, Sandy gave Karen a knowing grin. With that the tune began, along with Karen's commanding vocals.

Chris' proud smile spread through the entire booth. There was no doubt about it. Karen nailed it on the first take.

"Man! You're a quick learner, Karen," Jerry said admiringly.

Karen's snickering picked up where it had left off before the song. "I told you...I had really big motivation!"

"Wow," Charlie said as he and Chris came out into the main room. "I'm not prepared to do the next song so quickly. Let's discuss what we're going to do with it so we can start working on it."

"Yeah, we're going to need a strategy if we're going to take on Tom Jones," Jerry replied.

"This is such a powerful song." Karen bit her lip. "I sure hope I can do it justice."

"Karen, you need to have complete faith in yourself," Chris said while rubbing the tension out of her shoulders. "I certainly have faith in you."

Karen smiled nervously. "Thank you, honey. I feel my confidence building with each song, but there's still that little voice in my head making me wonder."

"It's the devil," Chris replied. "Don't listen to him, he's a liar. Listen to your heart. That's where God is, and He's the One who gave you the talent."

After everyone went over the particulars and got into their places, Karen readied herself for "It Looks Like I'll Never Fall in Love Again". As much as she used the message from Greg for motivation, when Karen pushed those thoughts aside she let the thoughts of her dad's message creep in. That uncertainty settled into her mind like a thick fog.

She knew her voice was shaky when the song began; she couldn't help it. Her concentration was broken. Barely into the chorus, she waved her arms toward the control room. Charlie stopped the tape.

"Karen, what's wrong?"

"I lost my focus. Please give me just a minute to compose myself."

"Sure thing," Charlie replied. "Why don't you go get a drink of water and be back in five?"

Karen took a walk to the water cooler right outside of the conference room. Everyone else stayed in the studio, and watched her go out. She knew they had to be wondering what was up with her, since she was wondering herself. *I was spot on with the first song tonight. Why am I suddenly falling apart?*

*****

Karen came back in, looking better but still not completely sure of herself. She took a deep breath as she stepped back up to the microphone.

Chris felt for her. He knew this feeling very well, and he also knew it was something you had to work out for yourself. Sometimes no amount of praise from other people would penetrate the mind; it was the inner voice that needed to straighten itself out. He silently sent up a little prayer to help Karen.

"I'm ready to try it again," she said.

Karen got through the entire song this time, but shook her head slowly as she finished. Rob fiddled with the tuning on his bass. "Did we jinx you with all of our compliments before, Karen?"

Karen shook her head, blonde hair flying everywhere. "No, I don't believe in that jinx stuff. I guess that little voice in my head decided to start shouting."

"Well, you are new to this," Charlie said. "I'll tell you what...you go ahead and rehearse this one over the weekend and we'll try again on Monday. We got the other song so fast that we're actually still on schedule."

"I'm afraid I'm going to have to," Karen said. "I feel like I'm letting all of you down."

"Don't sweat it," Jerry said. "You've been amazing so far, so you were bound to have a bad one. It happens to every singer I've ever known."

"Including me," Chris added from the soundboard. "No one's immune."

Everyone picked up his or her instruments and equipment for the weekend. Sandy approached Karen and gave her a hug. "Hey hon, why don't you and Chris go ahead so you can go spend some time together? I can fill the guys in on the Greg thing if you want."

"Sandy, that would be wonderful. I don't think I have the energy left to tell that story again today."

"I'll give you a call tomorrow," Sandy said. "I know it might be difficult, but try to relax, OK?"

"I'll give it my best shot," Karen called over her shoulder as she went over to Chris.

"Honey", Chris said. "Jerry's right. It happens, really."

"I know...but I have to get over it."

"We'll work on that over the next couple of days. Let's go get your things and get you settled at my place."

Karen nodded, but as she followed Chris out to the car she wondered if a couple of days would be long enough to tame the voice of doubt that threatened to derail her dreams, just as they were beginning to come true.

CHAPTER 19

Karen drove more slowly than usual to her house, as she made sure Chris' car stayed right behind hers all the way there. She dreaded what she might find. Thankfully, the place seemed quiet, with not even a blinking light on her answering machine. She quickly gathered her things as Chris kept watch on the house, then they both set off for Chris' home.

Karen pulled her car into Chris' driveway right behind his convertible and turned off the ignition. She couldn't believe she was going to wake up in the morning right on the California coastline. She wasn't just near the ocean, but right at its very edge. She had wished for this for ages; now it was coming true just like so many of her other dreams from long ago.

"Are you ready for the grand tour?" Chris asked while unloading Karen's things. "It's not exactly a Malibu mansion, but it's a great place."

"Truthfully, Chris, it could be a dump and I'd still love it because it's on the beach."

"Good…so I can stop keeping it neat and clean, then?"

"Very funny, mister. I didn't say you should turn it into a dump!" Karen chuckled. "I love spending time at the beach. This is so much more convenient, to walk out your door and be right there."

"Darn. I thought I was off the hook," Chris said with a wink. "Come on, let's take this stuff inside."

Karen picked up her guitar and briefcase, following Chris up the stone footpath to his beach house.

"I'm glad you didn't pack too much, honey," Chris said as he carried the makeup box and small suitcase to his front stoop. "We got it all in one trip."

"Just the necessities," Karen answered.

Chris glanced at the guitar in Karen's hand and smiled. "You and I think alike about necessities, I see."

"Hey, after starting to play again, I'd be lost without it. Besides, I have a little surprise for you myself."

"Really? What is it?" asked Chris.

"It's in the briefcase, but it will have to wait until tomorrow."

"Ah…paying me back by keeping me in suspense this time?"

"Of course," said Karen, giving Chris a little tap from behind with her guitar case. "After all, it's only fair."

As they came through the front door, Karen discovered she could gaze at the stars and the ocean from the entire length of the house.

"Chris, the view is breathtaking! I didn't realize there would be so many windows!"

"Oh, yeah. My one luxury right now is paying someone to come in and clean the windows. I'd never have the patience to do them myself."

"It's probably not cheap."

"Definitely not," Chris admitted, "but I must say it's worth every penny just to have this view of the world every day."

"It's so gorgeous now when it's dark," Karen said. "I can't wait to see it in the morning light."

"First things first, sweetheart. You've got to be exhausted after the day you had today. Let's take your stuff to the guest room."

Chris took Karen upstairs to a spacious room decorated in theater chic. Posters from Broadway musicals covered the walls, accompanied by a piano key border dancing merrily above them near the ceiling. It was mesmerizing, and too much to take in all in one glance.

"I hope this room will be to your liking," Chris said. "If not, we can switch. Mine's a little bigger. There are only two bedrooms in this place, but at least there's plenty of space in both of them."

"This one will be perfect. I love this décor. I've secretly been a theater fan for a long time. What made you decide to do a Broadway room?"

"Actually, there are two reasons. I've always been interested in Broadway myself. I was hoping I'd get to do some after 'Anderson Boys' was over, but producers had me typecast into the 'Grant' role so much that they couldn't see past it."

Karen sat on the bed and frowned. "So they didn't even give you a chance?"

"Not at all. It felt like I was going to be pegged as Grant for life. Now, I enjoyed my role as Grant, and I'm very grateful for it - but I'm more versatile than they gave me credit for."

"That doesn't make sense," Karen said. "That's why actors act – to play all different kinds of people. If you're an actor you can play more than one type of person."

Chris sat next to Karen and slipped his arm around her waist. "I sure wish the powers-that-be would think like you."

"So what's the other reason for this room?"

"This will be a surprise to you…and actually most of the rest of the world. Have you heard of Brian Holloway?"

"Of course. He's one of the best actors and singers on Broadway. He's won just about every theater award there is!"

"He's my brother - well, I guess technically he's my half-brother. After my dad wound up in jail, my mom divorced him and remarried. Then they had Brian."

"Oh my gosh, I never realized that! How is it that nobody's ever mentioned it?"

"First of all, with the different last name no one made the connection, and we don't look enough alike for it to be obvious. Second, it was decided not to publicize it, since I couldn't even get arrested on Broadway. I didn't want my 'Grant' persona to hold Brian back too."

"Wow," Karen said, "I can't believe all this time I never knew that Brian is your brother!"

"When he was growing up, we weren't close. My stepfather made sure of that. Unfortunately, my mom married a guy almost exactly like my father. My dad and I never really got along, then he became so jealous of my success that it was impossible. My stepfather couldn't stand my success either. He didn't treat Brian that well, and he was his own flesh and blood. So it was even worse for me. He didn't want Brian to be close to me either, and he did everything he could to turn Brian against me."

"How horrible!" Karen said. "How could anyone be so hateful?"

Chris seemed to have a far away look in his eyes, as if he was taking himself back in time. "I wish I knew. All I know is I had two father figures who were not good to me or good role models, and it was not a pleasant experience."

Karen shuddered at the thought of Chris' family life and upbringing. "So, are you and Brian closer now?"

"Yes, just in the last few years. We're trying to make up for lost time, now that we both realize that we shouldn't let the past keep us apart. He comes to visit when he gets a break between shows, so I fixed this room up especially for him. He's ten years younger than me, but it doesn't feel like there's any difference."

Karen heart danced within her at that statement. "Kind of like us, huh? I mean, considering that I'm the same age as Brian."

"Exactly like us. Age is just a number. The person you are is what matters."

"That's how I've always felt," Karen said. "All the time growing up, people would try to make me feel that how old you were mattered so much. Other than legally being able to do certain things at certain ages, what's the difference?"

"To me, none," Chris responded. "God's in charge. If He wants you to do something, He's not going to let a little thing like your age get in the way."

Karen took another look around the room. She knew Chris must love his brother a lot; the room was so complete that she couldn't think of anything else it needed. "I'm going to enjoy staying in this room. Maybe it will get my mind off of all this other stuff that's going on."

Chris hugged Karen tightly. "I'm really relieved that no one was waiting for you at your house when we got there."

"Me too. I'm thankful you were with me. It really helped me stay calm there."

"I know it's a lot to deal with, honey." Chris looked at her tenderly as his hazel eyes grew darker. "Is there something else bothering you besides this? You seemed so upset at the studio."

"There is. I had a message from my dad right after the one from Greg. I really just wish my dad would believe in me."

"What did he say?"

Now that she was talking privately to Chris, Karen didn't even try to hold back the tears. "It was a two-sided comment. On the one hand he hoped the session went well, but then on the other hand he hopes that I don't actually believe I can make a living at it."

Chris pulled her in even tighter. She felt herself calm down as he stroked her hair and spoke softly. "Oh, honey. I know that hurts."

"It was a short message, but add it to the other conversation I had with him. It's like he's pouring salt in the cut that he made in the first place."

"You know you have to trust your own heart, Karen. Right?"

"I know. I also know part of it is that he's trying to do what's best for me by wanting to keep me safe."

Chris moved back a little and looked right into her eyes. "Sometimes doing what's best for you actually means taking a chance – taking a risk that an opportunity will lead to a better life."

Karen nodded. "I agree with you. I have to tell you…my whole life, my parents were always worried about my safety. Maybe it comes with being an only child, but there were so many things they wouldn't let me do that other kids did, like play sports and stuff like that. They were always worried I would get hurt."

"But…you're not living life if you sit in your room all the time and don't try to do anything."

"Exactly, and it's taken me a long time to realize that, since their way of keeping me safe was all I'd ever known. Sometimes I still have moments of doubt."

"Honey, think of it this way. You're not skydiving, you're singing. You're not risking a trip to the hospital."

Karen managed a laugh. "According to my family, one is just as risky as the other. But that does make me feel a little bit better."

"Besides, the only one who can keep you completely safe is God. Parents have responsibilities with that, but

He's ultimately in charge. Pray that you do what's right for you, and also for His help and protection."

"I have been praying, harder than I ever have in my life," Karen said. "Every feeling I have about this leads me to believe this is part of God's plan for me."

"Then that's the feeling you should go with."

"I mean, I think about being a young girl, having the feelings I had about music and about you. Somehow I know deep in my heart and soul that God's been preparing me for this since way back then. Think about it…it's pretty amazing!"

"It's beyond amazing. All of the things that didn't work out for me in the past, well…I didn't understand why then. I'm sure I don't know it all yet, but I do know that God wanted me to wait for you to move out here so we could be together. Little did I know He was saving the best for me."

"Chris…" Karen raised her lips to his, kissing him through her tears. Chris brought his hands up to Karen's cheeks, holding her lovely face level with his. He looked so piercingly into her eyes that she was sure he could see right into her soul.

"Karen, I've never met anyone like you. You're a remarkable woman, and I feel as if I've known you for a lifetime. I know I'm not perfect, but I'll always strive to be my best for you. I love you so much."

"I love you, Chris, more than you could ever know. I've always known you were a special person, and I don't mean for being famous. You're special for being you. Heaven sent me that message a long time ago, even though we hadn't met yet. Now I get to see it for myself, actually being with you and getting to know you. It just confirms for me how wonderful you are. I love you with everything in me."

Chris was speechless, so he just kissed her again while they held each other as if their lives depended on it. When they finally came apart, Chris took Karen's hands in his, not able to completely let go of her.

"I never want to lose you, honey," Chris said tenderly.

"You won't. Don't worry about perfection. No one on earth is perfect." Karen's lips formed a sweet smile. "I can see your heart, and your soul. We can work out any imperfections either of us may have."

"I'm happy to hear you say that." Chris glanced over at the Phantom clock, whose hands continued to tick around its white mask. "Now if we want to work out some music in the morning, we'd better get some sleep."

Karen and Chris kissed once again, a brief kiss good night. Chris went down the hall to his room as Karen settled under the cozy red comforter and into a deep, dream-filled sleep.

*****

Karen didn't wake until the bright golden sunlight peeked through a small parting in the red velour curtains, which were regally trimmed with gold tassels and cord. She arose and slipped into her emerald green robe as she made her way over to the dresser mirror to brush out her hair.

As she worked the tangles from her fair tresses, she spotted a golden-framed picture of a dark-haired, smiling Brian Holloway with his first Tony Award, which he'd won right out of the gate with his first lead role on Broadway.

It was still only starting to sink in that Brian was Chris' brother. If she looked closely enough, Karen could see some resemblance between the siblings, mostly in their beautiful smiles. But Chris was right. It must be that Brian looked more like his own father than their mother.

Karen had never been fortunate enough to attend a Broadway show, though she always wanted to go someday. She secretly followed what was happening in New York and knew a lot about Brian and the other major Broadway stars. At least Karen had been able to see a few off-Broadway productions when they came to the big city nearest her little hometown. She always snuck off by herself to these shows, since none of her friends or family really seemed to be fans.

Karen glanced again at Brian, eyes shining as he stood clutching his Tony. She smiled, knowing she'd watched him accept it on the awards broadcast. She never missed a Tony Awards show.

The rhythm of Chris' knock came at the guest room door. "Karen, can I come in? Are you decent?"

"As decent as I can be," she said with a chuckle.

Chris opened the door and walked right over to Karen for a long morning kiss. "Good morning, sweetheart," he said, eyes shining.

"Good morning, honey. Now this is a wonderful way to start the day."

"You took the words right out of my mouth. Did you sleep well?"

"Did I ever. That is the most comfortable bed I've ever slept in." Karen sighed. "Either that, or I was just that tired."

"Probably both. You really needed the rest. I'm glad you got it." Chris brushed the hair out of Karen's face and smiled, eyes sparkling.

"I know it would be impossible for me to sleep at my house. I've frightened myself so much…"

"You have good reason to be cautious. It might be nothing, but Greg might also be a problem. This is one of the few cases where your dad would be right to worry. You can't take a chance with your safety when it comes to something like this."

"And since I'm staying here," Karen added, "it gives us a chance to work on the music together."

"I'm certainly pleased it worked out that way." Chris led Karen to the door so they could make their way downstairs. "I've got coffee on, so we can have some breakfast and get started."

Once they were downstairs, Chris didn't need to lead Karen to the kitchen. She followed her nose, breathing in the rich scent of cinnamon almond.

"Mmm…that smells heavenly," she said. "I didn't realize you liked flavored coffee."

"Oh, I like all types of coffee. Being the creative type yourself, you know we like to try different things."

"You're really right about that," Karen said, butterflies starting at the word "creative". Wait until I show Chris my surprise, she thought.

"Yeah, the other night I had to have the regular high octane stuff, just to be alert for the drive home, but I drink all kinds. I even try different teas."

"Tea sounds wonderful too. I learn more about you every day."

"Well," Chris said with a sheepish grin, "those are my vices now that I'm off the alcoholic beverages. Experimenting with different coffees and teas keeps me from thinking about those."

"Good." Karen didn't miss a beat, not wanting Chris to feel bad about his old issues. "Coffee and tea are my vices too, except I have a third – chocolate."

"Oh yeah…I forgot about that one!"

"See, honey? Who needs a drink anyway? We have enough somewhat safer addictions to keep us busy." Then Karen looked down at her hips, giving them a little pat. "Although the chocolate causes other problems."

Chris reached for her hands, grabbing them and pulling them away from her hips. "Now sweetheart, you look wonderful from head to toe. I wouldn't change a thing about you."

Karen beamed at him.

"Unless…"

The light was extinguished from Karen's eyes. "Unless what?"

Chris couldn't keep a straight face; the smirk gave him away. "Unless you eat chocolate for breakfast, lunch, and dinner."

"Oh, but of course." Karen laughed. "Plus between meals and some fudge for a bedtime snack."

"Sounds yummy." Chris rubbed his stomach while rolling his eyes.

"I think you'd have to scrape me off the ceiling after eating like that. One thing I have learned, though, is that if I overdo the chocolate or other sweets, my body just doesn't feel right, and it's hard to accomplish anything."

"Funny, that sounds just like having too much alcohol. What do you know?"

"Right now, though, that coffee is calling my name," Karen said.

"I think I can hear it," said Chris with a laugh. "Let's have some. You're going to love it."

"If it tastes anything like it smells, let me at it."

They went into the kitchen, brightly lit by the sun and ocean view. In addition to the brewing java, Karen discovered bagels, light cream cheese, and a huge bowl filled with fresh strawberries. All were set on a counter that was as blue as the water outside of the window.

"Chris, do you have breakfast like this all the time? I must confess, I'm guilty of grabbing something on the run in the morning."

"I try to sit down and eat most of the time, but sometimes I'm guilty of that too. I knew I'd be working on songs today, so I wanted to start with a good healthy breakfast. Luckily, I now get to share it with you."

"Excellent thinking, my dear," Karen replied. "Plus we need to go over the song you wrote that I'm about to record."

Chris thought about that as he poured coffee into two giant beige stoneware mugs. "We should probably also practice the one you started working on last night."

Karen's sigh was loud enough to be heard over the sound of the coffee maker. "I really did a number on that song, didn't I?"

"You had a lot on your mind, which can affect anyone," Chris said. "Believe me, Karen. No performer is immune from a weak session. You've been awesome so far at this; don't beat yourself up for one minor setback. And I mean minor. Don't sweat it. Just work the kinks out and everything will be fine."

"Thanks." Karen carefully took a full steaming mug from Chris' hands. "What I really have to do is stop thinking about what my dad said."

"Just remember, honey, it's hard for a lot of people to understand wanting to go after a dream more than wanting a secure job. They're too scared of the unknown."

"But those of us with the dreams are being driven crazy by those secure jobs. We can't just do that same mundane thing for the rest of our lives. The dream is too important; it would make us insane if we didn't go after it."

"Exactly." Chris stood on the opposite side of the counter from Karen and handed her a plate. "You have the right attitude, and I can tell by the excitement and determination in your voice that you can do it. Just think about the words you told me now whenever you want to dwell on other people's doubts. That inner voice of yours will pull you through."

"This means way too much to me to give up on myself," Karen said. "Guess I need to look to God to help me get to that point where His voice and mine drown out the negative voices."

"That's the spirit." Chris began spreading cream cheese on a bagel. "And I'm sure no matter what he said, your dad means well."

"Oh, I'm sure he does. He believes that what he thinks is what's best for me. Sometimes that can be true, but now I'm an adult and it isn't always the case."

"Sounds like you need to listen to his advice, but then take it with that proverbial grain of salt."

Karen laughed as she loaded juicy red strawberries onto her plate. "Maybe the whole salt shaker. But I do need to hear everyone's advice, let my brain process it, and take what I can use. God's the only One who gives perfect advice every time."

"That is the truth," said Chris, recalling his conversations with Father John. "We have to check with God to see what it is that He wants us to do."

Chris and Karen watched the waves roll in as they enjoyed their breakfast together. The morning sun created the appearance of diamonds dancing on the water. Good coffee, strawberries, and an ocean view with Chris…Karen savored every moment.

"Hey honey, want some more strawberries?" Chris asked, shaking Karen from her trance-like state.

"I think I'd better quit now before I turn red."

"Gotcha." Chris grinned as he got up from the table. "I'll put the rest away so we can get started."

The kitchen was tidied quickly, and the two of them took their coffee mugs into the great room, ready to go over the music. Karen sang "It Looks Like I'll Never Fall in Love Again" a few times, with Chris playing the melody on his baby grand piano.

"I think you've got it down for sure now," Chris said. "Are you ready to work on the new song?"

Karen gazed out over the ocean. "I have to come clean with you. I haven't even looked at it since you gave it to me on Thursday. It's still in my purse."

"Oh." Chris slowly pulled out his copy, placing it on the piano.

"I'm sorry, honey. I was so tired that night, I just went right to bed. Then everything else happened."

Chris looked up at Karen, running his hand through his deep brown hair. "Oh yeah…of course! Sorry, I don't know what I was thinking. I temporarily forgot that you've only had the music for a day and a half, with total chaos happening during that time. Forgive me, sweetheart."

"Forgiven and forgotten," Karen replied. "Let me go grab my purse."

"No, wait. Why don't you sit with me at the piano so we can go through it together?"

A relieved Karen slid in next to Chris on the long wooden bench. She read the music, working to truly understand the words and melody.

"This song is amazing," Karen exclaimed, her heart pounding harder with each line of "I've Always Known". "It's as if you reached into my soul, pulled out my feelings and put them on paper."

"And set them to music," Chris added. "Actually, your telling me of your feelings when you were growing up helped me realize something."

"What's that?"

"I realized that, in a way, I had the same type of feelings. I mean, the knowing that I was going to meet someone like you – the woman who truly cared about me…not just the celebrity, but the real me."

"Well, as wonderful as the character you played on TV was," said Karen, "the real person in front of me is even better."

"Thank you, honey." Chris placed his right arm around Karen, with his left hand still playing a few notes on the piano. "I sure wish a lot more people had bothered to get to know the actual person inside this actor. There may have been a little bit of me in Grant, but there was so much more to me than that."

"There still is," Karen said. "I guess for a young girl, I had pretty good sense. I always knew you were an actor playing a role. I watched and read interviews with you. Since I already knew about Grant, I wanted to get to know Chris."

Chris suddenly stopped playing. "You didn't read every interview, did you?"

"Why Chris," Karen said with a wink, "would that be a bad thing?"

"It's just that…well…"

"Don't worry. I was young enough that I didn't even know that anything beyond those teen magazines existed. If my parents knew anything about those other articles in the more 'adult' magazines, they certainly didn't inform me. They weren't going to let me grow up that fast. I probably still don't know everything."

"That's the thing," Chris said. "I knew I needed to do those interviews to show that I wasn't Grant in real life, but after I did them I worried that young kids would get hold of the magazines and become wise beyond their years, so to speak. I'm still glad I gave those interviews, because they were really meant for the adults to see that I could play other roles. I just hope that other parents were as responsible as yours."

"I think most of them were. Parents made sure kids stayed innocent back then."

"It's a really difficult line to walk," Chris said, "when you're in your twenties and a good majority of your fans are kids and teenagers."

"Now that I'm an adult," Karen said, "I can see what your dilemma was."

"I did what I had to do, but now that I'm older, I keep thinking if I had a kid, I'd be worried about stuff like that. Of course," Chris added with a smile, "it hasn't stopped me from being a wise guy."

"Really Chris? I hadn't noticed!"

Chris playfully messed up her hair. "I see you have some wise guy in you too!"

"That's probably part of what brought us together," Karen said.

"Well, let's move from the smart alecky stuff to the romantic," Chris said. "We'd better get going with this song."

Chris sang his composition for Karen, giving her insight along the way. "Of course, you're not going to do it exactly like me. You need to put your own heart and soul into it."

"I'm so used to copying the sound on your records," Karen admitted. "It might take a few tries."

Chris pulled her in closer. If there were such a thing as warm chills, Karen was feeling them now.

"So far, you've put your own spin on the songs you've covered in the studio. This is an original. You can make it completely your own."

Karen gave it her best, struggling to break the habit of imitating Chris Lassiter and Anderson Boys records.

"Remember, Karen, I sang it just to make you familiar with the melody. Now think of the song as if you wrote it yourself."

Karen thought of the tunes she did write herself that were sitting in her briefcase. "All right," she said.

Soon she was really feeling the words. It did feel as if this was her own creation.

"I like where you're going with this," Chris said as the excitement rose on his face. "Let's do it again."

Karen kept at it, knowing she was on her way to finding her true voice. Things were feeling incredibly right, and she only wanted them to get better.

"Honey." Chris stared at her, unable to say anything more.

"What? Did I really mess it up? Tell me what I did wrong!"

Chris slowly shook his head at her. "Karen, you did absolutely nothing wrong. It was…it was even better than I had hoped for when I wrote it. I knew you'd do a great job, but this…"

"Chris, I'm flattered."

"It's not just flattery. I'm really blown away by your range, and I love your interpretation. If I didn't know better, I'd say you really think like a songwriter."

"Funny you should say that," Karen said as she blushed bright red. "Remember how I said that I have a surprise for you?"

"Yeah, that's right. We got so involved with the music that I almost forgot!"

"I'll be right back." Karen ran upstairs to retrieve her briefcase, now eager to show its contents to Chris.

When she got back downstairs, she found Chris still sitting on the edge of the piano bench, bent down with his strong, gorgeous hands folded, anticipating what was in store.

Karen laughed to herself. After all of the surprises Chris made her sweat through, the tables were turned. "So, would you like to know what's in my briefcase?"

"Umm…briefs?"

"Ha ha, very clever. Not exactly."

"Then please tell me. You're making me anxious."

"Oh I am, am I? How badly do you want to see it?"

"Oh, come on honey! Now you've really got me!"

"Just paying you back for the many surprises you've given me, my dear," Karen teased.

"OK, OK, I get it. Now what is it?"

"Are you really sure you want to see it?"

"Yes!!!"

Karen spun the numbers to the correct combination, flipped the case open and pulled out a notebook.

"I take it the surprise is in there?" Chris said, not taking his eyes off of Karen's hands.

"You would be right. I've been working on something…something I used to do a long time ago, but stopped when the stresses of life got to me. It was time to start again."

Karen handed her notebook over to Chris, watching carefully as he flipped it open. She studied his eyes as they scanned that pages filled with her words and melodies.

"Wow, honey, when did you start working on these?"

"Right after we met. I had been thinking about starting before that, but kept putting it off with all of the late hours at work. When I stopped working so late I had the time, plus now I also had your inspiration."

Chris turned back to the first page again, this time really examining the words. "This first song…it's…"

"It's about you. You've been my inspiration for such a long time, even more so now. I just had to put it into words."

"It's beautiful," Chris said, as he started to tear up.

Karen reached over and brushed the first tear away. "Usually you make _me_ cry."

"You managed to turn that around on me too. You can't imagine how honored and touched I am."

Karen let out a huge breath that she didn't even realize she'd been holding in. "I'm happy you like it. I was so worried you wouldn't."

"It's incredible. How many songs are in here?"

"Eight. They've been popping into my head everywhere. At the beach, at home...I even thought of one while I was at work."

"Welcome to the wonderful world of songwriting. I once wrote some lyrics on toilet paper in a public restroom."

Karen giggled. "Really?"

"Well, yeah! I was afraid I'd lose the words before I had something else to write on."

"The fun part is thinking of a tune while I'm not near my guitar," Karen said. "I keep trying to save the melody in my head until I get home."

"You need a mini tape recorder. Just hum or sing what you thought of into it and play it back later."

Karen snapped her fingers. "See? That's why I need to hang out with the professionals more often."

"Which you're doing now."

"I almost can't believe this is all happening. It's everything I ever dreamed of...but beyond that!"

Chris smiled. "The Man Upstairs has a way of doing that."

"So," Karen said, "may I play your song for you?"

"Absolutely, honey."

Karen went behind the piano where Chris had placed her guitar the night before. She took it out, checked her tuning and sat down again next to Chris.

She was sure her nerves would have gotten her, but she made it through the song surprisingly well. Near the end she looked up to see tears streaming from Chris' gorgeous hazel eyes.

"It's even more emotional hearing you sing it," Chris said. "Behold the power of music."

At this point Karen found herself crying as well. Both of them just kept looking at each other, neither one able to speak for what seemed like forever.

Finally Karen found her voice. "Why don't we go for a little walk on the beach? We could both use the break."

Chris stood up from the piano bench and closed off the keys. "Excellent thought. Let's go."

The moment she and Chris stepped outside, Karen could feel the warm salt air fill her lungs as she breathed in deeply. Leaving their shoes behind, they held hands and began to stroll through the soft sand. A gentle breeze caressed their skins, heightening the pleasure of being together. Karen looked to heaven, thankful and completely sure of her place in the world.

"You know, Chris," she said, "for the first time in my life I feel like I really belong."

"Belong? What do you mean?"

"I grew up always feeling so different from everyone else. I was treated most of the time as if something was wrong with me, like I didn't fit in. Even the people who loved me always questioned things about me…you know, my interests and ideas."

"Like your family does with music?"

"Yes, exactly like that. I'm not sure I really had anyone who supported me in trusting my gut instincts. The friends I did have were cool enough about it, I guess, just not really enthusiastic. No one was actually encouraging me to go for it."

"You mean going for the things that really interested you?" Chris asked.

"That, and trusting what I believed was right." Karen paused, letting the breeze send her long, golden hair out behind her. "Now that I've moved out here, I have you, plus loads of support from the band and Charlie. I'm accepted for who I really am, inside and out."

"Karen, I'm happy to hear that, because that's exactly the way you make me feel. You're the only woman who has ever made me feel that I could be completely myself, good traits and bad, strengths and weaknesses."

"We all have bad traits and weaknesses, otherwise we wouldn't be human. Unfortunately, one of my weaknesses has been my tendency to let other people define me."

"When you grow up that way, it's a hard thing to break."

"Well," Karen said, stopping in her tracks to look Chris in the eye, "I'm going to break it. It may not be that easy, but only the Lord and I know completely who I am. Through Him, I understand myself more every day, and I'm going to work hard so I don't let comments from other people make me question that."

Chris hugged her tightly as their feet dug into the sand. "I'm proud of you, honey, and I'm so excited for your future."

"I am too, and that's saying a lot for me. The future never seemed very bright before; it seemed tedious and boring. But now I get goose bumps thinking about it."

Karen and Chris walked hand in hand again for a while, then made their way through the soft sand back to the house.

"Honey, I'm just going to run up front and grab the mail," Chris said. "I'll be right in."

Karen shook the glittery sand from her feet and went inside. Pulling a bottle of spring water from the refrigerator, she thought about all of the wondrous things going on in her life.

Chris came into the kitchen, tossing the pile of mail onto the nearly empty counter.

"Don't you want to go through it before we get started again?" Karen asked.

"Nope. I'm sure it's mostly bills anyway, which will only distract me from the music. It can wait until later."

Chris followed Karen back into the living room without even a glance at the mail. If he had looked, he surely would have noticed the strange envelope on top of the pile, postmarked Portland, Oregon.

CHAPTER 20

The decision to go to Chris' church together put Karen more at ease than she had been most of the week. She certainly did not want a repeat performance of what happened the week before at her church with Greg, and after his unusual phone call both she and Chris were concerned about her safety.

They were dressed and on their way out the door when Chris discovered that he needed to run back into the kitchen. "I'll be right back out," he said. "My car keys are on the counter."

As Chris snatched the keys from the edge of the counter, he noticed the pile of mail from the corner of his eye. *That's right,* he remembered, *I never looked at it last night. I'll have to check it out when we get back.*

Chris dashed outside to his car, where Karen was waiting for him in the passenger seat. "Hey honey," he asked when he started the engine, "could you remind me to open my mail when we get back?"

"Oh, sure," she said. "Looks like we got carried away with the songs last night."

"That has a way of happening. If I'm lucky it might all be junk mail, but it's probably not so I'd better go through it."

On the drive to church, Karen felt a familiar feeling of dread begin to come over her that she felt almost powerless to stop. "Oh, Chris," she sighed. "I hate the thought of even going to work tomorrow."

"You could still say you're sick," he suggested. "You are sick of that job."

"Yeah, except since I left sick on Friday, I have to get that report finished tomorrow."

"Well, I could meet you for lunch. I'd love to see your office."

"That would give me something to look forward to." Karen smiled, hoping a midday break with Chris would push the nagging anxiety out of her mind.

"Oh...wait!" Chris smacked his hand down on the steering wheel. "I can't do it tomorrow. I have a meeting with Charlie. How about Tuesday?"

Karen swallowed hard. "I can't on Tuesday. I have a doctor's appointment."

"You do? Is everything OK?"

"It's just a checkup," Karen said, hoping that's all it would turn out to be.

"That's good," Chris said through a relieved sigh. "You had me scared for a second. Wednesday, then?"

"Wednesday would be wonderful. But what about your sessions?"

"Did I forget to tell you? I have only afternoon sessions this week. Charlie had already booked the studio for the mornings before we came along."

"Oh, OK. I guess that gives you a little bit of a break."

"And the band too. They've been going all day with me and all evening with you."

"How I did not think about that?" Karen said. "It never dawned on me just how many hours they were working. How selfish of me."

"Don't worry. You know they're glad to do it. Musicians are used to long hours when it's session time."

"I know, but I'm really happy that they're getting at least some sort of break."

"Well, you'll see some of them at Mass, I'm sure. A few of them belong to this church."

Chris parked the car just in time to see Jerry getting out of his ancient blue pickup truck. "Hey," Jerry said. "I'm glad to see the two of you here together today."

"Why, thank you," Chris said. "Karen is letting me have the honor of escorting her to Mass today."

Karen laughed. "Yes, and it's nice to have my own personal bodyguard for church."

"Oh yeah," Jerry said. "Sandy filled me in on your, um...unwanted attention."

"It's driving me crazy. I've got to figure out how to get rid of him. I can't have him following me around everywhere I go."

"We'll help you all we can," Jerry said. "If you need anything, just let me know."

"Thanks, Jerry. You never know, I just might take you up on that."

"Jerry could really come in handy," Chris added. "He used to be a bouncer at a nightclub. He could probably bounce Greg all the way back to Indiana."

Jerry raised his eyebrow at Chris. "What do you mean, probably?"

As the three of them laughed, the steeple bells began to chime. They scrambled to get inside and find seats. Chris and Karen wound up at the end of one row, with Jerry directly behind them in the next.

The service began, with both priests saying different parts of the Mass. Father Timothy performed most of the duties, but Father John was up on the altar with him, making a slow but steady return.

Jerry tapped Karen on the shoulder. "Do you have an extra songbook?" he whispered. "Someone must have ripped some of the pages out of this one."

Father John spotted Chris and Karen just as she turned around to hand Jerry a new book. Chris was thankful that Karen missed that moment. The scowl on Father John's face let Chris know that he was not pleased.

Chris sighed, reaching to hold Karen's soft, smooth hand in his. *Why can't Father John be happy for me, instead of trying to plant doubts in my mind?* he thought. *Shouldn't he be happy that she loves the Lord and came with me to church?*

As the Scripture readings went on, and all the way through Father Timothy's sermon, both Chris and Karen noticed some strange looks from the older priest. As they glanced at each other, Chris began to wonder if they wouldn't have been better off dealing with Greg at Karen's church.

Once it was close to time for communion, Chris figured that Father John would be a little too busy to worry about them. Since they were in Father Timothy's communion line, he let his muscles relax. Still, he sensed he was developing a nice little tension headache from all the anxiety.

Father John seemed to have removed his focus from the couple by the end of Mass. Chris tried to keep calm, hoping they had been forgotten now that Father John had other things to do.

The guitar choir played and sang the closing hymn and Mass was ended. They all began to leave their pews and walk slowly toward the front of the church. As they got closer to the altar, Jerry leaned in toward Chris' ear.

"Hey, man," he whispered. "Was it my imagination, or was Father John looking funny at you guys?"

Chris nodded. "I know he's a priest, but he's really starting to get on my nerves."

Karen finally let out a sigh. "I was hoping he would have been over this by now."

"Apparently not." Chris looked toward the doorways to follow Father John's activities. "He went out the left side of the church. Let's go out the right. I think we'll be better off greeting Father Timothy today."

As they exited the church, Chris glanced back to make sure Father John wasn't coming toward them. Out the right door they went, with a smiling Father Timothy there to receive them.

"Jerry! Good to see you. Hi, Chris. This must be the lovely Karen."

Karen blushed as she shook Father Timothy's hand. "It's good to meet you, Father."

"And it's wonderful to meet you as well, Karen. I've heard a lot of good things about you."

Chris tried to hide his nervous laugh. "Obviously you've heard them from the band, since I'm sure it didn't come from Father John."

Father Timothy looked kindly at the couple, his eyes filled with sympathy. "Well Chris, I have to admit that you are correct."

"Karen is the best thing that's ever happened to me, Father," Chris said. "Why can't he just be happy for me?"

"I wish I knew." Father Timothy shook his head. "I think he thinks that he's being helpful. I did tell him I believe he's carrying this a bit too far."

"What did he say?" Chris asked, shocked at Father Timothy's boldness with his superior.

The priest's eyebrows rose, forming a deep furrow in the middle of his forehead. "He just keeps on repeating that it's his duty to stop you from making a terrible mistake."

"But he doesn't spend enough time with us to really know what's going on," Karen protested. "Who is he to say it's a mistake?"

Jerry looked over his shoulder with a start. "Hey guys, looks like you-know-who is coming our way."

"Oh man," Chris said. "I don't want to get into an argument with him, especially here."

"Just go," said Father Timothy. "I understand. Better go now, before he gets within shouting distance. I'll talk to you later."

"Thanks, Father," Chris said with a grateful smile. He, Karen, and Jerry hurried away to their cars.

"I'll see you two tomorrow," Jerry said. "We'd better take off; he just might be determined enough to come out here."

"You're right. See ya, Jer." Chris pulled out of the parking lot as Karen managed a fast wave to Jerry.

Jerry waited until they were safely down the street. He started his truck and began to back out of his parking spot. Then he heard a familiar voice yelling.

"Jerry, wait!" Father John was running as well as he could, attempting to flag Jerry down. "Jerry, where are they?"

"They left, Father!" Jerry shouted as he backed out the rest of the way and started to drive off.

*****

Karen and Chris pulled up to the beach house, simultaneously letting out a huge sigh of relief. Chris turned off the engine and looked over at Karen. "Why is it," he said weakly, "that I kept expecting to see Father John running behind our car all the way here?"

"I know what you mean…although he would have to be the Bionic Man or something."

"True, but I would never underestimate a man on a mission. If he has his mind set on something, he could be capable of more than anyone could know. He's been so determined about this. It scares me."

Karen looked back down the road they had just traveled; nothing was there but the pavement glistening from the sun's rays beating down on it. "Well, it looks like we don't have to worry about that, at least this time. But what do we do next time? We can't avoid him forever."

Chris closed his eyes, hoping to shut off the picture in his mind of Father John running after them. "I know that. It's just...I was hoping he'd be able to see that you and I are right together, before it came to a confrontation."

Karen nodded as she let out another deep breath. "I guess that's the way I am with my dad. I avoid conflict if I can help it, which is good sometimes. But other times it's just because I hate the thought of him being upset with me because we don't agree on something. Ever since I was little, I tried to do everything perfectly for him, just so he would be happy with me."

"Looks like we have similar weaknesses," Chris said. "It's hard for you because it's your dad, and it's difficult for me to have it out with a man of the cloth – another man I'd hate to disappoint."

"Let's go inside, Chris," Karen said, taking hold of his shaking hand. "We'll get something cold to drink and try to calm down."

Karen went straight to the kitchen and found a glass pitcher. As she grabbed lemons from the refrigerator to make lemonade, Chris spotted the pile of mail on the counter.

"I guess I'll finally go through this," he said. "I'd rather see all of my bills right now than think about what happened at church."

Chris set the mail on the kitchen table, then went to the living room to locate his checkbook. Spotting it in the middle of the coffee table, he picked it up just as his cell phone rang.

"Hello…Jerry! Did you escape too, I hope? What? You're kidding! No…I know you wouldn't joke about that. We're on our way."

Chris ran back into the kitchen to find Karen slicing lemons on the thick wooden cutting board. "Karen! We've got to go now!"

"What's wrong?"

Chris slowed down long enough to catch his breath and explain. "Jerry called. Father John is in the emergency room. He kept running after Jerry as he was pulling out, and he fell."

"Oh, no! Is he OK?"

"Jerry's with him, and so is Father Timothy. They don't know anything yet. He's being examined by the ER doctor."

"Then we should get down there." Karen placed the cut lemons in a plastic bowl, snapped on the lid and placed it in the refrigerator.

"I know, we have to get there right away." Chris picked up the car keys from the spot on the counter where he had thrown them, and glanced up toward the ceiling. "I just hope the sight of us doesn't cause Father John any extra stress that he doesn't need right now."

Karen leaned over the counter. "I guess we should have had our face-off with him there. Maybe it would have saved him a trip to the hospital."

"Yeah…now we know better. Of course it's after the fact," Chris said with a catch in his voice. "Come on, honey. Let's go."

*****

Jerry and Father Timothy wearily looked up to see Karen and Chris dash into the waiting room. They didn't even bother to catch their breaths before they spoke.

"How is he?" the couple asked in unison.

"He's stable, but the doctor is still running tests on him," Jerry said.

Karen's hand shook as she brushed her hair back out of her sweaty face. "He's not unconscious, is he?"

"No," said Father Timothy, "but they're worried that he could possibly drift in and out of consciousness."

Chris threw himself into a chair, sinking all the way back until his head touched the pristine white wall behind it. "This is all my fault. I didn't want to face him…just wanted to be a coward and run away."

"Please don't blame yourself, Chris," Father Timothy pleaded. "Don't forget, I'm the one who urged the two of you to hurry up and go."

"It's not your fault either, Father," Jerry said, putting his arm around the young priest's shoulders. "You were only trying to help."

"But it didn't help. It only made things worse." Father Timothy leaned forward with his elbows on his knees, holding his head in his hands.

"I'm afraid none of us handled this well." Karen slipped her arm around Chris. "You were right, honey.

We underestimated Father John's determination. His mind was set on getting through to us." She sighed. "Unfortunately, his body is not as strong as his mind."

Father Timothy, still leaning on his elbows, propped his chin up in his hands. "I wish I knew why he's so adamant about this. Why does he oppose the two of you being together?"

"He keeps telling me he doesn't want me to get hurt, which has happened to me in the past." Chris shook his head sadly. "I just can't get through to him that Karen isn't like those other women. I'm tired of having the same argument with him over and over again. It's really draining."

"I'll bet," Father Timothy replied. "He's talked to me about it, but not in great detail. I know it's got to be a hundred times worse on you than it is on me."

A handsome blond gentleman in a white coat came through the exam room door. "Are you the group here with Father John?"

"Yes," Jerry answered. "Are you his doctor now?"

"Yes, I'm Dr. Halvorsen. The other doctor's shift ended, so I'm the one on duty now. We're waiting for some of the results to come back, but we do know for sure that he has a mild concussion."

"Is he still conscious?" Father Timothy asked.

"He is, but right now he's sleeping. We've moved him into ICU for now, at least until we find out the other test results. We have to monitor him while he rests because of the concussion."

"Do you think he will be sleeping for a while?" asked Karen.

"Oh, definitely. He's been through a lot of tests and examinations. If you want to get something to eat, that's fine. I can have someone come get you in the cafeteria if anything changes."

"Thank you, Dr. Halvorsen," Chris said. "We probably should go eat something. I know we woke up late and didn't eat breakfast, or lunch for that matter."

"Same here," Jerry said. "Are you hungry, Father Timothy?"

"I guess I am. I had breakfast but it's getting to be late afternoon. With all of the commotion, I never noticed I was starving until now."

"Go ahead," Dr. Halvorsen said. "Father John's in excellent hands. I'll talk to you in a little while."

The famished foursome took the elevator down to the basement cafeteria. Karen wasn't sure what to get, but after being looked up and down by a slim redhead, she headed for the salad bar.

"You're still going to be hungry after you eat that, sweetheart," Chris said. "You haven't had anything all day."

"But I want to have something healthy," Karen protested.

"Well, make sure you toss some protein on there. I don't want you to pass out later. One person I care about in the hospital is more than enough."

Karen went back through the salad bar and added some chunks of grilled chicken, along with a few slices of hard-boiled egg.

Once she and Chris paid at the cash register, they found the table where Jerry and Father Timothy had already begun to eat.

Jerry took a swig of his cola as they sat down. "It sounds like they'll probably have to keep Father John in here for a while."

Father Timothy nodded. "I'm sure it's better for him anyway. Maybe the nurses can keep him calm and we won't have to be nervous about him falling again."

"Let us know if you need any help, Father," Chris offered. "You're going to be holding down the fort for quite a long time by yourself."

"Thank you. I know once we have a diagnosis, I have to let the Bishop know. He'll send another priest temporarily to help me, but I may still take you up on your offer."

Everyone finished eating their meals and made their way back up to the ER. A nurse came into the waiting area just as they arrived. "Oh," she said. "Looks like perfect timing. Father John is awake now."

"Can we go see him?" asked Chris.

"Well…yes and no. I assume," the nurse said with a glance at Karen, "that you are Karen, but which one of you three gentlemen is Chris?"

"That would be me," Chris answered.

"I'm afraid that you and Karen are not allowed to see Father John right now. He keeps mumbling something about you two and getting himself upset. Dr. Halvorsen thinks it would be best if, for now, he didn't see both of you. We don't want to cause any more stress to his system than he already has at this time."

"Oh," Karen said, "of course. We don't want to make him feel any worse."

"Jerry, you go ahead in with Father Timothy," Chris said with a heavy heart. "We'll wait out here for you."

After Jerry and the priest followed the nurse through the doors, Chris turned to Karen. "I know we might not have acted the best in this situation," he said, "but why am I starting to feel like we've committed a mortal sin?"

"I feel that way too," Karen said as the tears rolled down her cheeks. "We're going to have to learn to be patient with this."

"I just wish Father John wouldn't get so bent out of shape about us. He's doing himself more harm than good."

"We can only hope that this stay in the hospital will give him a new perspective. Maybe then we'll be able to talk rationally to him."

After about half an hour, Father Timothy and Jerry came back to the waiting room. "The doctor gave him a sedative to keep him calm," Jerry said. "We got to visit with him for a little bit, but he stayed pretty quiet. He's asleep again now."

"The more rest he gets, the better," Chris said. "I guess Karen and I should take off, since we can't really visit him yet."

"Good idea," said Father Timothy. "Jerry said he would bring me back to the rectory later this evening, so we'll call you to give you an update."

"Thanks, Father." Chris took Karen's hand, leading her out of the hospital and back to the car.

*****

Back at the beach house, Karen opened the fridge and pulled out the bowl of lemons. She picked up where she had left off earlier, concentrating as hard as she could on getting the lemonade ready so she wouldn't think about Father John.

Chris sat down with the mail. "All right, now I really need to focus on these bills. It's been a heck of a day."

"Looking at bills to relieve stress." Karen let out a tiny giggle. "That's a new one."

Chris stared at the envelope on the top of the pile. "This is strange."

"What's that?" Karen asked.

"It's a letter from Oregon. I don't believe I know anybody in Oregon, at least not anybody who knows where I live."

Karen smiled. "Maybe it's a fan letter from someone who was able to track down your address."

"Could be…wow, I haven't gotten one of those in a long time. That would be kind of cool."

Chris picked up the envelope and began to slice the top with his letter opener.

CHAPTER 21

Karen looked up from the kitchen counter just in time to see the color drain from Chris' face.

"Honey, what's the matter? You look as if you've seen a ghost!"

Chris didn't answer. He kept reading the letter, his face getting whiter as he went down the page.

"Chris, you're scaring me," Karen pleaded. "Please say something!"

Chris slowly looked over at Karen. "I…he's…I might…"

"You might what? Who is he?"

Chris closed his eyes and took a deep breath. "He's a twenty year old kid. He lives in Oregon. I might – he says I'm his father."

"What?" The glass of lemonade Karen had just poured slipped from her hand, shattering as it hit the floor. The sound of the breaking glass caused the letter to fall from Chris' hand onto the table.

"Sorry," Karen said, slowly stepping back from the fresh mess on the floor. She was trembling all over.

"It's all right. My nerves are pretty much shot now anyway."

"This kid thinks he's your son? If he is, then why did he wait so long to contact you? And why didn't his mother get in touch with you?"

"I have no idea. I know for a while it probably seemed like I fell off the face of the earth, but not right away. I was still trying to keep my career going for a couple of years after the show ended. She could have reached me easily while she was pregnant or even once she had the baby."

Karen leaned on the kitchen counter, at the far end away from the puddle of liquid and glass. "You would think that an old girlfriend would want to let you know if you had a child."

Chris swiftly turned from Karen's gaze and stared out the window at the ocean. "Well, she may not exactly be an old girlfriend. You know it was the seventies. A lot of people were into one-night stands. I had girls literally falling at my feet. I let all of the fame and everything else go to my head. I wound up using my popularity to sleep with as many women as possible, thinking I somehow earned the right to whatever and whomever I wanted."

Karen stood there, unable to look at Chris either. She stared directly above his head, through the doorway at the piano in the music room. *I know he feels awful,* she thought. *I know some of this kind of thing went on back then. But I didn't think Chris had been quite so involved in all of that…not to this extent.*

"OK," she finally said in a low voice. "So, you may have a child with a woman you may not even remember?"

Chris stopped looking out the window. He folded his arms on the table and buried his face in them. "I hate to admit that may be the case. This boy, Brett…he included his mother's name, but I don't recognize it."

Karen turned away and bent down to pick up the pieces of broken glass.

"Let me help you, honey." Chris got up from the table and came over to her with a broom. "I don't want you to cut yourself."

"I can do it myself, thank you very much!" Karen snatched the broom from his hand without even looking up.

She could sense Chris was standing there for a moment and watching her, but she couldn't stop the tears from falling. "Oh," he said. "Well then, I'm going for a walk." She glanced up to see him strolling with his head down into the living room.

Karen didn't know where the dustpan was, so she swept the glass into a pile and found a plastic cup to scoop it into so she could dispose of it. Now she only wished it was that easy to pick up the pieces of her freshly broken heart.

*****

Chris slipped off his shoes and socks, shoving one sock into each shoe and leaving them at the door. He rolled up the legs of his jeans and started walking.

His mind felt like a bunch of pieces from a jigsaw puzzle, all mixed up. He didn't know how to put them back together. He even thought that a couple of them might be missing.

Why did it take so long for Brett or his mother to come forward? Plenty of thoughts kept coming at him, one after another in rapid fire fashion. *How did Brett get my current address?*

Chris stopped, staring out into the middle of the bright blue ocean. *Could he really be my son?*

He sat down right where he was on the hot sand, continuing to gaze out over the water. He knew Karen was really angry and upset, and he also realized she had a right to be after such a shock. How could he convince her that he wasn't like that anymore, and hadn't been for a long time?

Chris felt the knot forming in his stomach, tightening up more with each thought. He hoped Karen would be calmer when he got back, even if only a little bit. He had to make her understand.

*****

Karen lay on her bed in the guest room, trying to control the shaking that refused to stop. She was glad she'd gotten rid of the glass without even a scratch. The last thing she wanted to hear was an "I told you so" from Chris if she had been cut.

She reminded herself that Chris was upset as well; he had to have been taken totally by surprise. But she never knew just how crazy the "Wild Seventies" had been for Chris. Maybe it was because she had been so young when it was actually going on. When she was older and heard about it, the information amounted to just a few sentences in an article without much detail. *If you haven't lived it or witnessed it,* she supposed, *then it's hard to grasp.*

Still, it was hard to fathom that he wouldn't even remember the woman. Karen knew that if she would have ever slept with someone, she would remember his name. She stared at the "Phantom of the Opera" posted on the wall. Were there two sides to Chris as well? Did he have a mask that he was hiding behind?

Tears soaked the red bedspread where Karen was resting. She wondered if there was any man she could actually trust. Her doubts about the opposite sex began with Greg, and since then no boy or man had given her any reason to think differently.

That is…until Chris. Karen felt at home with him, safe with him. She had been so sure of Chris. What was she to think now?

The sound of the sliding glass door opening downstairs shook Karen out of her thoughts. She heard Chris calling her name, looking for her. *Maybe he'll think I went for a walk too,* she thought. She stayed silent as her tears now fell onto the golden throw pillow.

After a while, the sound of footsteps echoed on the stairs. They came closer and closer, and when Karen lifted her head from the pillow she saw Chris standing in the doorway.

"You know what's funny in all of this?" Karen sighed. "Father John is actually worried about <u>me</u> breaking <u>your</u> heart." The tears started again.

"Karen, honey, I am so sorry about all of this. This is really bothering me too." Chris looked like he was about to throw up at any second, color still drained from his face.

"I know this is no walk in the park for you either," Karen shot back. "But at least you already know about your past. You knew this could be a possibility!"

"I really didn't think about it being a possibility, even though I should have. And the past is exactly that – the past. I quit that lifestyle a long time ago. You

253

know, I thank God every day that I made it through the seventies in one piece!"

"You're still tempted by alcohol, aren't you? Maybe you could still be tempted by other women too!"

Chris appeared be thinking of an answer that would satisfy Karen, as he opened his mouth to speak but then stopped. Finally he opened it once again. "I guess we both need some time to cool down and think. I'm going to see if Charlie will let me into the studio for a little while tonight." He turned and walked out of the room, down the stairs to the entryway.

Karen waited until she heard the front door close and the convertible drive away. She sat up and took a good look at herself in the mirror. Her tear-streaked face was beet red; her eyes were so puffy that she almost couldn't see out of them. And her hair – it was all mangled and sticking out on one side. She was officially a mess.

What am I going to do? I can't stay here while I think everything through. And I can't go home…Greg could be there.

Karen walked over to the mirror and combed her hair. After staring at her blotchy face for a few more minutes, she picked up the phone and dialed.

"Hi Sandy. Umm…what's wrong? Oh, I just had a huge fight with Chris. Can I come over? Thanks. I'll be there in about half an hour."

Karen hung up the phone and threw everything into her makeup bag and suitcase. She took them to her car and then went back inside. She placed her guitar back in its case as she glanced at the piano. She found all of her sheet music and put it in her briefcase.

Karen took a long, last look at the ocean. She slung her purse over her shoulder, grabbed the briefcase and guitar, and set off for Sandy's house.

*****

Sandy opened the door to find a Karen she barely recognized. "Oh, sweetie. It must have been one doozy of a fight."

"It was." Karen walked in, letting her purse fall off her shoulder onto the nearest chair.

Sandy put her arm around Karen's shaking shoulders. "I'm so sorry. Is it something you can tell me?"

Karen shoved her hair behind her ears, revealing even more of her tear-stained face to Sandy. "I don't know. It's a bigger deal than what happened last time…much bigger."

"Oh. Well, sit down hon. Do you want something to drink?"

"You know, just some water would be good right now. I think I've cried all of the water right out of my body. There's probably none left."

Sandy brought the glass of ice water and handed it to Karen.

"Thanks," said Karen, taking a sip. "Plain old water has never tasted so good in my life."

"So what's going on? Sorry hon, but you don't look so good."

"That's OK. I know it. I don't feel so good either. I honestly don't know if I can work through this one."

"Karen, what could be so bad that you couldn't get past it?"

Karen looked at Sandy as her next drink of water went down hard. She hesitated. "I'm not sure if it's something I should share with anyone."

"I understand if you can't. But maybe I can help you," Sandy said. "I promise not to let it leave this room."

"Well, Chris has…it seems Chris has a twenty year old son that he never knew about."

"Seriously?" Sandy asked. "A son?"

"I couldn't be more serious. Chris got a letter from this kid. I'm spooked but still skeptical. I know Chris is too."

"So that means Chris could also still not be the father."

"Yes, but whether he's the father or not is not the problem."

Sandy sat straight up in her chair. "It's not? Then what is the problem?"

"I asked Chris why an old girlfriend would wait so long to let a guy she used to date know about his child. He told me it might not have been an old girlfriend; it could have been a one-night stand."

"Oh…I see." Sandy leaned forward once again. "That makes it a little tougher."

"Then he proceeded to tell me that he'd had so many of these little flings that he can't even imagine who this kid's mom might be. He didn't recognize her name in the letter at all."

Sandy closed her eyes, taking in that last statement. "Well, I know it was a wild decade, free love and all, but I'm sure that doesn't make you feel any better."

"No, it doesn't. I was raised to commit to one person. How do you sleep with so many people that you don't remember who they are?"

Sandy shrugged. "I can't say that I know the answer to that one. I didn't have a lot of boyfriends. I was always playing music or drawing."

"I didn't have that many boyfriends either," Karen admitted. "It seems like every guy I met turned out to be a jerk."

"Yeah, I've had my share of those too. I have to say…I do remember names, whether they were great guys or scum. And these are guys I only <u>dated</u>. I never slept with them."

"Exactly. Even if you couldn't recall a name, if someone mentioned that person at least then it would ring a bell."

"You would certainly think so," Sandy said. "Maybe everyone doesn't think the same way we do."

"Apparently not." Karen downed the rest of the water and set the glass on a wooden coaster on Sandy's coffee table. "I just know the way my mind works. Trying to figure out Chris' thought pattern is starting to give me a headache."

"Well, you just try to relax here," Sandy said. "Are you still going to stay at the beach house, or are you going back home?"

"I don't know what to do. I can't stay with Chris right now…I need time to think. And I can't go to my house either. I'm still worried that Greg might show up there."

"Oh yeah," Sandy said. "I almost forgot about him, with all of this other stuff going on."

"Ha…I wish I could forget about him."

"Why don't you go get your stuff and come stay with me? I'd be happy to have your company, and we'd have more time to talk."

"That would be wonderful. But, well…" Karen suddenly stopped and blushed.

"But what?"

"I already have my things in the car. If I didn't figure anything else out, I was going to find a hotel room." Karen let out a heavy sigh. "I didn't want to go back to the beach house for anything, because if Chris came back while I was there, he would try to talk me out of it."

"So Chris wasn't there when you left?"

"No, after the argument he went to see if Charlie would let him into the studio. I wanted to get out of there fast, in case Charlie wasn't available and Chris came back right away."

Sandy nodded. "It looks like you both need some time to yourselves."

"We both have a lot of thinking to do, that's for sure."

"Then let me help you get everything out of your car and maybe you can try to calm down a little bit."

"Since you're letting me stay here," Karen said, "at least I have one less thing to worry about."

*****

Chris attempted to make the most of his time in the studio, grateful to Charlie for coming down and opening the place up for him.

"You look like you've had an awful day, Chris," Charlie said as he looked Chris up and down.

"You could say that again." Chris filled Charlie in on the Father John drama, but made no mention of the rest of the day's events. "I just needed to come in here and play with the sound…you know, to get my mind off of things."

"Good idea. Music is the best kind of therapy." Charlie gave Chris a light slap on the back. "It sure beats going to a shrink."

"Not that I could afford one of those now, anyway," Chris replied as he started flipping switches.

"I hear ya, buddy. Hey, take as much time as you need. Lock up when you're done; you can swing by my house and leave the key under the potted plant by my front door."

"Thanks Charlie. I really needed this." Chris got back to work as Charlie went out the front door.

Chris made some progress at first, trying out new ideas and deciding what worked best to get a jump start on the next day's songs. Then he saw the master tape of Karen's last session sitting on the shelf.

Chris pulled out the tape and loaded it to play. That beautiful, crystal clear, soulful voice came on over the sound system. Chris got chills with each and every line.

Karen had made "You're No Good" her own. Chris leaned his head all the way back and stared at the ceiling. That song was probably what Karen was thinking about him right now.

Chris was tipped so far back that he almost fell backward with the chair. He grabbed the edge of the control panel, pulling himself up just in time.

What am I going to do?   Chris thought about how he could make Karen understand. *I need to find out more about Brett. Maybe I'm not even really his father. But what if I am?*

Chris stopped the tape. Karen was the best thing that ever happened to him. Was his colorful history going to screw up his present – and his future?

Chris put Karen's master tape back in its proper place and shut everything down for the night. He had to get back to his house and talk to Karen.

He did his best not to drive too fast, but he really wanted to make things right, if she would let him. At least Charlie only lived ten minutes away from the recording studio. Chris left the car running and ran up Charlie's front steps. Tilting the heavy planter, he slid the key underneath.

Chris didn't even bother to open the driver's side door. He jumped over it into the convertible and sped home, eager to plead his case with the woman he'd come to love more than anything in the world.

When he pulled into his driveway, he realized Karen's car wasn't there. *Maybe she didn't feel like cooking in a strange kitchen,* he thought. *She probably went out for something to eat.*

Chris hurried into the house, thinking Karen had probably left a note for him. He began looking around the kitchen, remembering how easily Karen had found her way around earlier in the day. *She likes this kitchen. That wouldn't be the reason she left.*

He left the kitchen and made his way into the living room. He walked toward the piano, stopping in his tracks when he saw that the sheet music was gone…and so was Karen's guitar.

Chris' heart immediately sank. He raced upstairs to the guest room, hoping to still see the rest of Karen's things in there. But they were gone.

Does this mean she went back to her house? Chris dialed the number, but the phone kept ringing until the answering machine picked up.

Chris hung up and dialed Karen's cell phone. She didn't answer and it went to her voicemail.

"Karen, it's Chris. Honey, where are you? I'm back home now and I'm worried about you. We need to talk. Please call me back. I love you."

Just as Chris hung up, his doorbell rang. *Maybe she came back,* he thought hopefully. *That could be why she didn't answer her phone.*

Chris went to the front door and opened it, ready to beg Karen for forgiveness. The sight of the figure in front of him stunned him.

CHAPTER 22

"Hey, big brother! How's life been treating you?"

"Brian! This is a surprise!" Chris' smile spread across his face as he reached across the threshold and wrapped his brother in a huge bear hug.

"I know," Brian said. "I usually let you know ahead of time that I'm coming to visit. There was a delay in the new production and we don't start rehearsal for about a month, so I thought I'd surprise you this time."

"You sure did!" Chris swung the front door all the way open to give Brian more room. "Come on in, bro!"

Brian stepped inside, carry-on over his left shoulder and suitcase in the opposite hand. "Well, Chris, I'm impressed. I thought with me dropping in on you, your place would be a mess!"

"I've been keeping up with it much better now," said Chris. "I kind of have to…you know, for company."

Brian's astonished grin formed quickly, spreading from ear to ear. "What kind of company? Why Christopher, are you blushing?"

"No, I'm not blushing," Chris answered, knowing fully well that if he felt this hot from the inside, he had to look the part on the outside as well.

"You are. This must be female company that you're talking about. Come on, you've got to tell me about her."

Chris felt the heat begin to leave his face as he spoke. "Her name is Karen. She is so beautiful, a real sweetheart…and incredibly talented." Chris gave Brian the full story, from their first meeting all the way until the work at the recording studio.

"She sounds like a gem," Brian said. "So when can I meet her?"

"Well…"

"What's the problem? Have you told her awful things about me?"

"No, actually it's the opposite. She's a Broadway fan and was quite surprised to learn that we're brothers, but certainly nothing bad was ever said."

"OK," Brian said, "then what is the problem?"

Chris flopped himself onto the couch so hard that it slid over and bumped the end table, shaking the tall porcelain lamp perched upon it. "We just had a hell of a fight. I can't even reach her on the phone right now."

"You want to drive by her place? I'll go with you," Brian offered.

"I guess we could." Chris sighed. "You see, she was staying here for a while, but I just got back before you arrived, and all of her stuff was gone."

"She was staying here? You work fast, brother."

"Brian, you know I'm not like that anymore. She was staying in the guest room because there's a problem at her house. It's a long story."

"I know you don't live that life anymore," Brian said apologetically. "I'm just giving you the business, you know."

"Sorry, it's just a sore subject right now." Chris moved the couch back into place and straightened the lamp shade. "Really sore."

"Is that what the fight was about?"

Chris hesitated for a moment as he sat down. "Yes and no. I'm sure it would have eventually come up, but something brought it to the surface a lot sooner."

"Like what? Did an old groupie show up at your door?"

"No," Chris answered. "Worse."

Brian sat down on the couch next to Chris. "What could be worse than that?"

"How about a kid I didn't know I had?"

"Are you serious?"

"That's what this guy claims, anyway," Chris said. "I got a letter in the mail that I just opened this afternoon. This twenty-year-old is telling me that he's my son."

Brian stared straight ahead for a minute, looking through the front window and into the street. "Do you think it's true?"

"That's the thing. It's certainly possible, but why did he or his mother wait so long to contact me?"

"Well, you did lay low for quite a while, Chris."

"I know, but I was still somewhat in the spotlight for a good two or three years after the show was done. Wouldn't you think she would have wanted something from me, you know…support money, whatever?"

Brian scratched his head so hard that Chris could actually hear it. "That's true. It had to be hard to raise a child on her own, especially back then."

"So…I'm left wondering what the deal is here."

"And Karen is upset that you may have a child."

"That's not really it," Chris said. "She's not totally naïve. She knows that this happens to people sometimes. She's more upset that I've slept with so many women that I can't even remember who they are."

"Oh, I get it now," Brian said. "You said she's my age, right?"

"Yeah, she's a couple of months older than you."

"Think about it. I remember what it was like to learn about your life as a teen idol and all of the fringe benefits, so to speak. It's pretty mind-blowing if you've never experienced it."

"Brian, it's still mind-blowing even if you <u>have</u> experienced it."

"OK…but if you haven't personally gone through it, it's hard to comprehend, especially at first."

"Yeah," Chris said. "I do remember you having a hard time with it when you found out."

"And I'm just your brother. This is your girlfriend we're talking about here. Don't you think it has to be even rougher on her?"

"You're right. I feel awful for putting her through all of this. I think if we'd known each other longer when she found out, at least she'd be a little more secure in the fact that I don't live that life anymore, and wouldn't want to even if I had the opportunity."

"That's what you have to get across to her. You didn't just stop doing it because the opportunities dried up when you were out of the spotlight. You really don't want to live that way anymore. Karen needs to know that even though your career is making a comeback, that lifestyle isn't coming back along with it."

"I love her so much," Chris said, voice cracking as he grabbed Brian's arm. "I have to make her understand. I just have to!"

"I understand," Brian said, "but you also have to deal with this issue of someone claiming to be your son. What are you going to do about that?"

"I don't even know where to begin," Chris admitted. "It's not that I'd have a problem with being a dad, I just would have liked to know before he became an adult."

"Of course. If he is your son, you missed out on a lot of his life."

"Then there's the other possibility," Chris speculated. "This guy could be trying to scam me. He could be thinking that I have all kinds of money at my disposal, and he's desperate to get his hands on some of it."

"So," Brian said as he placed his hand on Chris' shoulder, "you have to investigate before you contact him."

"I'll talk to Jerry. His cousin is a detective for the Santa Monica Police Department. Maybe he can give me some idea of where to take this."

*****

Karen sat quietly in Sandy's kitchen, running her finger around the mouth of her coffee cup.

"Sweetie," Sandy begged. "You need to eat something."

"I don't know if my stomach can handle it right now."

"Please, at least a little bit? I don't want you fainting on me." Sandy set a plate of cheese, crackers, and fruit on the table right in front of her.

Karen inhaled slowly, then let out a long, deep breath. "I'll try."

"Good. What did you last have to eat, anyway?"

"A salad."

"That's it? What else did you eat today?"

Karen thought back over the day. "Just the salad. We got up just in time to get ready for church, and then after Mass I had a salad at the hospital."

"Hospital?" Sandy's eyebrows closed in tightly together to form one. "How did you wind up at the hospital?"

"Oh, yeah, said Karen. "I guess I haven't told you about that yet."

"What else is going on?"

"Father John wound up in the emergency room again." Karen wearily relayed the day's other major event to a stunned Sandy.

"Why in the world is he getting so worked up over you and Chris?"

"I guess he's afraid of Chris getting hurt, but I find it rather ironic that I'm the one who's hurting at the moment."

"Umm, yeah, that is kind of funny…not really funny, I mean strange funny."

"My head is spinning over all of these things." Karen stared at the plate full of food. "It seems like everything is conspiring against us."

"Listen, hon. Every time I'm with you and Chris, I can tell that you two belong together. Don't let all of the crazy circumstances get to you."

Karen picked up a grape and popped it into her mouth, chewing and swallowing until it was gone. "Just how am I supposed to get past this?"

Sandy took Karen's hand and squeezed it gently. "All I know is that Chris is a good guy – not because I work for him, but I've seen him in action. He definitely does not act like a spoiled rock star."

"Well…I know that's true. I've spent a lot of time with him, and I can tell," Karen said. "But still, this throws a wrench into everything."

"I know, hon. I guess you'll just have to talk to him some more about it."

Karen smiled weakly. "It'll have to wait until tomorrow after work." She looked over the varieties of cheese that were spread before her, deciding on a thin slice of Swiss. "I have no more energy today to deal with drama."

*****

Chris and Brian pulled into Karen's driveway, with Chris jumping out as the car as soon as he put it in park.

"Hey Chris," Brian called out, "I'll wait in the car for now. You need to talk to Karen before you spring me on her."

"Good idea. I know her car's not here, but I really hope she's here and just parked down the street somewhere because of Greg."

Chris ran up to the door and rang the bell. He waited for a response, but there was none. He rang the bell three more times, while simultaneously knocking on the door.

"Any luck?" Brian yelled from the car.

Chris ran back to the car and jumped in. "No. It's getting late, but she could be walking the beach. She does that sometimes when she needs to think."

"Just like you do," Brian responded.

They drove to the part of the beach closest to Karen's house, while Chris tried to reach her on her cell phone. "Karen, sweetheart, please pick up. I'm worried about you. We really need to talk. I love you, honey."

Brian and Chris both got out at the beach, walking as quickly as they could along the breezy shoreline. "I'm not seeing anybody out here at all," Brian said, "which is unusual in itself."

"Where could she be?" Chris began sprinting over the sand. "Karen!"

The two brothers searched as long as they could, shouting Karen's name as they ran. Chris finally collapsed onto the sand, exhausted.

"I hate to say it, brother, but maybe she just really doesn't feel like talking to you yet."

"Maybe not," Chris replied. "I'm praying that she didn't get into some kind of accident. She was really upset."

"You'll have to call her at work tomorrow, I guess."

"Well, then I can forget about sleeping tonight. I won't feel better until I actually hear her voice."

"Let me drive us home," Brian pleaded. "You're in no shape to drive right now."

"You're right about that." Chris' shaking hand held the keys out to his brother. "Look at this. I have to be driven home, and there's not even any alcohol involved."

"Yeah, it is kind of strange," Brian admitted. "Looks like there's more than one way to be impaired."

Once the two of them got back to the beach house, Chris dragged himself inside. He landed on the couch, his mind still racing. Was Karen just avoiding him, or was she hurt somewhere?

Chris hoped she wasn't alone, especially if she was hurt. He knew she didn't know many people in town, especially people she could go to with a personal problem.

Suddenly he had a feeling of where she might be. He pulled out his cell phone and dialed. "Sandy? It's Chris. Does Karen happen to be with you?"

"Yes, she's here," Sandy whispered.

"Sandy, I can barely hear you."

"I know. Karen's sleeping. I don't want her to wake up and hear me talking to you."

"She's sleeping already? I was hoping to talk to her."

"She fell asleep on the couch. You know, it's been a rough day for her."

Chris let out a deep breath. "It's been rough all around. I'm just relieved that she's safe with you."

"Don't worry about that, Chris. It sounds like you already have a lot to worry about."

Chris leaned back on his couch and ran his hand over his throbbing forehead. "It came out of nowhere."

Sandy glanced over at Karen, who thankfully was still sound asleep. "What are you going to do?"

"I'm going to meet with Jerry's cousin Roger in the morning."

"The detective?"

"Yeah. I have to find out if this kid is legit."

"What about Karen?"

"I have to explain things to her as soon as possible."

Sandy closed her eyes. "Well, it can't be tonight. She's too exhausted for any more of this right now."

Chris' voice quivered. "At least I know where she is and that she's safe. I'll figure out the rest somehow."

"You need some sleep yourself, Chris." Sandy tried to lower her voice even more. "Maybe everyone will be able to think more clearly in the morning."

Chris swallowed in an attempt to prevent the lump forming in his throat. "I certainly hope that's the case, Sandy. I pray that you're right."

CHAPTER 23

"Why am I even here anymore?" Karen couldn't help thinking out loud as her fingers flew across the keyboard. She felt like she could do these reports in her sleep. Luckily for her, nobody else was around. Jim and all of the other company big shots were at a conference. Except for a couple of junior architects who were new to the firm, Karen was alone in the building.

She actually knew the answer to the burning question she just asked. She needed the health insurance. Her annual mammogram and other tests were tomorrow, and without coverage they would be really expensive.

Like I need something else to worry about, she thought. *Isn't there enough on my plate right now?*

Karen tried to get her work done, knowing there was no one else there who could help her with any of it. She was furiously typing an urgent quote when she heard a knock at her doorway.

"I'll be with you in just a minute," she called out.

"Take all the time you need, Karen."

Karen's fingers froze over the keyboard. She knew that voice, and it didn't belong to anyone at her company. She slowly turned her head, locking eyes with Greg Richards.

"How – how did you find me here?" Karen felt her body slowly sinking further down in her chair.

"I remembered you saying that you worked for an architectural firm. I started calling local firms looking for you, and I got lucky that this was the second place I called."

Karen couldn't believe his nerve. "Why on earth would you track me down to bother me at work?"

Greg's smile began to fade. "I really didn't want to do this at your job, but every time I left messages on your machine you didn't return them. I even tried to swing by your house a few times, but it seems that you're never home."

Karen looked skyward, silently thanking God for telling her to trust her instincts. Greg had looked for her at her home. She asked for God's help now to deal with the problem immediately in front of her, still feeling shaky and unsure.

Then she turned back to Greg. "I had no desire to call you back, and I've been staying with a friend."

"Why are you staying with a friend?"

"Why does it matter? It's not any of your business anyway."

"I care about you, Karen. That's why."

"What? Where do you get off saying that? When we were in each other's lives before, you treated me like a dog. No, wait…lower than that. You treated me like what comes out of the dog's behind."

Karen was now on her feet, no longer shrinking with fear. If Greg had wanted to get a rise out of her, he certainly succeeded. All of those years of frustration were now coming out and would not be held back.

"Karen, that's part of the reason I needed to see you. I…" Greg's face turned crimson, just like Karen's used to at school long ago. "I wanted to apologize to you for the way I acted back then. You did not deserve that at all."

A dumbfounded Karen found even more emotions bubbling to the surface. "Why, Greg? Why were you so crappy to me?"

"I didn't want to be." Greg sighed as his face grew redder by the second. "I really didn't."

Karen threw up her hands. "Then I guess I don't understand."

"Well, if you remember correctly, I didn't start out treating you badly."

Karen leaned her shoulder against the wall, shaking her head. "Actually, I remember every minute of it. At the time, I thought maybe we were becoming friends. That's why it hurt so much when all of a sudden you turned on me."

Greg stepped further into Karen's office, closing the door behind him. "I know, and believe me, I don't want to disrupt your work. I just have to explain."

"Then start explaining." Karen looked down at her watch. "In fifteen minutes I have to meet with the junior architects. You have to be out of here by then."

"OK, I understand. Thanks for giving me a chance."

"Now I'm curious. Go ahead."

Greg pulled out the chair that was next to Karen's desk and sat down. "We were becoming friends. I always liked talking to you and joking around with you."

"I know it all hit the fan when you found out I really had a crush on you," Karen said.

"That just made me snap. Nobody even suspected before then that you had a crush on me, and then within twenty minutes half of our school knew." Greg leaned on Karen's desk, frowning.

"Was it that awful for me to have feelings for you? Most guys would be flattered by a girl's attention."

"No, that wasn't it at all! It was just a big shock, and then all of the guys starting giving me a hard time. I didn't even get a moment to process the information. They were all over me before I had any time to think."

Karen tilted her head back against the wall, trying to blink the tears back into her eyes to keep them from falling. "I guess I was just so hideous that you couldn't stand the thought of me having a thing for you."

"No, Karen, that wasn't true. I actually thought you were really cute."

Karen swallowed the lump in her throat, the one that felt just like it did the day this all had originally happened. "Then I don't get it, Greg. What was the big deal?"

Greg focused his eyes on the linoleum floor, unable to look at Karen. "When the guys started in on me, it wasn't just about a girl having a crush on me. It was about...well...it was about your weight."

"What?" Karen said. "Say that again?"

"They all made me feel like there would have to be something wrong with me. You know, if I were to feel that way about you...because you weren't thin."

"I'd heard something to that effect…but my weight never stopped you from talking to me before that day."

"You're right. Your weight never bothered me; you really weren't all that heavy, just bigger than most of the other girls. Of course, they were all sticks to begin with. I didn't let any of that even enter my mind – until other people put it there."

"You shouldn't have let them get to you, you know."

"Yeah, I do know that now," Greg said. "They were shallow, and so was I for letting them tell me how I should feel. But it was eighth grade. I was just as insecure as anyone else in our class, maybe even more."

"Really?" Karen snorted. "You certainly never acted like you were insecure. You were always so sure of yourself. That's part of what drew me to you in the first place."

"In some ways I was sure of myself," Greg agreed, "in sports and stuff like that. But if someone said something to me that made me question myself, that confidence went right out the window."

"I guess some of this, as I look back, was typical junior high stuff," Karen said. "Even so, you still hurt me, more deeply than you could ever know." She felt the tears falling even as she tried to hold herself together.

"Karen, I'm so sorry."

"You started making fun of me after that…not just my weight, which I was used to from other people. There were other comments that I was shocked to hear coming from you."

"I have to admit, I laid it on really thick, just to show the guys that I agreed with them." Greg finally looked Karen right in the eyes. "Except that I didn't."

Karen had a puzzled look on her face, as if trying to unscramble a coded message. "You didn't what?"

"I didn't agree with them. I had a big crush on you too."

Karen quickly stood up. "Are – are you serious?"

Greg smiled, though his lips were trembling. "I've never been more serious in my life. After that day, I missed our talks and joking around. I really missed seeing your smile."

"Well, Greg, you sure could have fooled me. You're the reason my smile went away."

Greg shook his head at his own stupidity. "Every one of those guys made me feel like I had a problem if I liked a girl who wasn't rail thin. They were so adamant, I started thinking if they all said the same thing, then there really <u>must</u> be something wrong with me. So I bent over backwards to prove that I was just like the rest of the guys. I wound up turning into a real jerk, and I'm not proud of myself."

"Greg…"

"You don't know how many times I wished we could have gone back to the way it was before that day," Greg admitted. "I wanted to go back to talking with you in the hall, cracking jokes…being friends. I wanted to be able to look at your pretty face without everyone else questioning me."

Karen was completely sobbing now. Greg went over to her and put his arms around her.

"When I wound up moving out here," he said softly, "and then I ran into you at the store, I felt like I was getting that second chance to make things right. I can't take back everything that happened, but at least I finally confessed it all to you. Hopefully you can understand, and maybe even forgive me."

Karen, as she realized that Greg was holding her, made her own confession. "You know, back then I would have given anything for a moment in your arms."

Greg smiled. "And if I hadn't fought my feelings and been such an idiot, it might have happened."

Karen was now also aware that there was a puddle of tears soaked into the shoulder of Greg's dark blue shirt. "I've made a mess of you," she said. "I'm sorry."

"No, Karen." Greg brushed a stray tear from the tip of Karen's chin. "I'm the one who's made a mess of everything. I am so, so sorry for everything I put you through."

Greg hugged her tightly again, with Karen laying her head right back on the wet shoulder. "I can't believe I'm still getting so upset over something that happened when I was thirteen," she said.

"Well, obviously it still bothers me too, so don't feel bad about that. It's just something that neither of us got a chance to deal with or get over."

"Until now," added Karen.

"So what do you say?" Greg asked, lifting her chin. "Can we start over and take things where they should have gone?"

Karen released herself from Greg's arms. "Wait a minute. When this apology started, you asked me to forgive you. You said nothing about taking it to the next level."

"Well, I thought…"

"Whatever you thought, you thought wrong. Come on, Greg. For one thing, I have a boyfriend, and for another…I haven't even said if I forgive you."

Greg took a step back and stared at Karen. "I'm sorry. I guess I jumped a little too far ahead."

Karen's eyebrow went up. "A little?"

Greg sighed. "OK – a lot. I've been thinking about you for such a long time. I got way ahead of myself."

"All right, Greg. I guess I understand. You were really starting to freak me out. We never even had a chance to develop our friendship."

"So," Greg shyly asked, "can I at least ask if you forgive me?"

Karen thought it over for a minute or two, which must have seemed like an eternity to Greg. She could see that he was anticipating her answer.

Karen took a deep breath. "I forgive you, Greg. We were barely teenagers. We sure didn't have all of the answers back then."

Greg let out a little laugh. "I guess we still don't."

Karen smiled at him. "Besides, I know it had to be difficult for you to admit all of this to me."

"Not as difficult as it was keeping it all inside of myself. It was torturing me, knowing you were out there somewhere and I wasn't able to tell you. I feel so much better already just getting it off of my chest."

"I feel better now too," Karen said. "In the back of my mind, I always wondered if you ever thought about me and if you ever grew up."

"Yeah, I know what you mean. Too bad I didn't find you sooner."

"Sooner? Why?"

Greg gently placed his hand on Karen's shoulder. "Maybe I could have found you before you met your boyfriend."

*****

Chris tried to concentrate during his meeting with Charlie, but he couldn't stop thinking about Karen. He knew he wouldn't be able to get rid of the jitters until he saw her later tonight.

He was also waiting for a call from Jerry's cousin. Chris had spoken to Roger first thing that morning, and Roger said he was going to check into Chris' supposed long lost son. Chris had given Roger all of the information that he had, which really wasn't much. Still, the detective was hopeful that he would be able to find out more about the mysterious young man.

"Chris?" Charlie's hand waved back and forth in front of Chris' face. "Chris Lassiter, are you with me?"

"Sorry, chief. I was thinking about something else."

"I knew you had to be. I just asked you the same question three times."

"Sorry," Chris said again.

"What's on your mind? Anything I can help with?"

"It's a long story." Chris tried to give Charlie the short version of all that had happened on Sunday, but he wound up spilling the entire story completely from beginning to end.

"Wow," Charlie said. "You had one hell of a day there, Chris."

"Tell me about it. I'm trying to sort it all out. I'm glad my brother's in town, otherwise it would be awfully lonely at my place right now."

"I can imagine," Charlie allowed. "How come Brian didn't come with you?"

"I kept him up kind of late last night, and he's still jet-lagged. I talked him into sleeping in this morning, but he'll be here later to hear Karen's session."

Charlie took the pencil that he'd been chewing on out of his mouth. "Do you think she'll still show up tonight?"

"I hope so," Chris said, leaning back in his chair. "I hope she doesn't let all of this other stuff interfere with her session. Hers is one voice that definitely needs to be heard, no matter what's going on between us."

Chris' cell phone rang. "Maybe that's Roger. I'd better take it."

Chris grabbed the phone off the table and looked at the number, answering as he walked out into the hallway. "Oh good…it is you, Roger."

"It took a little while, but I did get some information," Roger replied. "It's pretty interesting."

"Interesting? How?" Chris thought he might possibly throw up, wondering just what Roger meant and what it would mean for the rest of his life.

"Well, Brent has a record in Oregon. Breaking and entering, three counts. He also set up a phony construction company and tried to scam a bunch of senior citizens."

"Wow."

"He doesn't have anything here in California – yet. I'm still looking into some other things. I'll keep you posted."

"Thank you, Roger. I appreciate your help." Chris closed his phone, just as he realized that he had broken into a cold sweat.

*****

After work, Karen drove to a nearby sub shop where she got a turkey and cheese and diet soda to go. She ate it in her car, parked outside the sub shop while she tried to decide whether she should go to the recording studio that evening. Chris was sure to be there and she wasn't sure if she was ready to face him yet. She wondered why every day of her life seemed like a soap opera lately.

Karen took a sip of her soda to calm her whirling thoughts. *Who would have thought that Greg Richards would apologize to me after all these years? I guess people really can change. I don't know why I'm so surprised by that. After all, I've certainly changed since high school, and God knows, I haven't always chosen to do the right thing in my life.*

Karen thought about that for a minute and realized that her conscience was telling her that she needed to give Chris the same grace that God gave to her. She owed it to him to hear him out and give him a chance to prove that his explanation about how much he had changed since the seventies was true.

Karen picked up a napkin and wiped away the tears that were forming in her eyes. *Come on Karen,* she told herself. *You won't be able to drive to the studio if you don't get yourself under control.*

She finished the sandwich and stuffed the wrapper into the empty bag. It was time to go to the session and face the music…in more ways than one.

*****

As it got close to the time Karen was expected to arrive at the studio, Chris urged Brian to hide in the men's room.

"Come on, brother," he said. "I have to talk to Karen first before I surprise her with you. It's just like you said last night. Her nerves are already shot as it is."

After Brian thought about it he finally agreed. He made himself at home in the restroom, patiently waiting for the right time to come out and meet Karen.

The band had just re-tuned and was ready to go when Karen walked through the door. Chris walked up to meet her and spoke softly. "Honey, I'd like to talk to you before you start. You don't need any distractions."

"I know," Karen said, "but Charlie's waiting for me to get started."

"I cleared it with him. He agreed that we should take care of this now so you can be as together as possible for the session."

"Oh good, I'm glad he thought the same way...because I need to talk to you too."

"Karen, I'm sorry about all of this. I guess my past mistakes are coming back to haunt me. I'm really not that way anymore. I've learned my lesson."

"Stop right there, Chris. I'm sorry too. I should have let you finish explaining yesterday, but my mind went to the worst possible scenario right away."

"I can understand why. Maybe I should have told you more about my past sooner, but I was afraid I'd lose you."

"And I shouldn't keep punishing you for what happened a long time ago." Karen added. "I may have been infatuated with the Chris of the past, but I fell in love with the Chris you are now."

Chris let out the breath that he didn't even know he was holding. "I think we both need to make a promise."

Karen stood up a little straighter. "What kind of promise?"

"A promise to each other." Chris put his arms around her. "That when the going gets tough for either of us, we don't follow that first instinct to run away and hide from it. We face it together and support each other."

Karen smiled. "I like that idea. We've both been hurt, so we're a little nervous about relationships. But if we keep God with us through any crisis, I'm sure we can make it through and work it out."

"As long as we ask for His help," added Chris.

"I have something else to tell you," Karen said. "Greg showed up at my office today."

Chris thought he might actually jump out of his skin from the shock. "He what?" Are you OK?"

"I'm fine. It all turned out all right, but it would take too long to explain right now. I don't want to keep everyone waiting too long."

Chris hugged Karen tightly, secretly wishing he had the power to just make everything OK. "Well," he said, "I have a surprise for you too, and I must say it's a much more pleasant one than yesterday's."

"A pleasant surprise? I could sure use one of those for a change."

"My brother Brian arrived last night after you left. He's here at the studio and eager to meet you."

"Brian's in town? Did you know he was coming?"

Chris shook his head. "No, not this time. Usually he plans his visits, but he surprised me with this one. He wants to hear you sing, especially after hearing my rave reviews."

"Wow!" Karen sounded enthusiastic, but looked like she suddenly wasn't feeling well. Chris realized that even though Brian was his brother, he was also a Broadway star with a legendary voice. Karen had to be thinking about that.

"Don't be nervous, sweetheart," Chris soothed. "Pretend it's only me in the studio. He'll understand."

Karen laughed. "For a minute there I thought you were going to give me that old standby. You know, just pretend everyone is out there in their underwear."

"You could do that." Chris winked at her. "Just know that I look better in my underwear than Brian does."

"Chris!" Karen blushed as she reached out and smacked his arm. "How would I ever concentrate on my song then?"

Chris winked again and laughed as he hurried to the men's room to retrieve Brian, pulling his handsome sibling from his boredom. They went back to the office, and as the door opened Karen smiled.

"Karen, this is my little brother Brian. Brian, this is the one and only Karen."

Brian reached out his hand and shook Karen's. "I'm so happy to meet you. Chris has told me so much about you."

"It's a pleasure to meet you too," Karen said, making note of the fact that the two brothers truly did share the same killer smile. "I'm sorry about all of the drama you stepped into when you got here."

"No problem, Karen. Life would be boring without it. It's not like you caused it yourself."

Chris nudged his brother playfully. "Well, you definitely know about drama. With all of those awards you keep winning, I'm going to have to start calling you Tony."

Charlie poked his head into the office. "Are you all set, Karen? Band's getting restless."

"OK," Chris said. "We'll be there in five."

Karen grinned at the older gentleman. "We're ready, Charlie. Just let me get my mind into music mode."

"You've got it, dear. I'll tell the natives to cool it." Charlie walked back toward the main studio, with Chris and Brian following suit.

"See you on the other side of the glass!" Chris smiled his biggest smile at Karen, and then they were gone.

*****

Karen closed her eyes and prayed for focus. When she felt ready to sing, she strode into the studio and gave each band member a big hug. "I promise this song will go better than last time," she said.

Jerry and Sandy both gave her a big A-OK sign. "No matter what, Karen, we've got your back," Jerry said.

Karen got herself ready at the mic, then gave Charlie the thumbs-up. Even though she'd received an apology from Greg, she decided to put herself back in those old feelings, just for the moment. She knew the song would sound better if everyone believed that her heart was really breaking.

As the first take ended Karen could tell that Charlie was pleased, but he decided to change up the arrangement a little bit and try it another way. He ran his ideas by the band and they agreed to give it a go. They did two run-throughs to make sure everyone was familiar with it, and then Karen stepped up to the mic for her turn at the fresh approach.

*****

She'd nailed it. Charlie and Chris both felt their hair standing on end, and Brian sat in his seat with his mouth hanging open. "Brother, you weren't kidding! She's phenomenal!"

"I told you! I'm not just the boyfriend hearing what I want to hear, I only call it like I really hear it. Karen has the voice, no doubt about it."

As the song ended, Charlie stopped the tape and got on the intercom. "Karen, that's a keeper. The first three members of your fan club are in here and can't wait to share you with the world."

"Hey," Jerry called out, "what about us? We want to sign up for the fan club too!"

"Does membership come with a huggable, kissable poster of Karen?" Rob teased. "You know, just like Chris' old fan club?"

Chris nearly tripped over his stool as he was laughing. "I don't think fan clubs work that way anymore, wise guy!" Then he turned to Karen. "Baby, you've got soul!"

Karen blew him a kiss, then looked over at Brian for his reaction. Chris' little brother stared at Karen, eyes sparkling as he finally broke into applause. "That's quite a set of pipes you've got there. I'm beyond impressed."

*****

"Thank you!" Karen exclaimed. She was pleased that not only did Chris love her voice, but Brian did as well. *It never hurts to have two positive professional opinions,* she thought. *And Brian is just a little bit more impartial.*

"Why don't we take ten?" Charlie suggested. "We've made up some of the time we'd lost. Then we can work on that brand new song."

"Sounds good," Karen answered, still wondering whether she and Chris had spent enough time on it before all of their problems showed up.

"Hey, honey." Chris poked his head out through the door into the studio. How about we use the break to go over the song again?"

Karen smiled at him as her shoulders relaxed. "You must have been reading my mind."

As the others left the room, Chris and Karen went over the ballad. "Do you remember what we tried on Saturday?" asked Chris.

"I do, but I just want to go over it one more time to be sure. Saturday suddenly seems like such a long time ago."

The ten minutes flew by and it was time. Karen hoped she would be able to do justice to Chris' powerful words.

Jerry had gone over the music with the rest of the group before Karen had arrived for the evening, and they began what they had rehearsed many times already. Charlie shut his eyes, listening intently. He had a few ideas of his own going around in his mind, so he needed to pay extra attention to what everyone was doing.

"Well gang, I've got it on tape, and it was really great," he said, "but why don't we try out a few variations, just to see if it makes a difference."

By 9:30, a few of the band members looked exhausted, with Karen attempting to stifle a yawn. "Hey Charlie, can we call it a night?" Jerry asked. "The coffee we drank wore off a long time ago. It's to the point where nothing even sounds good anymore."

"I hear you," Charlie agreed. "Do we all have a date for tomorrow evening?"

"We certainly do," said Karen, as her mind began to drift to other events, namely her appointment at the hospital in less than fifteen hours.

"We wouldn't miss it." Rob high-fived Jerry. "I think we have some different directions to think about, don't we?"

"We can all brainstorm over the next several hours," Chris added. "Then it will be easier to work it all out tomorrow night."

"Sounds like an excellent idea," Karen said as she tried to convince herself that she'd be in the mood to brainstorm the next day.

"All right, I'll see all of you tomorrow night," Charlie said. "And Chris, be ready for your session on Wednesday."

"You've got it, chief!" Chris gave Charlie a quick salute and a silly grin.

Chris, Karen, and Brian decided to go back to the beach house. Once there, Chris wasted no time. "All right honey…you have to tell me more about what happened with Greg."

"Do you want me to leave you two alone?" Brian asked.

"No, it's OK," Karen said, "as long as it's also OK with Chris."

"It's fine with me, Brian," Chris said. "Maybe a third opinion on this guy will help us out."

Karen filled Brian in on exactly who Greg was, and then she launched into an account of the morning's happenings. Karen face flushed all over again as she thought about the surprise attack visit.

"So he tracked you down where you work?" Brian asked.

"Yes – and I was not happy about it. I'm very glad that my bosses were at a conference for the day."

"I'm still not thrilled about this guy," said Chris. "It just feels like he's stalking you."

"I know," Karen said, "but Greg was on a mission, and at least it was a good one for a change. He actually had his mind set on apologizing to me for being awful to me when we were in school."

Chris frowned. "You know, I'm happy that he apologized, but couldn't he have left that message on your answering machine? That way maybe we wouldn't have been so nervous about all of his actions."

"I guess he could have, but I think he felt that he needed to do it in person."

"I understand that…I'd rather do something like that face to face myself," Brian said. "But I can also see why you two flipped out, just getting that original message from him without ever giving him your phone number."

The three of them sat quietly for a few minutes as they mulled over the situation. Karen grabbed a pillow and hugged it tightly as she processed the scene in her mind all over again.

Finally Chris spoke. "Well honey, I'm still not crazy about the way he went about it, but I am really glad that you got an apology from Greg. You've deserved one for a long time."

"Thank you," Karen said. "Now…what about Brett? Have you found anything out about him?"

"As a matter of fact," Chris said as he ran his hands through his dark brown hair, "I've talked to Jerry's cousin, who happens to be a detective."

Karen dropped the pillow and her eyes widened. "And?"

"And he ran a check on Brett this morning. We don't know anything for sure, except that this kid's already got a nice long criminal record."

"So he might be lying to you," Karen pondered hopefully.

"Maybe. He could still be my son, but also still be a criminal. And of course he could be making this whole thing up."

"What do you think?" Karen asked.

"If I had to speculate, I'd say he's lying right through his teeth – or through his pen, in this case."

Karen sighed. "That's the way I'm starting to feel about it."

"But we have to find out more," Chris added. "We'll have to wait and see what else the police find out."

"That," Karen said with a sigh, "still makes me very nervous."

CHAPTER 24

Karen sat in the chilly mammography room in her pastel blue hospital gown, waiting for the technician to come and say she was ready for her. She took a few deep breaths in an attempt to slow her pounding heart.

I should be used to this by now, she told herself. *I've been through all of this so many times, I should be able to run my own tests.*

The technician knocked on the door. "Are you all ready, Karen?"

"I'm as ready as I'm going to be," Karen said with a smile as a gray haired woman opened the door and came in. Her bright pink nametag identified her as Renee. Karen got up and walked over to the machine, and Renee got her into the right position. "It's going to be a little uncomfortable, dear," she said.

"Oh, I know. I've done this before."

"Oh…all right. Hold your breath until I tell you to relax."

Karen held her breath, marveling at how the lab techs always called it "a little uncomfortable". Who were they kidding? It hurt like crazy.

Renee swiveled the machine around to take another view of the breast. Once that was complete, they began the same process again for the other side. Karen repositioned herself, thankful for at least one thing. Since she'd been through this before, she knew how tight she'd be squeezed and was better prepared to handle it. The first time she had a mammogram, she swore she saw stars and came close to passing out.

After they were done, Karen put her gown back on and tied it shut. "Sit tight, dear," Renee said. "Let me make sure these films took, then we'll move on."

"OK." Karen said with a faint smile. "Thanks."

It was only a few minutes, but as Karen shivered it felt more like an hour. *Can't somebody invent a better hospital gown? Something more like a winter coat, since there's always cold air blowing on you, no matter where you sit?*

Thankfully Renee was back in a relatively short amount of time. "Everything took, so let's go down to the ultrasound room."

Karen followed Renee down the hall to a very dark room. She got up on the table and lay down in the proper position without any instruction.

"You really have done this before, haven't you?" Renee said.

"Oh yeah…just not in California."

"Where did you live before?"

"Indiana."

"Does our hospital have your most recent set of films for comparison?"

"They do. I sent for them when I scheduled the test."

"Very good. Now, just try to relax as much as possible."

Karen felt the sensation of the warm gel pour onto her breast and lay very still as Renee started moving the ultrasound scanning device around. After she got all of the images needed, the process was repeated on the other breast.

Karen noticed that Renee kept moving the device around the same area over and over. "Is everything OK?" she asked.

"I'm just trying to get the clearest image," Renee replied.

Even with those reassuring words, Karen couldn't help but feel nervous. She knew the technicians weren't really allowed to say anything one way or another; they had to let the doctor look at the images and give whatever news there was to give. She tried to hold her emotions in check while Renee completed the ultrasound. Finally, she handed Karen a towel. "You're all finished, dear. You can wipe the gel off and get dressed. We'll get these over to your doctor today."

"Thank you." As Renee slipped out, Karen cleaned herself up and put on her clothes.

On her drive back to work, Karen ate the roast beef sandwich she bought at the hospital deli with one hand as she steered with the other. She said a fervent prayer to God for everything to be normal with her tests.

Soon she was back at the office, throwing herself into her work as she hoped to keep her mind from thinking about her mammogram and ultrasound. It still wandered into her thoughts every now and then, even though she tried hard to push it away.

"Karen," Jim called out, "I have another proposal for you to start."

"OK, I guess I'm ready," Karen replied. "I just finished the one I had."

Jim walked into her office and handed her his notes. "Karen, are you feeling all right? You look a little pale."

"I'm fine. Just having a weird day…nothing to worry about."

"Good. I'll be in my office, so give me a call if you have any questions."

Jim strode out and headed down the hall to his desk, leaving Karen alone with his notes and her thoughts. *Why can't I keep my mind from racing right to the worst possible scenario? It was only my routine checkup, that's all.*

Karen closed her eyes. She knew why. There was a time when her checkup was anything but routine. She hoped she wouldn't have to go through that all over again.

Karen opened her eyes and focused on Jim's notes. *Try not to think about it,* she told herself. *Don't start worrying unless you're actually given a reason to worry.*

She got right back to work, and somehow the rest of the afternoon flew by. Karen shut down her computer for the evening, grabbed her purse, and left for the studio.

Karen was thankful that she wouldn't have to eat in her car for the second time today. Charlie had decided that he was treating Karen, Chris, and the gang to dinner. It was just pizza, but at least Karen wouldn't have to stop for something on her way there. Besides, pizza sounded good after the anxiety filled day she'd just had.

Her cell phone rang just as she pulled into the parking lot. She didn't recognize the number, but she answered anyway.

"Karen O'Neil?" asked the male voice on the other end.

"Yes, this is she."

"Karen, this is Dr. Robertson from Santa Monica Hospital."

Karen felt her heart sink straight down into her stomach like a giant boulder. "Yes, doctor?"

"I've been looking over your films, and I did notice something that we're not completely sure about. We're 90% sure that it's nothing to worry about, but we need to have it removed in order to totally rule out any problems."

Karen felt the tears coming. She could have recited the doctor's speech word for word. It sounded exactly like the last time this had happened.

"OK," she said, attempting to keep her voice from breaking. "When will the surgery be?"

"I'm scheduling it for Thursday morning. It's better to get it done quickly, just in case anything is wrong."

The day after tomorrow, Karen thought. *That is quick...although it was pretty fast the other time. Just not this fast. Last time I had five days to prepare.*

Karen and Dr. Robertson discussed all of the particulars; she would have to go in for pre-registration in the morning. Her head began to spin with all of this coming down on her at once, and she reached into her purse for some Tylenol before the call was even finished.

As Karen hung up she tried to steady herself, slowly getting out of her car and leaning against the door frame. She didn't feel like singing tonight.

She went in to find everyone eating pizza and joking around. Just seeing their smiles and hearing their laughter made her burst into tears, and she fished around in her pocket hoping to find a Kleenex.

Chris' eyes locked onto her, and the smile on his face immediately disappeared. As he ran over to Karen, the others became aware of her presence and stopped laughing.

"Honey, what's wrong?" Chris took both of her hands in his. "Please tell me why you're so upset."

Karen cried even harder, which embarrassed her deep down inside. She tried so much to keep this kind of thing private. Now, not only would she have to tell Chris…she'd have to share it with everyone else in the room. They would want to know why she was crying.

"I have to have surgery," she blurted. She dabbed at her eyes with the tissue, but it was already saturated with tears and unable to hold any more.

It seemed as if Chris was frozen in place. "I thought you were just having a routine check-up today."

"Well, kind of," Karen said. "It is a yearly check-up that I have to have, but now it turned out to be more than that."

"Hey guys, let's take some time before the session to chill," Chris said to the group. "I think I should talk to

Karen alone for now. Maybe you guys could work on that instrumental track for the next song?"

Karen felt her muscles loosen up a little bit. At least she could tell Chris first, then he could tell the others so it would be a little easier on her.

"Now," Chris said after everyone had gone, "what exactly is going on?"

Karen was trembling so much that it shook Chris' hands as he held onto hers. "Please, honey," Chris begged. "It's just me here now. You can tell me anything."

"I had a mammogram and an ultrasound today," Karen said, still shaking. "The doctor called me right before I came in here. There's something on the films that has to be removed to be tested. He doesn't think it's anything bad…but he can't completely rule it out, so I have to have it removed to be sure."

Chris rubbed the top of her hands with his thumbs, hoping it would help her relax enough for the shaking to subside. "Do you have a lump?" he asked quietly.

"No. I check myself every month and haven't felt anything out of the ordinary. I have to get tested yearly since this runs in my family."

"You mean your mom?"

"My mom, my aunt, and my cousin. I lost all of them to breast cancer. My other cousins and I have to remain vigilant because of it, and make sure we get our annual checkups."

"Wow," Chris said softly. "I can see why you're so upset now."

"It makes me so anxious, even though I've been through this before."

Chris looked like he wasn't sure he'd heard right. "You have?"

"I had one of these removed a year and a half ago. Thank God when it was tested in the lab, it came out benign." Karen sighed. She knew she would have to tell Chris sooner or later; she just didn't think it would be this soon. It was such a load to dump onto someone who'd only been her boyfriend for a short time. What if he couldn't handle it?

"So you're OK from that one?" Chris' beautiful hazel eyes melted Karen's heart with their caring and sympathy. She knew in that moment that she had to share one more thing with him.

"I am…except for the scar." Karen slowly pulled down the neckline of her shirt, just far enough to show what was right above her bra line. She revealed a deep pink scar about an inch long, well on its way to healing but still very noticeable. "I guess I'll have another scar to add to this one, only lower and to the left."

"Oh, honey…" Those hazel eyes now began to fill with tears as they focused on the short pink line.

"I understand if this bothers you, if you can't be with me because of my scars and my family history. It's almost like having a scarlet "C" etched into my skin, reminding me that I have to always keep an eye on things. It would always be there to remind you as well."

"Karen." Chris took his hand to his lips, kissed his fingertips and gently brushed them over her scar. "None of that matters to me. We all have our scars, some on the inside and some on the outside. And as far as family history, cancer may run in your family, but major life mistakes and addiction run in mine. I call it even."

Karen threw her arms around him, sobbing. "It's bad enough that I have to worry again about this, but it would make it unbearable if I lost you."

"Sweetheart, I'm not going anywhere. My only concern is for your health. Whatever has to be done in order for you to be healthy, I can deal with. I want you around for a long time. I love you."

"I love you too." Karen let herself lean on Chris as he pulled her in close. "You know, most guys would have a hard time with this. They always want women to have a perfect figure."

"You're already perfect to me." Chris lightly rubbed her back. "And I'm not like most guys."

Karen somehow found the strength for a little laugh. "Chris Lassiter, you're certainly right about that. You are one of a kind, and I thank God for that every day."

The two of them heard a faint knock at the door. It opened to reveal a very nervous Sandy, who quietly shut the door behind her and put her hand on Karen's shoulder. "Hon, is everything OK?"

"Well," Karen said with a sigh, "let me run this by you too. It always helps to talk to another woman about this stuff." She gave Sandy a condensed version of her situation, promising to tell her more later on. Sandy joined Chris in a giant hug for Karen, enveloping her in love and support.

"When are you having the surgery?" Chris asked.

"It's the day after tomorrow. The doctor wants it done right away, you know, just in case." With those last three words, Karen let loose with a fresh set of tears. "Sorry, guys. When I let my mind go, it goes right to the worst case scenario."

"Hey, sweetie, it's all right," Chris said as he smoothed her hair. "If it is the worst, which I hope it's not, God will help you through it. Besides, the doctor said it's probably not a problem, right?"

Karen nodded, and her tears began to subside as she took a slow, deep breath.

"Well hon, don't let your mind go there," said Sandy. "Deal with one thing at a time. Don't go there unless you find out that you have to."

"I keep telling myself that," Karen said. "Now, if I could just get myself to believe it."

"Believe, honey. It's going to be all right," Chris said.

"All I know right now," Karen admitted, "is that I'm not in the mood to sing tonight."

"I know." Chris wiped a single tear from Karen's flushed cheeks. "Sandy, would you take Karen back to your house? I'll talk to Charlie and explain it all. Don't worry, honey. He'll understand."

"Everyone will," Sandy added. "I'll drive. We can come get your car later."

Karen threw her purse over her slumped shoulders, hoping it wouldn't keep sliding down her arm. Sandy picked up Karen's briefcase. The women went outside, with Sandy's arm around Karen's waist to steady her.

Chris brought all of the men out of their hiding places and informed them of Karen's predicament. All of them were surprised, but also very sympathetic. "Well, of course," Charlie said, "she absolutely should not sing tonight...or tomorrow for that matter."

"I hope everything turns out well for her," Jerry said. He packed up Sandy's keyboard, planning to take it home with him for now. "Is there anything we can do to help?"

"Just lend your support," Chris said. "Say some prayers; let her know you're there for her. That's what she needs right now."

"I can see why she's nervous," Rob said. "Anyone would be nervous if it ran in their family."

"The thing is...just because someone in your family had it doesn't mean you will," Charlie answered. "Plus, there are a lot of women with no family history who wind up with it. You just never know."

"That means everyone needs to be checked," Chris said. "Even men can get it. Nobody should think they're immune from it."

"Well, I'm sure Karen doesn't want us all pouncing on her tonight," Rob said. "Just let her know we're on her side, and maybe tomorrow we'll be able to talk to her. That way she can get some rest. It's been a long day for her."

"Will do," Chris answered. "Thanks, guys. I'll talk to you later." Chris headed out to his car so he could meet up with Karen and Sandy.

"Hey, where's Brian?" Jerry asked. "He didn't come to the studio today."

"He had an interview with a local TV producer today, about the possibility of guest starring on his show," said Charlie. "Then he was just going to go back to Chris' place to rest tonight."

"We need to let him know what's going on." Jerry tapped his fingers on the counter. "Chris is on his way to Sandy's, and I'll bet he's not thinking clearly enough to call his brother."

"Let's ride over there," Rob suggested. "He'll be worried about Chris and Karen, so we can keep him company. I know I hate to be alone when I'm worried about something."

"Good idea, boys," Charlie said. "You all head on over and I'll catch up with you after I shut everything down here."

As Charlie started putting the equipment away, the rest of the men divided themselves into two of their cars and took off for the beach house.

*****

Chris arrived at Sandy's to find Karen resting comfortably on the couch, snuggled peacefully under the afghan and sound asleep.

"She's doing a little better," Sandy said. "We prayed together and that helped to relax her."

"Good," Chris said, feeling the tension begin to leave his own body. "The less stress she puts on her system, the better off she'll be for her surgery."

Chris sat down in Sandy's kitchen as she brought him a glass of water. "It's a shame that someone so young has to be put through something like this."

"Yeah, I know. It can happen to you at almost any age, and I'm not getting any younger myself." Sandy looked upward toward the ceiling and made the Sign of the Cross. "I guess this reminds me that I need to take better care of myself and watch out for stuff like this."

"I sure hope it's like the last time she had to do this…that it's benign." Chris leaned his elbows on the table and buried his face in his hands. "Karen's so wonderful, and she has such a bright future ahead of her."

"God will help her, and so will we," Sandy answered. "That will get her through anything, even if it's rough."

"I just love her so much. It would be nice if she doesn't have another obstacle to overcome."

"I understand," Sandy said. "I don't want her to go through it if she doesn't have to either, but of course you know how we all have to go through stuff in this lifetime. And there's only one sure way to get through it."

"Yes, I know." Chris glanced skyward to where Sandy had just been looking. "With help from the Man Up There."

*****

Brian heard the doorbell ring, but he had a hard time tearing himself away from Chris' piano. After a couple of knocks on the door, he called out, "I'll be right there!"

He finished the final notes of the song he was playing and strolled over to the front door. He found what appeared to be most of Chris' band standing there.

He felt the sweat break out on his forehead as his stomach did a flip.

"Oh God," he cried, "what happened to Chris?"

"Oh no, Brian," Rob said. "It's nothing like that. Chris is fine. We didn't mean to scare you."

"Oh, OK." Brian leaned against the door and relaxed. "Good. I didn't know what to think when I saw all of you here."

"We should have thought of that beforehand," Jerry said. "But we do have something important to share with you."

"Sure. Come on in, guys."

As they all began to come inside, Charlie pulled up in his car and got out. "I'm here…hold on a second!" He dashed up to the doorway and was the last one in. He shut the door firmly behind himself, joining the rest of the group in the living room.

Brian brought in chairs from around the dining room table, hoping he had enough seats for all of the men. Jerry started to sit on the floor, but it turned out there were just enough chairs so everyone could sit at the same level.

"So what's going on?" Brian asked. "You're still making me nervous."

"Well," Charlie said. "It's Karen – she has to have surgery."

"What?"

The guys took turns explaining Karen's entire situation to Brian, making his head spin more with each comment from each different man. "So let me get this straight," he finally said. "Something showed up on Karen's tests that needs to be taken out to see if it's cancer or not?"

"That's right," Charlie said. "The doctor thinks it's probably benign, but without removing it he wouldn't know for sure."

"When is the surgery?" Brian asked.

"Day after tomorrow," Jerry answered. "Her doc doesn't want to have any delays, just in case something would be wrong."

"Boy, that doesn't give her much time to prepare," Brian said.

"Yes, but it also gives her less time to think too much about it," responded Jerry.

"True." Brian leaned back on his chair, balancing carefully. "I take it Chris is with Karen now?"

"Chris and Sandy took her back to Sandy's house," Charlie said. "There was no way we were going to force Karen to sing tonight. She wasn't in the right frame of mind, and she would have felt even worse if she thought she was wasting our time, not able to get anything productive out of the session."

"What can I do to help, other than being there for my brother?"

"We've been trying to brainstorm on the way over here," Rob said. "Karen's such a great person, and she's living out here without any family nearby…there's got to be something we can do."

"We figured you could help us think," Jerry said. Besides, with Chris being so worried about Karen and going with her, we kind of thought he might not have thought to call you yet."

"You're right. I haven't heard from him." Brian stood up, rubbing the back of his head as he began to pace. "Thanks for thinking about me."

"Hey, since Chris and the rest of us are like one big family," said Jerry, "it's like you're our brother too."

"And we knew you'd want to help," added Rob.

"Absolutely." Brian looked at the entire group of men gathered around him. "Now, what can we do?"

CHAPTER 25

Karen sat silently in Sandy's sunny kitchen, making an attempt to eat the breakfast her friend had prepared for her. She was truly grateful for Sandy's help and support, but the knot in her stomach prevented her from taking a bite more than every few minutes or so.

"How's it going hon?" Sandy asked, as she walked by the table and saw Karen's plate still completely filled with scrambled eggs, fruit and toast.

"It looks wonderful," Karen said, wistfully playing with her fork. "But I'm afraid my nerves and my stomach are not cooperating with each other."

"Well, even if you have to eat slowly, at least eat some of it. After 9 o'clock tonight you have to fast, remember?"

"I know. I'll probably be starving at 8:45."

"So what did your boss say when you called him?"

"I could tell he was shocked, but he also seemed pretty understanding." Karen took a sip of the tea Sandy brought her. "He's scrambling to figure out how to get everything done because of the short notice, but he'll have to make it without me until Monday."

"I'm sure he'll manage," Sandy said. "Stuff like this comes up sometimes and can't be helped. What matters is your health."

"I was finally starting to calm down," Karen said with a sigh, "until I had to make that call to work this morning."

"Well sweetie, at least you got it over with," Sandy said. "Now you can concentrate on yourself for a change...no worrying about work. Right?"

"Right," Karen said. "Work is secondary to my well-being. Taking care of myself comes first right now."

*****

Chris paced at the airport gate, looking for a tall gentleman with salt and pepper hair wearing a purple shirt. As much as he wanted to meet Karen's dad, he had hoped it would be under much different circumstances.

Karen had given Chris the phone number, asking him to fill her dad in on everything. She was in no mood to do it herself; she knew how awful he would feel that he couldn't afford to come out there and support her. She couldn't take hearing his worried voice over the phone, which would only make her own anxiety rise.

Little did she know, but this is where Brian, Charlie, and the band came in. Brian booked Mr. O'Neil on a flight to California, footing the bill himself. While Chris was at the airport, Charlie and the guys were making up the guest room at the beach house, filling the kitchen with groceries, and getting everything else ready to make Karen's dad feel at home.

Chris held a hand-lettered sign up with the name Kenneth O'Neil. Within a few minutes, a handsome older gentleman in a deep purple golf shirt approached him.

"You must be Chris Lassiter. I must say, I still see the resemblance to the young man my little girl had a crush on a few years back."

"Pleased to meet you, Mr. O'Neil." Chris reached out to shake the older man's hand. "And I must say more than a few years have gone by since then."

"Well, I'm thankful to you and your friends for getting me out here. How's Karen doing?"

"She's nervous, but trying her best to take it in stride," Chris said. "She actually seems to be holding up better than I am."

"You really do care about my daughter, don't you?"

Chris placed his hand firmly on Mr. O'Neil's shoulder. "I love her with all of my heart. It's killing me that she has to be put through all of this."

"That makes two of us." Mr. O'Neil sighed. "Once was more than enough. I feel so helpless. I wish I could do more for her to keep her safe."

"Unfortunately, none of us are in control of that," Chris replied. "We have to leave that up to God."

*****

Karen got through all of her pre-registration and tests without breaking down, much to her relief. The nurse taking care of her was so sweet that the knot in Karen's stomach began to loosen up. Maybe once she got back to Sandy's, she'd do a better job on her lunch than she did on breakfast.

Karen was already in Sandy's driveway when she finally thought to check her cell phone. She dialed in and gave her password so she could retrieve her messages. There was one from one of the architects at work who needed her to call him back; there was an important question about one of the proposals. Karen punched in the familiar number and asked the switchboard operator to connect her with Ralph.

"Hi Ralph, it's Karen."

"Oh good, I'm glad you called back. There are a couple of things I need to ask about the Phillips proposal."

Karen filled him in on the details, wondering why he hadn't just asked Jim, who was right there and had all of the same information that she did. Still, she told him everything he needed to know.

"Thanks, Karen. Enjoy your time off."

"Uh, Ralph…it's not a vacation. I'm having surgery."

"Yeah – OK," Ralph replied, adding, "You know, that's the most creative excuse I've ever heard to get a few days off. You're good."

Karen felt her cheeks growing hot and her pride wounded. "Ralph, it is <u>not</u> an excuse. I am honestly having surgery tomorrow morning."

"Sure you are," Ralph said. "Anyway, have fun."

Karen slammed her phone shut as the rage built inside of her. How dare Ralph think that she would make something like this up! Feeling her stomach knot up again, she whipped Sandy's front door open and strode into the house.

"Karen! What's going on? You look mad as hell!"

Karen walked toward the couch, throwing her purse down on the firm, leather cushions. "I don't think it's possible for me to be any angrier."

"What's wrong? Did they mess up something for the surgery?"

"No, all of that went fine. It's what happened afterward that infuriates me." Karen relayed every single word of her conversation with Ralph to Sandy, whose jaw dropped lower with each of Ralph's words.

"Who does he think he is!" Sandy exclaimed. "You shouldn't have to take that crap from him!"

"When I go back to work on Monday, he's going to hear more about it from me," Karen said. "That will give me enough time to plan exactly what to say." She folded her arms in front of her. "Let's see..."

The ringing doorbell interrupted Karen's train of thought. Sandy went to the door and opened it.

Karen heard Chris's voice come through the doorway. "Can we come in?"

We? Karen sighed. *Who did Chris bring with him? I really don't want to see anyone except for him and Sandy right now. I can't believe he didn't check with me first.* She timidly peered around Sandy to see who was there, and suddenly all was forgiven.

"Dad!" Karen ran to the doorway and threw her arms around her father. "I didn't think you'd be able to make it out here!"

"I didn't think so either," Mr. O'Neil replied. "Thanks to the generosity of your boyfriend, his brother and his friends...I'm here. They even set me up to fly first class."

At the word "boyfriend", Karen felt herself blush, just like she had years ago when her father used to tease her about liking Grant Anderson, and the man who played him. It seemed like some things hadn't changed.

Mr. O'Neil gave his daughter a kiss on the cheek, squeezing her even tighter. "You looked so mad when we got here. What's up?"

Karen's deep green eyes flashed once again. "It's a phone conversation I just had with someone from work."

"Jim?" asked Chris.

"No – this one architect named Ralph. He was extremely obnoxious."

"Why?" Karen's dad asked. "Was there some problem at work?"

"Not really. He needed to go over a proposal, which was fine, but then he decided to accuse me of making up this surgery just so I could have a few days off from work."

"Well," Chris said indignantly, "you set him straight, right?"

Karen swallowed hard. "I tried to, but he acted like he didn't believe me. Why would I ever make up anything like this to get time off?"

"Maybe he's thinking that," her dad mused, "because he knows it's something <u>he</u> would do. Devious people always believe that everyone else thinks the same way they do."

"That could be, but I sure didn't appreciate it! I have enough stress going on right now!"

"Maybe I should go have a little talk with him," Chris said.

"Yes!" Mr. O'Neil chimed in. "I'll go with you. That man needs to learn compassion, let alone some manners."

"Wait." Karen put her hand up to signal a stop. "I'm glad you want to do that for me, but I need to take care of this myself."

"But Karen," the two men protested simultaneously.

"No. No buts." Karen's face suddenly lit up like a child seeing a Christmas tree for the first time. "I think I know how to take care of this, but it will have to be after the surgery. Just be patient."

"Are you sure, honey?" her dad asked.

"Very sure." Karen smiled slyly. "Don't worry – he'll get what he deserves. I have to rescue myself this time."

*****

Karen sat up in the hospital bed, watching CNN to pass the time so she wouldn't make herself too anxious. Her nurse once again helped to keep her calm with her sweet smile and pleasant voice. It also helped that her name was Helene, just like Karen's mom. It made Karen feel that her mom was there with her, watching over everything.

Karen already knew there was a delay. Helene told her that Dr. Robertson's first surgery of the day was taking longer than expected. The start time of her own procedure would now depend on when the other one was finished.

Since only one person at a time could be with a patient in the surgery prep area, Chris and her dad had taken turns keeping her company. Now they both went to get coffee so Sandy could come up to see her. Karen closed her eyes and said a prayer during the few minutes it took between the men going to the cafeteria and Sandy arriving in the waiting area. "Dear God, please be with me as You always are, and watch over me throughout this surgery. Please protect me and give me the strength to get through all of this."

When Karen opened her eyes, Sandy was there taking hold of her right hand. "How's it going, hon?"

"I'm doing all right." Karen squeezed Sandy's beautifully manicured hand, vowing to herself to finally get her own mani/pedi when this all settled down. "I guess I'm calmer than I thought I was going to be."

"Well, try to stay that way. We're all praying too, sweetie."

Karen took a deep breath and smiled. "I'm sure that all of this praying is the reason I <u>am</u> so calm."

*****

Chris sat in the hospital cafeteria with Mr. O'Neil, having coffee and a blueberry muffin to keep from getting weak or light-headed. He had to remain strong for Karen and her dad. "Thank you, sir…for breakfast this morning," he said.

"You're quite welcome," Mr. O'Neil replied. "It's the least I could do, considering your brother paid for my flight."

"Luckily Brian's career is in full swing. At least mine's on its way back, but I'm so happy he was here to take care of the plane trip for you."

"Well, you are letting me stay at your house, which I appreciate very much. You guys are all taking good care of me, and Karen as well."

"We all have only her best interests at heart," Chris said. "And I would never do anything to cause her any pain."

"In that case, I have a question for you."

Chris felt his insides tying themselves together, possibly even crocheting themselves into an afghan. "Yes, sir. Go ahead."

"Do you really think Karen has a future in music?"

The knots began to loosen and unravel. "Yes, I do. There's no doubt she has the voice – and I'm not the only one who has noticed it."

The older gentleman set his coffee down and sighed. "You know, when I was younger I always wanted to be a singer. When I was in the Army, I was part of a band that we had on base. People told me I should keep it up once I got out."

"Wow! Why didn't you?"

"I met Karen's mom, and before I knew it I had a family to take care of. I kept feeling that it would be irresponsible of me to try music, rather than have a more secure job to put food on the table."

Chris wondered whether he should ask the obvious question. Finally he swallowed hard and just said it. "Is that why you're so hard on Karen about this?"

Mr. O'Neil nodded sadly. "I worry about her...about her future. I don't want to see her become one of those starving artists."

"But – you would like for her to be happy, right?"

"Absolutely."

"Music makes her happy. I know she's not enjoying her job anymore, that's for sure. And not only does Karen love music, it loves her back. She has real talent."

Mr. O'Neil shook his head. "I haven't heard her sing for such a long time, and it was usually her singing along to the radio or a record. I wouldn't even know how she sounds now."

"I'll tell you what," Chris said. "Tomorrow, when Karen's resting, I'll take you down to the studio. I know Charlie would play Karen's session recording for you. Then you can hear for yourself."

"I'd like that," Karen's dad replied, his blue eyes shining for the first time since he arrived in Santa Monica.

"Good." Chris stood up. "I need to go outside for a couple of minutes to get some air. I'll be right back."

"That's fine. I'll stay here in case the nurse pages us."

Chris went out, turning his cell phone back on once he was out of sight from the automatic sliding glass doors. He had a message from the detective. Chris dialed him back, with Jerry's cousin answering on the first ring. "This is Roger speaking."

"Hi Roger, it's Chris. What have you found?"

"Brett is in jail in Oregon. Seems he tried this same scenario out on a well-known businessman up there, saying he might be <u>his</u> son."

"Are you kidding me?"

"Nope. On top of that, the police there interviewed his mother, who said she has never even met you or this other man. She's very distraught over this. She's divorced from Brett's actual dad, and Brett has known his father his whole life."

"Wow." Chris felt relief for himself, but he also couldn't help but be heartbroken for Brett's poor mother, who was now dealing with her son attempting to involve her in his illegal activities.

"I'm sure we'll still need a statement from you," Roger said, interrupting Chris' thoughts.

"Sure. Are you in a hurry for it? My girlfriend is having surgery today, so I don't think I can get down there for a while yet."

"That's fine. If you can stop by sometime tomorrow, that would be great."

*****

Chris and Sandy kept Mr. O'Neil company in the surgical waiting area as all of them said prayers for Karen. Chris got up and began to pace the floor, thinking that it felt like a lifetime ago that she was wheeled into surgery. *At least we all got to see her before she went in,* he thought to himself. *She actually seemed pretty relaxed, all things considered.*

As Chris continued to wear a path in the waiting room carpet, he sent up a silent prayer of thanks to God for revealing the truth about Brett. He also made sure

321

to say another prayer for the young man's mother, that God would help her get through her rough road ahead.

Chris knew that no matter what else was going on, the most important person in his life was in the operating room right now. Karen was the best thing to ever happen to him in his lifetime…better than the fame or hit records. All that really mattered now was her health, and Chris prayed even harder for the woman he loved.

The sound of the receptionist's window opening broke into his thoughts. "Excuse me…I understand a friend of mine is having surgery today. Karen O'Neil?"

Chris turned to see a dark haired man with glasses standing at the window. He was very tall, and looked to be in his early thirties.

"Hello," Chris said to the man. "I'm Karen's boyfriend, Chris. And you are…"

"Greg Richards." Greg put out his hand to shake with Chris. "It's very nice to meet you."

Chris was shocked to meet Greg here, but on the other hand, life had been full of surprises lately. What was one more? "How did you find out about the surgery?" he asked.

"I was in the area near Karen's office, so I stopped to say hi. Some guy there told me, but he was acting really weird about it. Kind of like he thought it wasn't for real."

"That sounds like that obnoxious jerk Ralph," Chris said.

"Ralph who?"

"I don't know his last name, but he works at her company. He gave her a hard time, telling her she was making this up just so she could have some time off."

"Why would she do that?" Greg asked. "I know it's been a while, but I also know that Karen is not the kind of person who would do something like that."

"I know. She was livid when it happened."

"Then this Ralph guy must be a real piece of work," Greg said. "It takes a lot to get Karen angry."

Chris nodded. "He sure is. Anyway, enough about that lowlife scum. Karen's told me a lot about you."

Greg's face resembled a beet as he tried to laugh. "I'm sure being a lowlife scum has come up when she talked about me."

"Well," Chris started slowly, "she didn't exactly give you a glowing report in the past. On top of that, you gave both of us a scare for a while there."

"I know," Greg said with his head bowed. "I'm really sorry about all of that. All I really wanted was to make things right with Karen. I guess I wasn't thinking clearly. I had a one-track mind. If I were you, I would have been nervous about me too."

"I understand now," Chris admitted. "I didn't at the time, but I know what it's like to be desperate to make someone get where you're coming from, so much so that it's the only thought you have."

"I'm just glad we worked it out," Greg said. "And...at least I know enough to be sure that Karen would never lie about surgery."

Mr. O'Neil, having just opened his eyes after prayer, looked toward the receptionist's window to see Chris speaking to a man about his daughter's age. And this guy looked so familiar.

"Greg!" Mr. O'Neil walked over to where the two men were standing. "I remember you. You were the boy who broke my daughter's heart."

Greg took a step back. "Ouch." He shakily offered his hand. "How are you, Mr. O'Neil?"

"I've been better," he sighed. "Sorry about that greeting. I'm a little stressed right now."

"It's all right," Greg answered as his stiff muscles began to relax a bit. "I guess I deserved that."

"Still…I could have done better," the older man admitted. "So what brings you to California? I didn't know you were out here."

Greg offered Karen's dad a condensed version of his situation. He didn't think there was any need to upset him any more; there was already enough going on right now.

Sandy came over to join the men. "So, you're the Greg Richards?"

"Man," Greg said. "Sounds like I'm well known around here…certainly more than I thought I would be!"

"Well," Sandy said, "Karen's a good friend of mine. You definitely came up in conversation lately."

Soon after Greg had done his best to convince the group that he had changed for the better, Dr. Robertson came through the double doors that led to the operating room.

"Chris?" Dr. Robinson said. "Are all of you with Karen?"

"Yes, doctor." Chris introduced everyone who was there to the surgeon.

"Well, you'll all be glad to know that the surgery went as expected. Karen is in the recovery room."

"Can we go see her?" asked Chris.

"Not quite yet. One of the nurses will come and let you know when it's OK. We're just waiting for the anesthetic to wear off."

"So she's all right?" Greg said.

"From the surgery, yes. The tissue that was removed still has to be tested. We'll know about that in a few days to a week."

"The waiting's always the hardest part," Mr. O'Neil said.

"I know," the doctor replied sympathetically. "Karen said you've been through this before. Hopefully my gut feeling is right and Karen will be fine."

"Thank you, doctor," Chris said as Dr. Robertson shook his hand and headed back through the doors into the operating area. He turned to the rest of the group. "I'm going to run down the hall and call my brother, so he can let the guys know. There has to be a phone down there somewhere, since we have to have our cell phones shut off in this area."

"You were reading my mind, boss," Sandy said, as Chris took off in search of a pay phone.

"Karen has a really great support system here, doesn't she?" said Mr. O'Neil with a calm smile.

"She truly does," Sandy replied. "Karen's a wonderful person. We all care about her so much."

Karen's usually stoic dad wiped a couple of tears away. "I've always worried about her. Maybe that comes with having an only child…that really protective feeling."

"All parents are protective of their children," Sandy said, placing her hand gently on the older gentleman's arm.

"I know, but maybe I overdo it. I can't help it. I was scared for Karen when she left her family and friends to move out here. I was afraid she'd be all alone."

Sandy smiled. "That's one thing you definitely don't have to worry about anymore."

"I'm here too," Greg put in. "I'm not here to disrupt Karen's life, but I would like us to be friends – something that would have happened a long time ago if I hadn't been so stupid."

"Well Greg, you were just a young kid at that time. Obviously you've grown up since then." Mr. O'Neil put his hand out to Greg. "I'm glad you're on Karen's side now."

Greg shook the hand offered to him. "Thank you, sir. I've definitely learned my lesson."

By the time Chris returned, they had all made amends and resumed waiting. A few minutes later, the nurse walked out through the double doors to address them. "Karen is still a little groggy, but you can see her now," she said. "I just ask that you limit it to two visitors at a time and keep it brief."

"Sure. Thank you," Sandy said. "Chris, you and Mr. O'Neil should go in first."

With that, Karen's two best guys followed the nurse back through the doors to the recovery room as they tried to relax their nerves before reaching her room.

*****

Karen opened her eyes to find her dad standing on one side of her hospital bed, Chris standing on the other, and each of them holding her hand. "Hey," she said wearily.

"Hey yourself," Chris said softly with a smile. "How are you feeling?"

"Like I'm trying to wake up from the world's deepest sleep, and I can't make myself come out of it."

"That's the anesthetic still in you." Karen's dad squeezed her hand. "It's not all out of your system yet."

"I know. It just feels like it's taking so much longer to wear off than the last time."

"Maybe they had to use a bigger dose this time," Chris offered.

"Well…I was told they had to go deeper than what was on my records from that last surgery. I guess I probably was given more anesthesia."

"Honey, if you feel you need to shut your eyes, it's OK," her dad said. "We are here for you. You're in the hospital…it's not like you need to entertain us."

"Just relax," Chris said. "Your doctor said the procedure went well. The anesthetic will steadily wear off and you'll be fine."

"OK." Karen felt her eyelids getting heavier as the words both of them said hit her.

"You have a couple more visitors," Mr. O'Neil said. "We're going to go out and let them in for a few minutes. They only want two of us back here at a time."

"Oh…OK," Karen said, wondering in her altered state who else would be here to see her. As her eyes closed, she figured Sandy was still in the waiting room, but who else? *Maybe Jerry or Charlie stopped by,* she thought to herself as she drifted off.

The next time she opened her eyes Sandy was at her side, just as she had thought. But on the other side of her was – Greg? *Wow,* Karen thought, *I must still have too much medication in my system. It can't be Greg. He doesn't even know about the surgery.*

"Hi hon," Sandy said. "Did you have a nice little snooze?"

"I guess so." Karen gave her friend a weak smile.

"Hi Karen," Greg said, taking her hand and ending all speculation.

"It is you. How did you know I was here?"

"I stopped by your office and someone there told me."

"Oh…all right." Karen was still too weak to give more than a passing thought to why someone at work disclosed personal information about her to someone.

"Anyway," Greg said. "I just want you to know that I'm on your side. If you need anything, I would be glad to help you out."

"Thanks," Karen said, starting to snap out of it a little bit more.

"Well sweetie, I think in a few minutes the nurses are going to get you sitting up so the rest of this can wear off. You may be able to go home in a couple of hours. Sandy squeezed Karen's hand a couple of times. "We're going to go out to the waiting room so we won't be in their way."

"Home sounds wonderful," Karen said as she began to drift off once again.

CHAPTER 26

The next morning, Chris bolted up out of bed upon the realization that he should have gotten up much earlier. He just remembered that he promised to take Karen's dad to the studio to hear some of her recordings, and he hurried to get ready as quickly as he could. It had been a long night, getting Karen settled back in at her house, and he'd wanted to make sure everything was all right before he went home.

"I'm supposed to pick Mr. O'Neil up at nine," Chris told Brian. "But I have to stop by the police station first and give my statement about Brett."

"You could do that after the studio," Brian offered.

"No, I can't do that. Karen's dad will want to know why I have to go to the police station. I'm just starting to get into his good graces. I don't want to ruin it."

Chris went to the station, praying that he had enough time so he wouldn't be late for his studio date with Mr. O'Neil. *Please God, I want to stay on his good side.* Thankfully he didn't need to talk to the detective for very long, and he headed over to Karen's house.

Karen had decided that her own house would be the best place to recuperate, and now that she longer had to be afraid of Greg, it was safe to go back. Everyone agreed with her, so her dad and Sandy went to stay with her to keep an eye on her. They didn't want her to be by herself while she was still on pain medication that made her sleepy.

Mr. O'Neil answered the door at Chris' knock. 'Hey Chris! You're just in time. Ready to go?"

"Almost. First I want to see how our lovely patient is doing."

"Hi honey." Karen smiled from her place on the couch, propped up by several pillows so she wouldn't pull against her stitches. "I feel some soreness, but I'm trying to use the pain medication sparingly. It makes me feel so out of it."

"That's a good idea. The less of that stuff you need, the better," Chris said as he leaned down to kiss Karen's cheek. "Have you been able to eat much?"

Karen laughed softly. "Yes, once Dad and Sandy cleaned my refrigerator. While I was away a few things went bad."

"Oh yeah," Sandy said. "It was getting pretty colorful in there. All the colors of the rainbow, except nothing was the color it was supposed to be."

"And talk about a smell!" Karen said. "Sandy went to the store to get me restocked while my dad scrubbed the whole fridge down. Now it's safe to eat around here!"

Chris grinned, and with that Karen felt that all was right with the world. "Good," he said. "You relax and get some rest. Your dad and I will be back soon."

Mr. O'Neil kissed his daughter on the forehead, and then followed Chris out the door to his car. Karen and Sandy sipped apple juice and talked.

"I sure hope my dad likes the recording," Karen said with a sigh.

"Now, come on," Sandy said. "He's gonna love it, hon. We all do, and he's your dad. There's no way he could not love it."

"But he was so against my being a singer. It's not a "secure" job," Karen answered, forming the quote marks in the air with her fingers. "He wants to be sure that I'm going to be safe and sound."

"Well, he and Chris had a talk, and I think he understands more now. After he actually hears your tracks, I think he'll <u>really</u> get it."

Karen put down her empty juice glass and looked back up at Sandy with a puzzled look on her face. "What I'm even more worried about right now is that someone at my office told Greg about my surgery. I know I'm on better terms with him than before, but my colleagues wouldn't know that. They don't even know who he is! Why would they give out personal information like that?"

"Yeah, well…" Sandy hesitated, not sure if Karen was ready for more information yet.

"Sandy, do you know who told him?"

"I think so. We didn't want to tell you yet while you're recovering, but –"

"It was Ralph, wasn't it?"

Sandy took a deep, steadying breath. "From what Greg said it sure sounded like it. He told us the guy he spoke to acted like he would be coming to the hospital for nothing, that you wouldn't really be there."

Karen's cheeks were burning now. "That does it. I need to straighten this idiot out now!"

"Now Karen, calm down. You are not in any shape to do anything yet."

"Maybe not," Karen said. "But I can plot my defense. Come upstairs with me so I can show you something. I've got an idea."

*****

Mr. O'Neil walked around the studio with Chris, amazed by everything he saw as Charlie explained how things worked.

"Can you tell this is my first time in a studio?" he joked. "I think I'm getting whiplash...there's so much going on here."

"It's a pleasure to show you around, sir," Charlie said. "Now, let's go into the control room. You can see the various bells and whistles in there while I set up Karen's tapes."

The three of them went in, with Chris explaining everything as Charlie loaded Karen's first session tape. "Wow," said Mr. O'Neil, "there's all of these levers over here, more buttons over there and a whole bunch of knobs. How do you guys keep all of this straight?"

"It doesn't take long; you get the hang of it pretty quickly," Chris said. "Go ahead and have a seat. I think Charlie is ready for us."

"I am indeed," Charlie replied. "Here we go!"

Mr. O'Neil heard the intro, realizing he already knew this song well. Then he heard his daughter's voice singing a perfect rendition of "Can't Take My Eyes Off You".

"This is really Karen?" he exclaimed. "She's wonderful!"

"It's absolutely, one hundred percent Karen," Charlie said with a smile. "We can always add background vocals later if we want. We decided to lay it down with just her and the band…just her voice right now."

The second track began with Karen's powerful acapella vocals on "Can't Help Falling in Love" taking over her father's ears. "I don't even know what to say," he said softly, tears streaming down his face.

"I think you've said it all without words." Chris put his hand over the top of the older gentleman's shaky one. "I'm happy that we brought you in to hear it for yourself."

Mr. O'Neil blinked back the remaining tears, trying his best to look strong and composed. "Are there any more songs?"

"There are a couple more, but we thought we'd save those for when Karen can come in here with you," Charlie said. "Maybe tomorrow or Sunday. I know she's supposed to take it easy for a couple of days."

Chris nodded. "We know she would love to see your reaction as you listen to her sing. Your opinion means a lot to her."

"Then let me buy the two of you lunch," Mr. O'Neil offered. "It's the least I can do, seeing how you've just made my year."

*****

Greg Richards made his way up and down the sidewalk, looking for help wanted signs posted in the windows. It was time to find a job.

It took Greg a while to come to this realization. He hadn't been sure whether or not he was going to stay on the West Coast, considering that things hadn't worked out with his girlfriend. He knew he shouldn't have followed a girl across the country that he wasn't sure about, and became angry with himself for doing something so stupid.

But now things were different. Now he had a reason to stay.

Maybe I'm being silly, he thought. *How much will I actually see of Karen? After all, she does have a boyfriend and other things going on in her life.*

Yet Greg couldn't help thinking that he was brought out here to make things right with Karen, to be here for her. God had used his stupid move for good. And it wasn't like he had anything that would make him want to go back home anyway. Now that he knew a few people in California besides his ex, he was feeling more comfortable.

Of course, by now his savings were starting to run low. Even though he had a good amount to start with, the cost of living in California was much higher than in Indiana and the money went faster than he could have imagined. He had to find work…anything he could for now until he found something that suited him in his regular line of work. This was no time to turn down anything due to pride. Pride wasn't going to pay his rent or keep him fed.

Greg's neighbor in the apartment across the hall from him said he saw a few places in the area that were hiring. So far though, Greg was not having any luck.

Maybe I should try another neighborhood, he wondered. *Maybe I misunderstood him and the jobs are in a different area.*

As he turned the corner, however, his luck began to change. He saw NOW HIRING signs in four different windows. He filled out an application at the bookstore, then decided to stop for coffee at The Daily Grind before going into the other businesses.

While he was waiting for his coffee, Greg saw the HELP WANTED sign posted behind the counter. Wow, he thought, if I hadn't stopped in for something, I wouldn't have even known about this.

As the barista behind the counter handed Greg his coffee, he asked her some questions. "Is your manager available? Could I please speak with him or her?"

*****

Sandy breathed a sigh of relief as she got back to Karen's house upon seeing that Chris and Mr. O'Neil had not come back from the studio yet. She went inside to find Karen watching TV.

"Thank God," she said aloud. "They would have never let me hear the end of it if they knew I'd left you here alone."

"Now Sandy, I told you to go. And it was only for half an hour."

"But still…"

"Come on, I'm fine," Karen said. "Besides, it's all a part of our plan. When will they be ready?"

"Tomorrow after five," Sandy answered. "I also warned them like you asked."

"Good." Karen's smile became brighter than it had been in the last few days.

"I really like this idea," Sandy said.

"Just do me a favor," Karen said. "Make sure none of this slips out to my dad."

"There's nothing bad about this plan. Why are you so worried about him knowing?"

"I know there's nothing bad about it, but he still wouldn't like it. One of us can get Chris alone and tell him. Since my dad's flying home on Sunday night, he won't even be here when we do it."

"OK," Sandy said. "I'll make sure I don't tell him."

"Thanks."

*****

Karen began to open her mouth to say more, but a knock at the door made her get back into visitor mode. She may have been smiling, but on the inside she was also glad that Sandy made it back first.

"Hi, honey." Mr. O'Neil walked over to his daughter and kissed the top of her head. "How's it going?"

"It's going." Karen smiled even brighter than before. "Sandy's been taking good care of me."

"So how was the studio?" Sandy asked, changing the subject quickly so her face wouldn't give anything away.

"Wonderful," Chris said with a wink to Karen. "Charlie showed your dad around the whole place."

"It's actually quite fascinating," Mr. O'Neil said. "And honey…your voice is amazing!"

Karen's mouth dropped open. "You really think so?"

"Absolutely! You know me, I always worry about you and I always will. One thing is for sure though…you have the voice to go for it, and…" Karen's dad paused, looking deep in thought.

Karen just stared at him until he was ready to continue. "I always wondered what it would be like to make a living with my music. I was too scared to try it, worried that I would let you and your mom down."

"Oh Dad," Karen said softly. "I never knew that."

"I know this is your dream, and I won't try to stop you." Mr. O'Neil's voice began to quiver. "I really don't want you to have any regrets. I don't want you to forget your dreams like I did. You need to give it a shot."

Karen's eyes began to water heavily. "Thanks, Dad. You know…this time I wasn't going to let you stop me anyway."

"I figured that." His tears began to form as well as he reached for her hand. "I'll just always pray that you make the right decisions."

"That's all I ask for." Karen slowly got up from the sofa to embrace her dad. "It really helps me feel better to have your vote of confidence."

*****

As father and daughter hugged, Chris and Sandy quietly ducked into the kitchen to give them a few minutes alone. "Chris," Sandy whispered, "Karen came up with a plan to put Ralph in his place. I'll let her tell you more about it, but I do want to let you know that she doesn't want her dad to know about it."

Chris felt like his heart skipped a beat. "Is it that bad that he can't find out?"

"No, it's nothing really bad, but Karen still thinks he wouldn't approve. You know how he hates to make waves, especially where her job is concerned."

"Understood. Now I can't wait to hear what it is."

"Well, it's Karen's idea, so I know she'll want to tell you herself. I just didn't want you to accidentally give anything away to her dad right now either."

"Hey," Chris said, "let's start making lunch. Then they won't wonder what we're up to in here and Mr. O'Neil won't ask questions."

*****

Before Karen knew it, Sunday morning was upon her. She felt stronger after a couple of days recovering from surgery, yet she knew her dad had to fly home tonight and she wasn't looking forward to saying goodbye.

"Honey," her dad called from down the hall, "Remember we're going to the studio after church."

"How could I forget?" Karen said, then began humming to herself as she got ready in the bathroom. She couldn't wait to play the rest of her demos for him, now that she knew he was pleased with her voice.

As they got ready upstairs, Chris was in the kitchen staring at his coffee cup. Since he found out the night before that Father John was out of the hospital he began to worry. *Will he be at church today? I don't want a scene of any kind with Karen's dad there. That would just make this an ever bigger mess than it already is.*

"Man," he said aloud as Sandy walked over to the coffee maker, "I hope there won't be another fiasco with Father John today."

"Will he be saying Mass?" Sandy asked.

"No, but if he's up to it he might come out to see everyone afterward. I don't know what to do about him. Karen's dad will be with us and it would be really bad if Father started yelling at us again."

"Have you told Mr. O'Neil that we're going to your church?"

"No…"

"Then why don't we go to Karen's church today? At least you wouldn't subject him to Father John. And Karen might be more relaxed there, since she's already been through a lot this week."

Chris perked up and straightened his slumped shoulders. "That's a great idea. I'll go upstairs and run it by her. She should be done getting dressed by now."

Sandy smiled. "I'm sure she'll like the idea too."

Chris sprinted up the stairs to talk to Karen, suddenly feeling about fifty pounds lighter than he had just a few minutes earlier.

Mr. O'Neil came down the stairs right after Chris went up. "Chris was moving pretty fast there, wasn't he?" he said to Sandy.

"Oh," she replied quickly. "I think he just wants to make sure Karen's all right so we won't be late for church."

*****

Finally seated in the church pew, Chris felt the tension go out of his muscles. *Thank you God,* he said silently, *for giving Sandy this idea. Now we can keep Karen and her dad from another Father John episode. I really, really appreciate it.*

Chris looked around as he prayed, impressed by the beauty of Karen's church. This wonderful feeling of joy spread through his body all the way to his fingertips. It was like being invited to come spend time with Jesus at His Father's private cabin, complete with gorgeous woodwork, rustic lanterns, and choirs of angels.

Then Chris looked to his right and smiled at the most beautiful angel of all. He took Karen's hand and squeezed it gently, hoping his angel would not have to go through hell to be healthy.

Just before Mass was ready to begin, a man slipped into the empty seat in the pew in front of them. Chris realized that it was Greg; he had temporarily forgotten that Greg went to Mass here. His stomach knotted for a moment until he also remembered that they were all cool with Greg now. *Greg is all right,* he thought as he closed his eyes. Anyway, he was certainly the lesser of two evils for the day.

*****

Greg got focused right in on the Mass, glad to have made it there before it started. He knew he had to thank God properly for helping him find a job so quickly. At least now he'd be able to afford his rent, and wouldn't just be sitting around all the time thinking about how badly his life was going.

As Mass went on, it dawned on Greg that maybe Karen hadn't even noticed him. He also knew that was just about to change. As the priest said, "You may now exchange the sign of peace", Greg shook the hand of the man next to him and then turned around.

As Greg spun around to the pew behind him he saw Karen. Not only that, but her dad, Chris, and Sandy were with her. *How did I not even know they were there until now?* he thought. *I must have been in my own little world.*

"Hi guys," Greg said as he stood there wide-eyed. "Peace be with you." All four responded and shook Greg's hand. When Greg turned back to face the altar again, he could see Karen breath a huge sigh of relief from the corner of his eye. He wondered if she was glad that he had refrained from hugging her this time.

Greg smiled as he faced forward, grateful to be on good terms with Karen again. It truly felt like a thousand pound weight had been lifted off his shoulders. If only he could have caught up with her sooner to apologize; now he wanted to make up for all of the lost time. Time that, he knew, was his fault for being such a stupid jerk and letting the other guys influence him all those years ago.

Once Mass was ended, Greg turned back around. "I can't believe I didn't know all of you were behind me!"

"Surprise," Sandy said with a laugh. "We wondered how long it would take you to notice us."

"I must have really been deep in thought," Greg said.

"Well, that's a good thing, especially at church," Mr. O'Neil remarked. "As long as you were thinking about God."

"Oh, I definitely was," Greg responded.

"Hey Greg," Chris said, "How about you come to lunch with us?"

"Sure," answered Greg, stunned yet pleased that they wanted him there. He saw Karen and Chris exchange smiles. Things were definitely starting to look up.

*****

As they all sat around the table talking and laughing, Greg began to feel at home. Though he was far from his and Karen's Indiana hometown, he was making some friends and was no longer unemployed. On top of that, any opportunity to spend time with Karen was completely fine with him…even if that time came with her friends and boyfriend attached.

"So, Greg," Mr. O'Neil said, "do you have a job out here yet?"

Greg swallowed hard, not expecting this question from Karen's dad. "Actually, I just finally found one. I start tomorrow."

"Really?" Karen asked. "What are you going to be doing?"

"Um…well, I don't want to jinx it," Greg said.

"What do you mean?" Chris said. "Are you superstitious or something?"

Greg tried to think quickly. There was no way he was going to tell them his job would be serving coffee. He'd just made friends with these people, and he refused to give them a reason to look down on him. Besides, he was sure Karen would not be impressed.

"I guess I am, a little bit," he answered. "Once I'm there for a while and more settled, I'll fill you in on the details."

"Well, good luck on your first day tomorrow anyway," Sandy said. "Hope all goes well."

Greg smiled nervously. "Thanks."

Mr. O'Neil turned to his daughter. "So honey, are you ready to go back to work tomorrow?"

"I am absolutely ready, Dad," Karen answered, with a grin that Greg recognized from childhood as Karen's "I'm-up-to-something" look. He also saw Chris and Sandy exchange what seemed to be a quick, knowing glance. He was starting to wonder just what was going on.

"I'm just sorry I have to go home so soon." Karen's dad took her hand. "You make sure you call me as soon as you hear anything from the doctor, all right?"

Karen nodded as her mind went back into worry mode and her grin disappeared. "I will," she answered in a whisper.

*****

Chris pulled out of the airport as fast as he could, before the officer coming toward his car could threaten

344

him with a ticket again. Karen sighed. "I'm sorry I kept you waiting out here so long."

"It's OK, honey. I know it was hard to say goodbye to your dad tonight."

"It was harder than I thought it was going to be. I know he has things to do back home, but it was so good to have him here for a few days."

Chris reached over and brushed a strand of blonde hair back from Karen's eyes. "At least now you know he supports your music."

"I'm forever grateful to you and Charlie for taking Dad to the studio and for letting me be there with him before we came here to drop him off for his flight. I'll never forget the look on his face when he heard me sing."

"My pleasure, and Charlie's too, I'm sure. Your dad needed to hear the songs, to really hear your talent and know that nobody is taking advantage of you."

"I could never thank you enough," Karen said. "It's one less worry on my mind, especially with everything else going on right now."

"You don't know how relieved I am to know that Greg's not a problem anymore either," Chris said. "I'm glad that's all straightened out; that's another stressful situation resolved."

"Me too," Karen said. "It was really great of you to invite him to lunch with us. I think he's kind of lonely, like I was when I first moved out here."

"Well, now that we know he's not a stalker, it's OK," Chris said with a laugh. "He seems like a nice enough guy…especially since he apologized to you."

"Even though we know he's all right, I'm still glad he didn't hang around too long after lunch," admitted Karen. "It worked out well that he said he had a couple of errands to run."

Chris turned the steering wheel and made a right onto Karen's street at last. "Oh really? Why?"

"I'm not necessarily ready for Greg to know about my potential singing career. Yeah, things are better now with him, but he already knows an awful lot about my life in such a short time. I didn't really want to get him involved with my health issues…but thanks to Ralph, it happened anyway."

"I understand," Chris said, "but that one's not actually Greg's fault."

"I know – and we'll take care of Ralph. But I want to see what kind of friend Greg can be without even an ounce of the possibility of my so-called celebrity status in his head."

Chris pulled in the driveway and cut the engine. "You think it would affect him?"

"Maybe not…but since I don't know for sure and don't really know much about what he's been like since junior high, I still don't want him to know yet."

CHAPTER 27

Karen and her entourage arrived at her office building a few minutes earlier than she usually would, giving them plenty of time to execute her plan. Flanked by Chris and Sandy, she strode purposefully toward Ralph's office with a large manila envelope in her hand.

When they reached Ralph's doorway, they discovered he was not there; his briefcase wasn't even on the desk yet.

"I'm not surprised," Karen said. "On most days he barely makes it to work on time."

"So what now?" Chris asked.

Karen walked behind Ralph's desk and sat in his chair. "We'll just wait for him."

"Waiting just makes me more nervous," Sandy said.

"I'm surprised I'm not more anxious about this," Karen admitted. "I'd almost gotten used to the panic attacks...but lately I haven't really had any, except for being nervous before the surgery."

"All of our praying really helped, didn't it?" Chris said.

"Yes," Karen answered. "That, and finally facing some of my fears, like talking to my dad about a singing career and making peace with Greg. And I really think it all started with not letting myself be taken advantage of anymore here at the office. It's nice to actually have a personal life and not feel like I'm chained to work 24 hours a day. There has to be balance. Sometimes the best way around it is to just go through it...and pray a lot while you are."

At nine o'clock on the dot Ralph appeared in the doorway. Karen was pleased to see the look of shock on his face.

"Karen!" Ralph exclaimed. Why are you in my office? And who are these people?"

"Good morning Ralph," Karen answered sweetly. "I thought you would want to welcome me back to work. My boyfriend and best friend both wanted to be here to see that happen."

"I don't understand," Ralph said, slowly lowering his briefcase to the floor without taking his eyes off the trio behind his desk.

"Oh, you will." Karen could not contain her fierce determination as she picked the large manila envelope up from the desk. "Do you really think I would lie about having surgery?"

Ralph sunk into the chair at the side of his desk. "Well, I…um…I thought…"

"You thought wrong." Karen opened the envelope, pulling out several large glossy photographs. "You seem like the kind of guy who needs some proof."

Ralph's eyes grew wide with horror as Karen shoved a photo right in front of his face. "Take a good look," she said as her voice went from sweet to angry. "These are the proof you need of my surgery in full color."

Chris and Sandy stared daggers at the floundering Ralph, who looked as if he was about to become very sick. He glanced around, trying to locate the wastebasket in case he needed it in a hurry. The bandmates thought it quite a shame that the cleaning lady had left it in the doorway when she emptied it. It was too far away to be of any use to Ralph.

"Have another look!" Karen forced picture after picture in front of him. With each one Ralph's face turned whiter.

"Now," said Karen as she unbuttoned the top button of her blouse, "if you need to see the actual scar..."

"No! Stop!" Sweat was pouring over Ralph's face and down his neck as he closed his eyes. "I believe you!"

"Good. Now don't you ever tell me or anyone else that I was not truthful about my surgery again! In fact, I never want to hear you speculate about my personal life at all!"

Karen gathered the photographs and strode out of Ralph's office with Sandy and Chris right behind her. It wasn't until they got to the end of the lengthy hallway that Karen began to shake.

"Are you OK, honey?" Chris asked. He put his hand on her shoulders to steady her.

"I am." Karen let out a long, slow sigh. "I'm just glad it's done."

"What would you have done if he still wanted to see the scar?" Sandy asked.

"I was pretty sure he wouldn't, especially after I saw him turn into such a mess," Karen said. "I probably would have laid into him about not being satisfied with the pictures, to keep from actually having to bare it all."

They walked over to Karen's office, where Jim stood waiting for her to arrive.

"Good morning, Jim," Karen said. "I'm sorry, I know it's a few minutes after nine –"

"That's all right, Karen," Jim said with a big grin. "I just heard what you were doing for those last few minutes."

Karen had no idea what to say. Even though Jim was smiling, she hoped he wasn't upset with her. She placed her purse on the desk along with the manila envelope, careful not to let the pictures slide back out.

"Good for you!" Jim continued. "Ralph deserved that. He's been a pain in the butt about this for days, ever since you first told us about the surgery. I admire your guts."

"Well, I have God for my strength and my friends for support," Karen answered with a sigh. "It doesn't get much better than that."

Jim's mind drifted off as he scratched his chin. "Now I'm wondering…Ralph took time off for a root canal a couple of months ago. Wonder if it was legit?"

Chris laughed mischievously. "If he thinks someone else would lie about medical issues, that probably means it's because he's done it himself."

"I think you may be right," Jim answered. "I'm going to check into that. Anyway…welcome back, Karen."

"Thanks, Jim."

As Jim headed back to his own office, Karen sat down at her desk. Though she still didn't feel like being there, she felt stronger than ever before. She looked up at Sandy and Chris, who were gazing at her with pride. "Thank you so much for being here with me for this."

"You're quite welcome, hon," Sandy said. "Besides, I enjoyed watching Ralph squirm."

"I can enjoy it more now that it's over," Karen said.

"Well, sweetheart, we'll let you get to work," said Chris as he blew her a kiss. "See you tonight at the studio."

"I can't wait," Karen said. "That's what's keeping me going today."

Once she was alone, Karen looked up toward the ceiling. "Thank you God, for giving me the strength to stand up for myself. I would love to quit this job and just do what I love, but I know I have to have the insurance right now. Please help me get focused on my work, and guide me in what to do next."

A few calls to Jim's office brought her up to speed on the happenings of the last few days. Karen threw herself into her duties, trying hard not to think about what the doctor would tell her when he called.

*****

With the first song of the afternoon session taking a couple of hours to get right, it was time for a well-deserved break. Chris and Jerry went outside to get some fresh air and sunlight.

"I can't wait for Karen to sing tonight, man," Jerry said.

"Me either." Chris took a sip from the ice cold can of soda he just retrieved from the vending machine. "After these last few days, it will be good for her to let loose in the studio. Nothing better than pouring out your heart in song to relieve stress."

"I'll bet it was a load off her mind when you told her that Brett kid was just trying to scam you."

"I could tell she was relieved, but…" Chris leaned against the studio's brick wall and closed his eyes.

"But what?" Jerry asked.

"This whole situation could come up again. Would she be able to handle another one of these reminders from my past? It's entirely possible."

"I guess that's just something you'll have to deal with if and when it comes up," Jerry replied.

"You know, when you're young you think you're invincible," Chris said. "You don't realize until much later that those things can come back to haunt you."

"Yeah, and when you're older you get it – just how stupid some of the things were that you did way back when," Jerry said. "I sure know what you mean."

"Karen didn't do all kinds of stupid things when she was younger," said Chris with a shake of his head. "Not like I did anyway. It might still be hard for her to understand, even though she's trying. She really doesn't have any experiences to compare to my earlier life."

"Well, it may not be on the same level as yours," Jerry mused, "but I'm sure she's done some stuff she's not proud of. She is human."

"I'm sure you're right," Chris said, "but let's go back in and start the next song. If I think about this for too long I'll drive myself crazy."

*****

Karen got back to her desk after lunch and checked her messages. There was one waiting for her from Dr. Robertson wanting her to call him at his office. Suddenly that tuna salad wasn't sitting so well in her stomach.

She went over to her office door and closed it, taking a deep breath as she walked back over to her desk and sat down. With trembling fingers she dialed the doctor's number.

It took a couple of minutes for the receptionist to get the doctor to the phone, but to Karen it seemed like hours. Finally she heard, "Karen?"

At the sound of the good doctor's voice, she felt as if someone were pulling the chair out from underneath her. "Yes, doctor, I'm here."

"Good. I'm sorry to keep you waiting. I already have the results back from the biopsy."

Karen braced herself against the sturdy desk, feeling that if she didn't, she would shake herself right out of her chair. She steadied herself as she prepared for whatever words she would hear next.

"Everything checked out fine," Dr. Robertson continued. "The tissue we removed was thoroughly tested and everything was benign."

Karen finally let herself breathe and relaxed her grip on the desk. "Oh thank God. Thank you, doctor!"

"I'm glad I was able to give you good news. The only thing I ask is that you schedule a follow-up mammogram in six months, just to make sure things are still good. And I'll need to see you in about a week to check that your stitches are healing properly."

"Oh, I have no problem with that," Karen said. "Thank you again for everything."

Karen hung up the phone and collapsed in a heap over her desk, sobbing. There was a knock at the door, then it quickly opened.

"Karen, are you all right?" Jim asked. "I knocked, but then I thought I heard you crying."

"Jim." Karen slowly lifted her head from the desk, attempting to support it with her arm. "I'm sorry I'm such a mess."

"Are you going to be OK?"

"I think so. I actually just got the best news from my doctor. There's no malignancy; all the tests came out fine."

Jim's face brightened as he heard the good results come out of her mouth. "Karen, that's wonderful!"

"I know...I guess I was so relieved that I finally let my emotions out. I'm sorry."

"Don't be sorry. In fact, since you've already had quite a day, why don't you take the rest of the day off?"

"Are you sure?" Karen asked, wiping clumps of black mascara from her cheeks. "I just got back from three days off, and I still have a lot to catch up on here."

"Karen, really...it's OK. I'm quite impressed with how much you've gotten done so far today. Take the rest of the day to sort everything out. I'll see you in the morning."

"Thanks, Jim."

After calling her dad with the happy news, Karen went straight home to her cozy, comforting Southwestern sofa and began softly strumming her guitar. She'd been playing mindlessly for quite a while when she took notice of the less than perfect pitch.

As she tuned up the instrument she found herself becoming in tune as well. All of her thoughts came tumbling out at one time. There was so much to think about.

She was beyond relieved that she did not have cancer. She was also content that the whole Brett saga was over, and that she and Chris did not have to deal with him anymore - he was in the hands of the police. She was thankful that her dad now understood her passion for music and her need to go for her dreams. And on top of everything else, she was getting along all right with Greg after all these years – and so was Chris.

The pile of mail that Karen had brought in when she came home was sitting on the coffee table before her. She grabbed the top piece and scanned the envelope. Once it was deemed to be junk mail, she turned it over in order to have a blank white space available.

She began playing her guitar again, but this time with purpose. She wrote on the envelope as she went along; the notes came easily, but the words filled up the space even more quickly as she wrote exactly what she was feeling.

Running through the rough version, Karen couldn't help but be glad that she hadn't laid down and taken that nap. She probably wouldn't have been able to sleep anyway, with all of those thoughts that had been going around in her head. They would have driven her crazy until she got them on paper.

She had barely enough time after completing the tune to make herself something to eat and change clothes before heading to the studio. *Hopefully,* she thought while working in the kitchen, *I'll get a chance to show Chris this new song after the session.*

*****

Charlie and the band were highly entertained by the story Chris and Sandy told them as they waited for Karen to arrive.

"Sounds like Karen gave Ralph just what he deserved," Charlie said with a wink.

"You should have seen his face," Sandy said. "I wish I'd had my camera for that – to capture that look on film for all time."

"Wow, I didn't know Karen could be that bold," Rob added. "I mean, she's on fire in the studio, but when she's not singing she seems kind of reserved."

"Well, she was nervous about it," admitted Chris. "But she was determined not to let this guy walk all over her. She was sick of being called a liar over and over, and having Ralph say it to other people on top of it."

At that moment Karen came through the door and removed her sunglasses. The thunderous applause from everyone in the studio caused her face to turn three shades of red, but her smile outshined the brightness in her cheeks.

"I guess you guys heard about my little performance this morning," she giggled.

356

"That was no little performance," Jerry said. "We're so proud of you for standing up for yourself."

Karen's grin grew even wider. "Thanks. I had a lot of help from above, to have the courage to go through with it. The Lord came through…and boy, it felt good!"

"So how was the rest of the day, hon?" Sandy asked. "Were you able to get much done?"

"Actually I got a lot done, up until the doctor called…"

The room fell silent; everyone stared at Karen anxiously awaiting her next words.

"It's good news, guys. Everything is fine. The tissue that was taken out is benign, so there's no cancer."

Shouts of joy filled the room as Chris nearly tackled Karen. He hugged her as tightly as he could with a tremendous flow of tears streaming down his face.

"Thank God!" he said. "Oh honey, I couldn't stand the thought of losing you, or for you to have to go through all of those treatments."

"Have you told your dad yet?" Sandy asked.

"I did. Jim came to my office right after I got the call, and he decided I needed the rest of the day off. I called my dad on the way home and we cried together. He's so relieved."

"You know," Chris mused, "your boss has been a lot more understanding lately. It wasn't that long ago when he was having fits when you couldn't always stay late to work."

Karen smiled with a sigh, her face softening further. "I've been thinking about that too. Maybe he finally realized how hard I work and what I've done for them, and that I need a life outside of the office so I can keep my sanity. At least that's what I hope."

"I'm sure glad he does realize it," Sandy said. "You deserve to explore everything life has to offer. You can't do that if you're chained to your desk 24 hours a day."

"So sweetie, do you have to follow up with the doctor at all?" Chris asked.

"I have to go next Monday, so he can make sure the stitches are healing properly. Other than that there's a six month follow-up to make sure everything's still OK."

"We'll have to celebrate after the session," Charlie said. "But for right this moment…are you ready to sing?"

"You bet I am," Karen beamed. "I have a lot of reasons to sing!"

Before Karen let go of Chris, she whispered in his ear. "I wrote a new song while I was free this afternoon. I'll tell you more later."

Chris released her slowly, revealing that famous grin once again. "I can't wait," he said, winking as he walked to the booth.

As Karen and the band got tuned up and adjusted, another person slipped into the control room. Chris felt a tap on his left shoulder. He slowly turned his stool around to see who was there.

"Hey brother!" he said as he looked up and focused on Brian. "I'm glad you made it up here."

Brian laughed. "I almost didn't. I got so involved studying my lines for the new show that I lost track of time. Good thing I looked up at the clock when I did!"

"A very good thing," Chris said. "And Karen got good news from the doctor – no cancer. She's all right."

"That's wonderful!" Brian said. "I thought she looked pretty relaxed when I snuck in the door. She didn't even see me."

"Yeah, she's in a super good mood. And she has every right to be," said Charlie as he turned on the sound system.

"Hey Karen," Brian called out over the now live speakers.

Karen looked up and waved as she spotted Brian in the booth, with a peaceful smile that shined all the way through her eyes.

"I heard your good news," Brian said. "I'm so happy you're OK."

"Thanks. It's a big relief."

"Now," Brian said with a wink, "just go right ahead and blow this song out of the water!"

Karen beamed as she gave Brian a big thumbs-up. She glanced over at Jerry to see if the band was ready and saw him nod to her. "We're good to go," he said. "And I second what Brian said."

The first take was solid, yet no one was jumping for joy. They all sat there thinking, trying to figure out just what was wrong. After a few minutes of silence, Charlie made a suggestion. "You guys remember that new direction we were thinking about the other day? Let's try that and see how it goes."

"Maybe that's what we need for this…a new vibe," said Jerry. "Let's do it." The band kicked it up to try the new way, with Karen once again pouring her heart and soul into the song.

Charlie shook his head. "It's better, but something's still missing. I just can't figure out what it is."

"Well, let's fool around with it some more, "Jerry answered. "Maybe we can figure it out from there."

"This might require some caffeine," Rob said. "If we run out of energy we won't even be able to think anymore tonight."

"You know, we could use a little pick-me-up," Charlie said. "Let's call in an order to the coffee shop. We can keep working until they get here with it."

"Since I'm not actually involved in this recording process," Brian said," how about you all give me your orders and I'll call it in? Unless you want some unsolicited advice from me."

"Well, you could call it in, and then give us a hand," Charlie said with a wink. "It certainly wouldn't hurt to get an opinion from a Tony winner."

Brian laughed. "Sounds like a plan to me."

Everyone in the group wrote down what they wanted; Brian took the list into Charlie's office and called the shop. When he got back he heard the musicians tinkering around with the sound.

"The manager said she'd have someone over here with the order in about thirty minutes," he said.

"Good." Jerry checked the tuning of his guitar one more time. "By then we'll need every drop of it."

*****

"Hey Greg, I'm going to let you run this order over to the recording studio. It's just a few doors down and across the street."

"Sure thing," Greg replied. He began to wonder – who was recording over there? It would be pretty cool to actually hear a record being made. Maybe it was some big star.

"Wow, this is a big order," he said, lining up the cups for his manager to mark and fill.

"They usually do give us a lot of business, but it seems that they have even more than usual this time," she said. "Must have needed extra musicians for today."

"All coffee, except for one herbal tea. Kind of odd."

"Some singers prefer the tea," she responded. "They think it makes their voices better, for whatever reason."

As they began preparing the drinks, the manager pointed over to the bakery case. "We made way too many biscotti today. Let's throw a bunch into a pastry box and give them to the studio so they don't go to waste."

Greg filled a large box with biscotti…the variety of almond, chocolate, and cinnamon confections smelled so good that he put one of each aside for himself to eat after the shop closed for the night. His manager helped him secure everything in his car to prevent spillage, and he drove slowly over to the studio.

*****

"All right, I think we may have it this time," Jerry said. "Ready, Charlie?"

"Sure am," Charlie said. "From the top, then."

Karen and the band got going again, sounding much better than the last few attempts. She allowed herself to get lost in the music and really let loose, feeling every single word and note as she sang.

The group gathered together in the main room to listen to the playback to determine if anything else would improve on what they had. In paying close attention to every note, they blocked out everything else in the room.

*****

Greg opened the door with one hand as he carefully balanced the first tray of coffee with the other. He heard the most beautiful voice as he made his way inside; it was better than anything he had ever heard in his life and he couldn't wait to see who it belonged to.

As he carefully walked down the hall, Greg heard Chris' voice. "Now that sounds like a hit if I ever heard one."

Now even more curious, he worked to keep the set of coffees steady in his hands as he moved quickly to the doorway. It was then that he caught a good look at the band.

"Karen?"

Karen looked up as Charlie shut off the tape. "Greg! What are you doing here?"

29935658R00204

Made in the USA
San Bernardino, CA
02 February 2016